Crossing America

An adventure in Life, Love, and Self Awareness

Any mention of named characters is completely fictional and are not based on any real people. Like any fictional story, any depiction of religious beliefs are for entertainment and have no real bearing on the author's or publisher's political views.

Crossing America

"What is that feeling when you're driving away from people and they recede on the plain till you see their specks dispersing? - it's the too-huge world vaulting us, and its goodbye. But we lean forward to the next crazy venture beneath the skies."

— Jack Kerouac

"A journey is best measured in friends, rather than miles."

– Tim Cahill

Preface

The buzz in her head made her dizzy. The pain in her eye didn't help either. The young girl made every effort to hold back the tears she knew would come. They always did. As she moved down the aisle looking for her boyfriend's favorite salad dressing, she heard someone say, "Are you OK?" The supermarket was crowded for a Sunday afternoon. When she first entered the store she was surprised, then realized that on this beautiful spring afternoon, everyone had the same idea as she or rather he, had.

Don, her live-in boyfriend of two years, nudged her at 6:15AM. "I'm only pulling a half shift today. I'll be home by 5PM. Let's barbeque." Mary moaned, "You had me up till almost daylight; why did you wake me? It's my one day to sleep. Leave me a note for what you want and I'll go to the market." She, almost at once, began to fall back to sleep. "I'm just as tired as you, in case you forgot that I was the one on top of you – doing all the hard work." As the last irritating words came from his mouth he poked her middle-back hard with his elbow. "I have to get up; so do you. I'm thinking, like a big salad, corn and

1

maybe ribs. Surprise me with something special. And, make sure there's dressing; the one I like." She heard his famous last words before he said them. *And beer.* "And beer."

The sound of his morning piss irritated her even more. Don never closed the bathroom door, subjecting her to all kinds of morning sounds. His motions as he started each day were ritualistic. First gas relief, then the tinkle of pee hitting the water as he stood over the toilet. She waited for the momentary silence. The manly pause of the non-ending stream that meant he would start again, usually missing a bit. His aim didn't matter; she would clean up after him.

Mary waited for the shower to begin its flow, making a new pitter-patter sound. His moan of pleasure from the steamy hot water followed as expected. She counted the seconds. "Hey babe. This is a great wake me up, why don't you join me?" Mary sat up, her mind blank for the moment. If she allowed her thoughts to process, it would only bring on her depression again. Memories of her dad bossing her mom around played in her head. Her mom did whatever he asked of her to keep the peace. Now, here she was. *The apple doesn't fall far from the tree.* She thought, what a cliché life has become.

"Hey! Are you deaf?"

The bathroom was steamed over, moisture dripped from the already peeling ceiling. The pink v-neck t-shirt clung tightly to her as she attempted to pull it over her head. *Don't do it; run, run far away.* Her mind spoke to her, but she ignored it as she joined her man.

No words were spoken, it had all been said before. What Don wanted, Don got. That used to be enough and Mary let herself be OK with that. He was demanding, but a decent provider. There were gentle and loving moments too. As time passed, two years now, the ratio of demanding to gentle and loving changed. They fought more and more now and it always ended in some form of violence. Sometimes Don would shove Mary or throw something at her.

"You forgot again! Move quicker when I call you! What, are you fucking stupid?"

Leaving him meant a quick and unexpected escape. Don never directly threatened Mary about leaving him but he did insinuate by example, what other men with disobedient, lesser halves would do. His mental and physical abuse is why Mary had such a low self-esteem. She was afraid, and told herself she hated him.

She envisioned him dead, lying in a pool of blood. The other problem she ignored was that, subconsciously, she loved him and thought she needed him.

Robot like, Mary faced the rear wall of the shower stall. Don embraced her from behind and kissed the nape of her neck. He whispered, almost tenderly, almost sincerely, "I love you. You know that, don't you?" She made no sound, no response. Doing so would only make things worse. He kissed her ear as his hands moved over her breasts and then lower down, between her legs. In a low gentle whisper, he told her, "Don't ever ignore me again." Then, he continued his whisper, a bit louder, and in a coarse tone, "NOW I'M GOING TO BE LATE FOR WORK." Those last words so cold, the hot shower seemed to freeze over.

His assault on her lasted all of two minutes. As he finished with her, he kissed her neck again and whispered in her ear, "Fucking whore." She sensed what was about to happen as his hand met the back of her head but she had no time to prevent the anticipated shove. Mary's face hit the shower wall. She just stood with the water hitting her back until her bastard lover dried off and left the bathroom.

Mary cried silently as she slowly and carefully wrapped a towel around her pained body. To her relief, Don was gone by the time she returned to the bedroom. The pain below her right eye throbbed. This was the first time he had pushed her hard enough to cause an injury that would most likely show. She needed to stop at the drug store and buy some cover–up.

Mary felt panic rising up – *where the hell is the bacon ranch dressing.* She frantically searched the two shelves of bottles, knocking several to the floor.

Oh, thank goodness. There it is.

Suddenly a barrage of cans and bottles fell to the floor. She held her head in her hands trying to control hysteria from overcoming her.

 "Excuse me miss. Are you alright?"

She heard someone speaking to her but her mind was so focused on the dilemma of the moment, her response was delayed. Mary turned abruptly; she had no idea that anyone was in the aisle; let alone, this handsome young man. She said, "Oh, yes; I'm fine." Her reflection in his dark, cool looking Ray-Ban's, said otherwise.

Wayne Lasner

Part One - Friends

Wayne Lasner

Chapter 1

Note to self:

Don't party when there's a work day ahead. Don't exchange telephone numbers with girls after a "One-Night-Stand."
Quit boring job, after finding better one.

Carlos stretched, opening his eyes slowly. The bright sunshine glared in through the partially open curtain of his single bedroom window. He was glad it had stopped raining. Three days of gloom was enough; it added to his already depressed state of mind. He sat up and checked the time on his iPhone 6 Plus. "Damn, 8:30; late again." Carlos Andres Martinez's subconscious mind planted the image of the last thing he recalled before he woke up. The list of things he needed to change so he could get his life back on track. The last one he remembered, *quit boring job*, really wasn't an option.

As he got dressed, he noticed the piece of paper on his dresser. Carlos picked it up and read the pencil scribbled note. "Jenifer – 555-531-1435, you better call me! Xoxo." Tiny hearts and kiss symbols framed her words. Usually that note would be left on his night stand from a girl he had met that night and brought home. This time he tried using better judgment. *Or not.* Jenifer bartended at the club he went to the previous evening. Carlos's friend called him after he had already arrived and cancelled for some lame reason. Carlos figured he would have a quick drink and head home. Jenifer poured that *one,* Patron Silver double over ice, and the conversation started. An hour later, they found themselves in a stall in the ladies room. Two hours later, after her shift ended, the rodeo continued back at his place.

Relationships and Carlos were a much needed work in progress. He never wanted any form of commitment. At least, not with intimate relationships. His work ethic on the other hand proved impeccable. His father once told him that good looks weren't enough. Education is the draw for women who mattered. Carlos had both. While he and his father didn't always see eye to eye, his dad made a good point. He was a magnet for beautiful women. His lack of commitment led him to countless, meaningless, one night stands.

By 8:45, Carlos had made his way down from his third floor walk-up to the street below. Bedford Avenue traffic was heavy, and he waited for the light to change before crossing over to the other side. The bus he needed to take to work traveled along Manhattan Avenue toward the Brooklyn-Queens Expressway. Today he planned to cut through McCarren Park to save time.

The grass glistened in the early morning sunshine; Carlos figured it must have rained overnight. His sneakers felt wet but he had shoes in his backpack, and extra socks. He referred to his backpack as something like the cartoon character from the 60's, Felix the Cat's Magic Bag of Tricks.

As he passed the basketball courts, he saw familiar faces shooting hoops. "Yo dudes. Isn't it kind of early?" He gave a chuckle and waved. The three men on the court looked at him for a moment then one of them said, "Carlos, brother. What's on? You all incognito or something." Carlos always wore his dark blue hoodie and sunglasses, even when it wasn't sunny out. He waved, "Something - Cruz. Later Guys."

The bus stop was directly across from the park exit. The usual cluster of waiting patrons stood around reading newspapers or making small talk with the person next to them on line. As Carlos began to cross the road, someone ran up behind him and grabbed his arm. He stopped and the cars started honking. One almost hit

Carlos and his unexpected escort. "Shit, bro. What is wrong with you?" The man let go of his arm, "Sorry, man. You got a five spot? I'll pay you back" Carlos made a serious face, "Again, Benny? I'm not a bank. And, you never pay anyone back." He already had the five in his pocket. Benny was an old high school friend who went down a bad path; not able to find his way back. "Here, get some food and coffee." Benny bumped fists with Carlos, "You the man – mucho thanks." Carlos' *friend* took off back to the park while dodging cars honking their horns.

The twenty-minute bus ride up Manhattan Avenue let him off at the corner diagonally across from his work place. The factory ran two shifts, 6:30AM to 3:00PM and 3:30PM to Midnight. Wisely planned, the thirty minute gap kept outgoing and incoming employees orderly during the change of shifts.

Chapter 2

How strange, Carlos thought, that there was just one single puffy cloud slowly drifting among the bluest sky he could ever remember seeing. He wanted to be up there riding on that cloud. He imagined looking down at the urban buildings and noisy people. A sad sight for sore eyes. But, there would be no sounds up there, only peaceful solitude.

The loud, irritating honk from the yellow cab's horn startled Carlos. It brought his attention back to earth, and the road he was only halfway across. He smirked at the cabby whose middle finger pointed upward. Carlos was sure it did not reference upward to the cloud he was so engrossed with. The front entrance to the building was on the adjacent street. Generally, that entrance was reserved for customers and other business related people. Employees entered via a separate entrance on the north side.

"Employees only." Carlos read the sign out loud and shrugged his shoulders as he grabbed the large steel handle on the red, steel, fireproof door. Normally there would be a line into the building as people swiped their

I.D. badges to clock in. Today, however, there was no line. Carlos was almost three hours late.

Most of the employees liked Carlos. They respected his down-to-earth persona. As he walked through the warehouse, some of them greeted him.

"Morning brother. Boss gonna have a piece of you."
"Hey, Carlos. Hot night last night?"
"Look at you, thinking you all fine and that. And, *you are* man."

Carlos thought to himself, *the guys act like my friends and the girls consider me, "So fine." It's like I'm not real, I'm not like them. But, I am.* He left the main factory and entered the office area where the billing and order processing is done. His own office seemed miles away when it was only three doors down on the left side of the wide hallway.

The morning hustle, long underway, had administrative people and clerks filing, talking on the phones taking orders, copying and various other business functions. Outside Carlos's office was another large copy machine and a reception desk. He tried to quietly make his way past both without drawing attention.

"Just a minute, mister; you stood me up for lunch yesterday." He almost made it. One date. A "one-night stand," like all the others. Now she considered him, hers. *Like all the others.* "Ginger, I got called into a meeting – last minute. I forgot. I'm so sorry." The pretty redhead did not smile. "You're unbelievable. Like you don't know what I do here, or something. Like I don't *arrange* your schedule and take your calls and *organize* your meetings." He was caught, and he knew it. *It happens.* "I'll make it up to you; lunch tomorrow. I promise." Ginger pinched Carlos's arm. "Ouch!" She seemed calmer all of a sudden; as if the brief pain she inflicted on him, satisfied her into forgiveness. "Not acceptable. Dinner out, then maybe back to your apartment for dessert. Chocolate something, – surprise me. You better not think I'm one of your 'One-night stand' conquests." Carlos was caught off guard big-time. He knew this was not going to play out very well. After all, Ginger was his friend and confidant. They shared an open friendship which meant they shared each other's secrets, and other details of their personal lives. This situation was a first for him. She was gorgeous, downright "hot," and a fireball in bed. "OK, Ginger. I'll check out what I have going on and get back to you." He told her this as he disappeared into his office.

Carlos knew he narrowly escaped that one for the moment; she would be a force to reckon with. He looked in the mirror, observing how cool and comfortable he was with his look. He removed his hooded sweatshirt, exposing his crisp blue Van Heusen shirt and striped tie. Off with the Ray-Ban shades and on with the mild prescription reading glasses. He didn't really need them, but his father insisted they made him appear more professional; *sophisticated*.

As Senior Account Executive, Inside Sales, Carlos managed two teams of sales professionals, or as their cards indicated, Account Executives. He had a total of eight men and one woman reporting to him. The rest of the two-hundred and forty employees reported to various managers who then reported to the president and owner, Carlos Martinez Sr.

The phone rang, the digital panel read "SLS Reception."

"Yes?"
"I'm still mad at you."
"Ginger – "
"You have a meeting in the conference room in ten minutes. Make sure you have your sales figures for the

month-to-date."

"Thanks, listen – "

The phone clicked loudly. Carlos rubbed his eyes, stretched for a moment, and got up out of his comfy desk chair. He hoped to avoid the reception area. Thankfully, his pursuer was not at her post. He figured that might be intentional, since she knew he would be heading to the meeting.

This meeting, like all meetings, went on for over two hours. He found it frustrating that each manager tried to impress his dad with big words and fancy charts. The information they each had to offer could have been e-mailed to the group. Or, explained and discussed in five minutes. Yet, for effect, they had to stretch it out.

"Ok, Carlos. What have you got for us? I hope some good news." Carlos stood up and cleared his throat. He was sure his father would be impressed with that. "Sales for the month so far are three hundred and fifty-three thousand. With nine more business days, I project our monthly sales to finish at about four hundred and fifty-eight thousand. That is eight percent higher than any month so far this year." The president asked, "What do you attribute the growth to?" Carlos smiled, "Luck." He felt the chill, no one got his sense of humor. "Good Fortune?" Not so much as a crack of a smile. "Ok, I don't have any fancy charts to waste precious time, but possibly, the addition of our new regional manager, Sam Westin. He brought ten years of sales connections to us. It's too early to tell, but I am confident we will see more sales as he gets out and presents us to his former clients." His dad stood, "Now, that *is* good news. Keep us updated." Carlos Sr. looked around the room and acknowledged his group. "Thank you, everyone. Good job."

Carlos was back in his office for ten minutes when his father knocked. "Busy?" Carlos looked up and smiled. "Of course; but not for you. What's on your mind, dad?" His father sat in one of the two quilted leather chairs facing Carlos. "You are a smart young man, doing a more than decent job. Why must you be so smug, and antagonize your peers? We are all members of the same team, with a common goal; to grow this business." "Dad, they are ass kissing weenies." His father stood up abruptly. "They are what keeps this business running strong. We need them and you should show them the same respect they show you. Someday this will be all yours. You will not inherit it; you will earn it. That is the only way your employees will respect you. Respect goes both ways, son. You were late this morning. Is everything alright?"

"Yes, Dad; I'm sorry."

After his father left, Carlos felt a bit hungry. The clock displayed 1:15. He sat back and considered asking Ginger to go to lunch with him. Clearly, the gorgeous assistant was seriously into him. Lunch would calm her down; or, lead her on. Carlos wondered if something was wrong with him. He decided; *"Lunch - Bad Idea. I need to mellow-out."*

Chapter 3

The rocket ship lifted off it's launch pad in slow motion. The fiery blast that would propel the missile-like capsule into outer-space spread wide across the grassy field surrounding the large platform now singed from burnt rocket fuel. It glowed bright as it headed up into the sky. The sun caused a blinding reflection as it turned in a semi-circle, forming a somewhat spiral effect. In the background, chatter from an excited mission control center could be heard. As fast as it had lifted off, it now began a downward spiral, leaving a trail of smoke and debris. The ground approached quickly; something like zooming in on the car's navigation system. Then, suddenly

-*Crash!*

"Mr. Glass, whatever you are doing with your pen, please put it down and answer the question." The daydream fantasy Daniel Glass had drifted into, cut him off from the goings on of the classroom. He had no idea what or how to respond to the professor's question. Daniel's face prominently displayed this with a bright red hue of embarrassment.

"Never mind, Mr. Glass."

Daniel loved fiddling with gadgets. As a young boy, around five years old, his parents gave him the deluxe Lego set. Within a day, he built structures the Lego company's owners probably never dreamed possible with their product. At age six, he appeared in one of their commercials showing how fast, really cool, and fun this new Lego set could be. That commercial ran for several years. The residuals helped to pay for Daniel's undergraduate schooling, and probably a lot more.

As the professor continued talking about the late 1980's and the emergence of personal computers, Daniel caught Randy Myers staring at him. He thought, *"As if I'm not embarrassed enough."* Then she smiled and gave what he interpreted as a silent laugh. His mind went *"Wow. She's not laughing at me*, she laughing *with* me." Daniel cautiously smiled back. He looked down at his note pad, *"Don't look her way again – resist; resist."* He failed; she caught his glance as he caught hers. Again, they both smiled.

"Thank you, everyone. Read chapters seven through nine and answer the chapter questions for each. We will discuss them on Wednesday." Daniel put his notepad in his back pack and looked around, hoping to see Randy. She was gone. He tried not to let disappointment get to him. Besides, what was he expecting anyway? The cute girls never paid him any attention; not anymore.

"May I have a moment, Mr. Glass? I'd like a brief word with you." Daniel's stomach ached, he didn't do well with confrontation. "Is there a problem you would like to discuss? I had you pegged for an "A" student. Yet, you seem distracted in my class. Am I boring you?"

"Oh. No sir. I enjoy your class immensely." *Actually, Professor, you do bore me, I could teach this course*. "I was distracted, as you so keenly observed. I won't let it happen again."

As a young boy, Daniel's outgoing personality was perceived as adorable by his family and his parent's friends. At parent-teacher night his various instructors would tell of his high intelligence and eagerness to learn. They also complained about his persistent, outspoken behavior.

High School presented challenges Daniel was not prepared for. Girls found him cute and smart. Eventually, the sports jocks caught on. They invited him to parties and soon coerced him into doing their homework and projects. For a while, he thought they were his friends. In eleventh grade he started dating a girl in his science class. She was a grade younger, but excelled in science. They talked about lots of things and worked on projects together. He really liked her. He finally had a girlfriend who was more than just a friend. By mid-term that year, she broke up with him for one of the senior jocks who he thought was his friend. Daniel was hurt and became distrusting of his classmates. The outspoken smart kid became introverted and paranoid of his peers.

Chapter 4

Established in 1930 as a combining of two other colleges, Brooklyn College brought an antiquated separation of the sexes together. Many of the buildings had retained their earlier architectural charm. Approximately sixteen thousand students are registered, resulting in a normally busy campus, with students and faculty hustling from one side of campus to another.

Today, the campus seemed a little quieter than most of the other times he visited. As Carlos made his way from the bus stop, crossing Bedford Avenue, he stopped at one of the food trucks parked along the street. The lines were short, as lunchtime had all but had passed by the time he got there. He pulled his phone out as he got on the line and checked the time. *Hmm, 1:35PM. I have to remember this is a good time to come here.* He checked his phone. Fortunately, there were no messages from the office. He wondered if anyone would confront him for taking an off-site lunch break, since he arrived to work late this morning.

"What's the special today, Jerry?" The dark-skinned man with a heavy Indian accent replied, "Same as

I tell you every time, my friend. Would you like to see the menu?" The chef pointed to the hanging plaque that said "Today's Menu." Carlos laughed, "Not necessary, Jerry. I'll have the tandoori chicken wrap and a cola." Jerry made an unpleasant face, "You order the same thing every time. Why do you ask about the menu? Maybe next time-" Carlos interrupted him, "Next time I will try something different." Carlos laughed again, Jerry shook his head. "Someday, Jerry; someday, I will get you to smile." With his back to the truck window and Carlos, Jerry mumbled, "Someday I will smile. I will be retired then. Then I will be smiling."

The morning clouds moved across the sky in uneven patterns, allowing bands of sunshine to escape. Carlos noticed the effect of the shadows from the trees and campus structures created a cool and animated illusion. The day turned out absolutely beautiful. A gentle breeze made the warm day comfortable for walking, or simply for hanging out. The bag with his lunch smelled delicious, and he felt hunger calling his name. As Carlos crossed the campus, he watched two guys tossing a baseball back and forth. The ball glided silently through the air between the two students. The rhythmic pop of the ball being caught had a mesmerizing effect. There were a few small groups of students sitting in circles, eating. Some seemed to be studying. To his left, a few boys and girls attempted to show their skills with a Frisbee. He found his usual spot in front of the East Quad, and sat against an old oak tree. Sometimes he would make his way over to LaGuardia Hall Library and sit on the small mountain of steps in front of the entrance. He would say "Hello" as students passed by. Carlos sometimes enjoyed the short interactions he had with them. In fact, one day he started talking with two female students that had stopped to ask him where they could find Ingersoll Hall. The student with cute blond hair noticed he held her favorite Stephen King book, "Insomnia" in his hand. She engaged him in conversation about what the author really wanted his readers to get from the story. Her friend, bored and mostly ignored, made an excuse and took off in search of their original destination of Ingersoll Hall. There were many women that had passed through Carlos's life. He could never remember important details; like, for instance, names. It had gotten him into trouble a few times. But this one really unnerved him. He and Catlin, her friends called her "Cat", *so she told him,* ended up back at his apartment that afternoon. Afterward, as they got dressed, he asked her what major she studied. *He found himself a smart one; and interesting too. Perhaps his dad's theory works in both directions.* Catlin was in her senior year, majoring in Biology. "I'm so glad I could help you study for finals." She actually laughed at his lame joke. He immediately liked her. She was smarter than his usual fling; beautiful, sassy and interesting. They sat and drank cola on his couch. He asked her about her family and where she grew up. All went down-hill from there. Catlin Messing's paternal grandfather was Miguel Santiago. Carlos's mother's uncle. Somewhere in that debacle of the family tree, Carlos and Catlin were related; third cousins once removed, or something like that. She was weirded out. Carlos thought it was kind of "Hot." He really liked her, but she couldn't let it go. That disappointment added to his fear of commitment. In his mind, and to protect himself, he would fend off any long term, intimate relationships. The less he knew about the women he met the better off he would be.

The tandoori wrap hit the spot. As Carlos took a sip of cola he heard a shriek. He looked across the field of green in the direction of the irritating sound. A girl sitting under that huge oak tree had just been struck by a Frisbee. One of the young men he noticed earlier, ran over to her to retrieve the flying disc. At first, she seemed angry. It looked like she might have been giving the guy a hard time. Then she handed the disc back to the guy, who took it and ran off toward his friends. Evidently she was alright, and it appeared she allowed herself to relax again. He watched as she leaned back against the big old oak tree; she had the right idea. Carlos adjusted his sunglasses and pulled his hoodie over his head and closed his eyes. Somewhere in the distance he heard guitar music playing. It was simple and relaxing. The brightness of the sun filtering through his Oakley shades made psychedelic images dance under his eyelids. The words were hard to hear, but the music sounded sad. The dancing images took an undefined form of a person strumming a guitar. Somehow this helped him to relax even more.

A fifteen-minute siesta before heading back to the factory.

Chapter 5

Winter finally gave up, allowing the warmth of spring to make its way to the East Coast. The freshman sat herself down on the great lawn facing the nineteen thirties architectural structure that now had thousands of students walk its halls on a daily basis. She leaned back against a large oak tree, probably as old as the building across the field of green. A gentle breeze moved the generations old branches and their leaves, back and forth. The quiet rustling sound and rocking shadows helped her to relax; making her sleepy. Randy closed her eyes. *The sun feels so good, so warm.*

Growing up in Kew Gardens, New York, there were always droves of children to play with. Randy's parents, both teenage progenies of the sixties generation, were outgoing party animals. They met in their early twenties and married soon after. Her dad often said, marrying her mom so young was the best stupid thing he ever did. In her pre-teen years Randy displayed introverted tendencies. Her parents called it shy, but the pediatrician said it might be a mild form of Asperger's. Her parents insisted she would grow out of it, and didn't consider that any medical follow-up needed to be done. Fortunately, they were right; mostly. Randy held onto her "shyness" throughout high school, and in social settings her peers considered her a loner. Guys generally thought she was cute and would try to talk to her. She remained polite but showed no interest in their attempts to make conversation with her. Eventually, her classmates ignored her. Randy was intelligent and academically she did very well. She participated in class discussions, and had a few friends she felt comfortable making small talk with, when *they* initiated the conversation.

Things opened up a little more for Randy when she started at Brooklyn College. Something about the maturity of her surroundings allowed her a new comfort zone. She managed to be more open with other students in her classes. Socially, she still avoided large groups, declining most offers to "hang out."

Randy thought about her morning computer science class. She liked computers and needed another elective for this semester. Computer science seemed like a good choice. Aside from herself and one other student who didn't major in some form of computer science, the rest of the class were computer nerds. Her love of history and reading put her in with another class of nerds. She laughed while pondering to herself, *I've got it covered on both ends. I'm good with that.* Then her mind drifted back to the morning course and Daniel Glass. *He had a nice smile, and he was looking at me.* Somehow she sensed a comfort level in that boy. She hoped that one day he would talk to her. She hoped that she, in turn, could engage in conversation with him.

Her eyes remained closed as the soothing hum slowly got louder. She sensed the approaching danger just before it hit her. Her eyes opened just in time to catch a glimpse of the bright green Frisbee as it struck her shoulder. Even though she saw it coming, she jumped and made the silliest sound; part screech and part indistinguishable words. Her eyes opened wide like an owl's, and her face flushed bright red.

"Are you OK?"
"I'm fine."
"Sorry, the wind must have caught it."

She recognized the young man from the library where she sometimes went before an exam to review her class notes. She would see him there, studying, every once in a while. He was good looking and tall; older. Probably a junior or possibly even a senior. She thought to herself, *look at him; make eye contact.* She knew he

31

was staring at her. Then, she realized the Frisbee was on her lap. She handed it to him; her eyes met his for a second before she inadvertently looked away.

"Thanks, and again, sorry."

Stupid, he thinks you are angry about the Frisbee hitting you and that you are RUDE! Randy looked over her shoulder hoping he might still be close enough to hear the apology she planned to blurt out in her usual awkward way. *Too late.* The young man already made it back to his group of friends. The Frisbee, already floating in the air in a direction away from her. Far away.

Trying to be indifferent to her surroundings, Randy, once again, closed her eyes. She allowed the warming sun to calm her as it did, prior to the *rude* Frisbee assault. For the next few minutes she found herself opening and closing her eyes looking for any incoming objects. She wasn't sure if it was the fear of getting hit again unexpectedly, or the hope that the Frisbees owner would come close to her again to retrieve his property. As Randy began to close her eyes, she noticed another young man had just sat himself down, about a hundred yards across the grassy campus area. She closed her eyes imagining the new mystery man with his cool looking dark sunglasses and hoodie pulled over his head.

Tall, dark, and mysterious. His face, likely hidden on purpose for privacy, faded as she drifted into a light slumber. A warm, gentle breeze rolled over her face as a soft hint of music played somewhere in the distance.

Serenity and bliss

Chapter 6

Sundays always seemed to be an easy day except for the one commitment he stayed with for the past two years; softball in the park.

Brooklyn's Prospect Park is a huge field of dreams for a conglomerate of ethnicities. People from many dissimilar cultures co-mingling in a beautiful and peaceful setting. Groups of young and old played volleyball using nets set up in several areas on the great lawn, just southeast of Prospect Park West. Surrounded by the areas of Park Slope, Gowanus and Carroll Gardens to the west and on the other side of the park, Prospect South, Crown Heights and Flatbush. The pungent and delicious aromas of the multi-cultural family barbeques teased the senses. The laughter of children romping on the grass echoed all around him. And, an endless variety of canine breeds barked in anticipation of a ball or Frisbee being thrown to them. Often, one could hear the grinding sounds of little wheels turning against the pavement as skateboarders and roller-blading daredevils zoomed by.

Motorists honked their horns as the young man rode his bicycle along Ocean Parkway making his way to the Grand Army Plaza entrance. He stopped at a light directly across from the park entrance. A gentle breeze caught the mist from the plaza fountain, moistening his forehead. He liked the sensation, and often stopped to rest on a bench by the great Bailey Fountain.

Joshua loved researching the history of places he visited, especially around his home town. Just recently, his curiosity provoked a Google search of his favorite rest stop. In 1929, Frank Baily and his wife hired architects and financed the construction of the fountains. The water spouting statues of Neptune, Triton and various others aside a ship, supposedly represented wisdom and happiness. The project was completed in 1932.

On hot days, the mist had a cooling effect. Today Joshua Cohen was late and had no time for a rest stop. The light turned green and the red flashing indicator began its methodical countdown to danger – 29, 28, 27. Joshua looked both ways and proceeded across the road and into the park. As he made his way through the entrance, the road split into three paths. The left would take him northeast around the outskirts of the park; more or less along East Drive and Flatbush. To the right he had two choices, a path into the park or another journey on the outer rim heading south, running parallel to Prospect

Park West. To save time, he chose the gravel-stepped path, allowing him to save time and avoid the longer outer paved paths. Like others with the same idea, he dismounted his bicycle and walked it down the short path. The overhanging tree cover and brush allowed for a momentary respite off from the blazing sun.

Back on a paved bicycle path again, Joshua made his way uphill toward the baseball fields which were located at the south end of Long Meadow. The day turned out beautiful despite the unreliable weatherman's prediction for a chance of rain. People were everywhere; playing catch and tossing Frisbees. The tangy aroma of barbeque made him hungry. He would most likely not be able to eat the food items that smelled so delicious. But, his imagination would have to suffice. His mind wandering with all that was going on around him, he almost crashed into a man rolling a large gray garbage can. Joshua squeezed hard on both hand brakes. He must have squeezed harder on the front brake which resulted in almost tossing him head first off his bicycle. Joshua's heart pounded. As the bike righted itself, Joshua jumped off, almost falling. Like the bike, he righted himself, avoiding a potentially ugly and painful fall. "Hey, brother. You best be watching where you riding that thing." Joshua grinned with embarrassment.

"Sorry, Sir."

"No harm, young man. You want a nice cold drink? I have water and cola. Besides, you look like you need it. Where'd you come from, up Ocean Parkway?"

"Yes, Borough Park."

"Ooh-wee, that's a long ride my friend. I got lots a family up that way, just on the other side of the park. You took off your heavy black coat today, did you? You lucky one of my brothers didn't take your wheels from you. Maybe that would have been all... right. Then you might not have almost run me down."

"I'll take a Coke."

"You know; I'm just fooling with you. One dollar."

Joshua paid for the can of soda and apologized again. The man told him, "You have yourself a fine and safe day."

Joshua arrived at the ball field ten minutes later. He was breathing heavily. To himself, he said, "There must be an entrance or someway into the park that is closer." His friend, really just a teammate, ran up to him. "Where have you been? We only have two hours and we wasted ten minutes waiting for you." Joshua wiped a bead of perspiration from his forehead, "Sorry, Moshe." He laid his bicycle against a park bench and pulled off his backpack. "Schlimazel! Where are you?" Panic ensued as he realized that he left his glove at home. He had taken it out to oil the palm and forgot to put it back in his pack.

"We chose positions, and since you were not here during the pick, you get outfield today. I hope your hands are tough. Don't get hit in the head." Joshua smiled like he did for most things pleasant and not so pleasant. He was a schlimazel, his mom reminded him of that all the time. She would say:

"Schlimazel, you know what that is? Come here and look in the mirror. You are so good looking, and a good soul. You just need to get some backbone and make better decisions. You're not a boy anymore; be a man." Then she told him in a quiet, softly spoken tone, "Your father was somewhat of a schlimazel when we met. He was so handsome, like you. I saw his potential and his good heart. Now he is successful and a good provider. He loves his family."

She always kissed his cheek, telling him she loved him. His mom would then potch his tush telling him, "Off you go."

Outfield can be lonely, but at times it could be the most heroic position; especially when a fly ball is hit, and it meant getting an "out" for the opposition. Without a glove, heroism was not likely. Fortunately, Joshua only had to field a few grounders. He was able to handle them by running to them and tossing the ball to his teammate at second or third base.

The game ended with a score of three to one. Joshua's team on the losing end; no surprises there. By the time he walked infield, most of his team had already grabbed their stuff and were leaving. He felt lonely and sad as he wiped his forehead with his sleeve. His yarmulke hung off to the right side of his head. He re-clipped it properly and then sat down in the middle of the green, grassy field. He laid back for just a minute to calm himself before the long ride home. He envisioned the elderly black man with the large trashcan filled with ice and cold beverages. Obviously, he was not living the dream. However, he was doing something productive. He provided a needed service. He was a smart man; perhaps down on his luck. He did seem content. Jewish studies often pointed out about the will to survive. After all, the Jewish people were one of the most oppressed throughout history. Yet, they never gave in and always found a way to find each other and regroup. Keep it positive. His mom would tell him that. "You will outgrow this boyish way and as a man, you will be an honorable and successful mensch." *And maybe not such a Shlimazel.*

His dad, a conservative Jew, met his mom at an engagement party at the local Yeshiva. His dad's Orthodox friend, the betrothed's brother, had invited him. "She was the most beautiful young woman I had ever seen. I knew she would be my wife from that first moment." His dad told that story and more many times. Joshua considered himself Orthodox, but on the much lighter side, due to his father's influences. He considered his religious following to contain the best of both worlds.

With a newly formed smile, Joshua sat up and looked around at all the people enjoying the day. Then, he stood up and started walking in the direction of his belongings while brushing off his black pants and partially unbuttoned white shirt. As he approached the bench he felt lightheaded; his eyes could not properly focus. No, he was OK. His eyes were fine. A man and his little girl sat on the bench, *his bench*. There was no bicycle and no backpack. Joshua looked all around, there were two other benches, both empty. This was the right one. His belongings were gone! ... *Shlimazel!!*

Chapter 7

"Hello, Aerotech. How may I direct your call?"
"Mr. Jones is in a meeting, would you like his voicemail?"
"Hello, Aerotech. How may I direct your call?"

The front desk receptionist had what most would consider a monotonous job at Aerotech Industries. Her repertoire repeated over and over again; day in and day out. Yet, she took pride in her job and did it as if every phone call was her first for the day. She was efficient and good at follow-up. As a first point of contact for the company, she set the example of how doing business with Aerotech would be. This manner of customer relations existed from day one; before Martinez Sr. even dreamed his garage start-up would become Aerotech Industries.

"And you have a most wonderful day as well, sir."

Carlos' father got his first job while in high school. He started working in the produce section at the local Associated supermarket. His upbringing taught him to always be on time and work hard to do the best job possible. It wasn't long before the food chain promoted him to a manager position. His family was very proud, and he felt good about taking pride in his job. His love for planes and rockets had him reading magazines whenever he had free time. He enjoyed looking at ads in the back of magazines, for parts and kits to build things. Eventually he started buying things he didn't need and then selling them. On occasion he sold an item for more than he paid. He had an idea to start a business out of his father's detached garage. Before long, his relentless "Knocking on doors" paid off, and got him started on the road to success. Companies he made a one-time sale to, started calling him for more items. He started hiring his school buddies to help, and took ads out in newspapers and trade periodicals. After a few years, the business started selling directly to various aerospace companies, commercial airlines and other airport related businesses. Today's operation is the thirty-year result of his father's earlier ambition to succeed. Aerotech Industries became the East Coast's largest parts supplier to airports for baggage carts, conveyor belt systems, and a host of other equipment. Forbes wrote an article, and mentioned them as one of the fastest growing companies, and having the best price for the finest quality cogs and sprockets.

"Carlos, your guys are in the conference room." "Thanks, Ginger. I'm on my way now." He could tell she was still angry with him. "Oh, can you grab the sales stats for me? They're on my desk in the blue folder." Her stare of death unnerved him a bit. "What, aren't you my administrative assistant? Is it OK that I asked you to do that?" *Oh no, why did you have to go there.* As Ginger turned toward Carlos' office she said, "I'll tell you what I don't have to do!" She stormed off, and out of sight.

The long corridor leading to the conference room hummed with chatter, but fell silent when Carlos entered. "Hello, team. I hope everyone is having a good week so far." He acknowledged each of the young men and one woman on his sales team with a nod and a handshake. One of the more important things his dad taught him was to keep it professional with his subordinates. Ginger was his only infraction to that rule. Joe, from the mailroom, knocked and entered the meeting room. "Hey Carlos, Ginger asked me to give this to you. She said you needed it ASAP and to tell you she was leaving early. Something about not feeling well." Carlos thanked Joe and took a quick look at the paperwork just handed to him. "Ok. Let's go over the numbers. Which, by the way, so far for the quarter, appear to be quite impressive."

The meeting lasted a little over an hour. At 4:30PM he wished his team a good night and thanked them for doing a great job. The blue folder in his hand reminded him of his uneasy encounter earlier that afternoon. Ginger was hurt and angry at him; this he understood. He thought, *its better this way, no more expectations. She deserves a raise. I'll have to talk to my dad.*

Chapter 8

Carlos, while following his typical daily ritual, found himself sitting on the soft, well-groomed campus lawn, eating tacos from one of his favorite food trucks. The still air had a heaviness to it. It felt more like summer than early spring. Yet, it allowed for a tranquility he preferred. The usual outdoor frenzy of activities seemed non-existent today, except for a few distant people lounging or studying by themselves or in small groups.

The beef taco tasted delicious; as it always did. The taco truck recently became his favorite choice for lunch. The chef on wheels created a unique food item by making his "Grande Tacos" large enough and packed with incredibly delicious ingredients to sate the hungriest appetite. Carlos' *grande* hunger tempted him to try something new. He also got a fish taco, which he found to be amazing; possibly his new favorite. Carlos usually preferred land born food for lunch to that of the sea; but, tastes change. Occasionally, he would go with some of his warehouse workers to Applebee's for lunch. One of the guys he went with loved that place. That would be George, or Speedy G, so nicknamed for his incredible ability to maneuver a forklift. He would roll down the narrow warehouse aisles at speeds that would even impress his idol, the former champion racecar driver Mario Andretti. Anyway, he would always get the fish tacos and rave about them. Carlos was sure they did not compare to his feast this afternoon. Today's menu featured them as the "Truck Stop Special of the day." Carlos found a new favorite to add to his fine fast food list.

The warmth of the sun felt good. A welcomed light breeze came about suddenly, rustling the leaves above him. With his tummy comfortably full, Carlos pulled his hoodie up and leaned back against the base of the big oak. His eyes closed, and he envisioned Ginger standing over him wearing a short skirt and nothing else. He tried switching channels, even thinking about his family dog that died when he was six years old. That only worked for a moment before he returned to the imagery of a breeze lifting her skirt; teasing his mind. He had hoped for closure for her, but it never occurred to him that he might be the one who needed closure.

"Excuse me, sir. Sorry to disturb you." Carlos opened his eyes but did not immediately sit up from his reclined position. Even with his dark sunglasses, the glare from the sun distorted the uniformed figure standing in front of him. It, for sure, wasn't Ginger. Although, right now he wished it was.

"Sorry. What?"
"Are you a student at this college?"
"Well, not exactly…"
"I'll need to see campus ID, Please."
"Sir, why are you singling me out? There are plenty of people here for you to harass."
"Let's just say you don't fit the average profile – you know, age wise."
"Are you profiling …"

Carlos's usual, easy going demeanor did a flip. He tried to control the arrogance building in him. Something about this wanna-be cop irritated him more than it should have. He sat up while slowly removing his sunglasses.

"Shouldn't you be working at the mall or something? I'd like your name and badge number."
"Sir, I need to ask you to leave the campus property now or I'll have you detained for the authorities."

The security officer's attention seemed to stray as he looked over Carlos' shoulder. "Dude, what's the problem here, why are you messing with my boy?" Carlos twisted his body while looking over his shoulder and to the right of the big oak tree. The officer asked, "You know this gentleman?" The young man grinned, "He's my friend, didn't I just say?" The guard stared at the newcomer for a moment and then asked him, "Hmm, really? And, what's your friend's name?" This was going to be awkward, Carlos stood and addressed the campus cop before the kid "put *his foot in his mouth.*"

"Carlos." His extended his hand as a gesture of good measure. "Sorry about the attitude. I was dozing off and you startled me. I was just hanging here waiting. We were meeting for lunch." Realizing his taco wrappers lay balled up next to his backpack, Carlos added, "Obviously, my good friend here was late; as usual." Carlos looked at the young man, "Sorry, buddy. My stomach made me do it." Both of them laughed.

The guard did not see the humor.

"Nickolas Caputo, philosophy major." He held up his student I.D., then looked at Carlos. "Sorry I'm late, bro." Carlos waved him off indicating that it was not big deal. Nick returned his attention to the security guard.

"So, are we good here, officer?"
"Just so long as you accompany him and there's no loitering."

The guard shook his head and walked off toward the library. Carlos offered his hand in gratitude, "Thanks, Nick. That was awesome!" They bumped fists and laughed. Nick said, "Man, you should have seen your face when you mentioned about meeting for lunch, and those freaking wrappers sitting right next to the pseudo cop's foot." Carlos nodded, "That was wild. I owe you lunch for real. How about tomorrow? Right now I'm late. I gotta run." Nick said, "Sure. Catch you tomorrow. I guess, here?" Carlos stated walking away, "By the food trucks; you can pick." They waved, both said at the same time, "Later."

Nickolas Caputo made a new friend. He didn't have many. Growing up on eastern Long Island, his parents, both business professionals, always put work before family. Their lack of family values left its mark on little Nick. He was raised by daycare in the early years and by nannies until ninth grade. His father traveled often and his mom always had meetings to attend. They alienated themselves from him and eventually from each other. By his thirteen birthday, they had divorced. His nanny cared more for him than his parents. Even before his parents' separation, he understood that both of them lead separate lives and had been involved in extramarital affairs. At that time, Nick started to act out. When being the class clown wore itself out, he took to bullying. He was never physical but his verbal abuse of many of his classmates eventually isolated him from the masses.

As Nickolas matured and realized his actions caused his loneliness, he tried to turn things around; but that too had consequences. Being on his own taught him to be strong-willed and assertive. He used that to impress young ladies. It worked for a while and caused some animosity among the other male students. Eventually, by his senior year in high school, he was alone again. Word of his arrogance spread, and students stayed clear of Nick.

When he started at Brooklyn College, he had the opportunity to start fresh. The problem, he found, was that he didn't know how to be a normal friendly student. He couldn't meet someone without making the conversation about him. Even worse, his compulsion to embellish his stories were so transparent. Often, he felt embarrassment after saying something that apparently could not be entirely true. Eventually, Nick became reclusive. It was safer and allowed him to have some peace with himself. But, he was lonely.

Today, he met this cool guy, Carlos. Admittedly, cooler than himself. He would try to be reserved and perhaps, he might have a friend. Nickolas Caputo needed to get through this day. Something changed for him, something he missed for so long. *He looked forward to tomorrow.*

Chapter 9

Time can be measured in many ways. The ticking of the clock on the wall or counting to one's self – one Mississippi, two Mississippi, three Mississippi. The position of the sun, and the shadows it cast, presents a good idea of the time of day. After all, the sundial represents one of man's earliest time pieces. Carlos sat in his chair in his office and tapped his foot while staring at nothing in particular. Twenty-five, twenty-six, twenty-seven. He had no idea why he was counting seconds. The boredom he felt, a rare event for him, made the afternoon move along slowly. The knock on his partially closed office door snapped him out of the trance-like mood he was in that afternoon. His foot stopped tapping and his lips paused from his murmured counting. As the door opened and his administrative assistant marched in, Carlos glanced at the modern *sundial* on the wall. Only 3PM, no meetings, no reports for the board of directors due; what could she want? *Oh, no, ME! He envisioned her closing the door, walking over toward him while unbuttoning her blouse. Her perfume, the same brand high school girls wore, aroused his senses.* "I have a date." She barely had one foot in the door as she blurted out her news. Carlos stood there trying hard to think of a cool reply. He had nothing. She walked up to him, her face close to his. He thought she was going to touch his lips with hers. "Bob, from accounting." In his mind's eye, he saw Elaine Benes flaunting this ridiculous information in Jerry Seinfeld's face. "What?" Ginger realized his attention was not focused on her words. "Bob from accounting asked me out. And, not back to his apartment; a real date." Carlos touched her arm gently, "Come on, it's – not like that." She pushed his hand away; her eyes were on fire. "Sure it wasn't; not for you. I'm tired of losers interested only in this." She pointed toward her legs. "And, not this or this." She redirected her pointing from her head and then to her heart. Whatever her intended point was, if it was to riddle him with guilt – it worked. "Bob is a nice guy, seems a tad on the quiet side. I'm sure you will have a very nice time." She looked at him with a pout that showed her disappointment in him. He continued despite his inner self, warning him to quit while he was only a little behind. "You and I, we are too much alike. I care about you; we are friends. I hope that won't change." Ginger had a tear forming, making Carlos feel even more uncomfortable. "You know what, Carlos? It did change; for me it changed." She wiped the tear with her sleeve. "You know what? Never mind!" As she turned and walked out of Carlos' office, her heart ached. She half expected him to stop her and pull her back into his office. She envisioned his arms around her, and him telling her that he loved her. Carlos watched her leave, he fought the urge to stop her. He wasn't prepared to commit to a serious relationship. As she disappeared down the hall, he admitted to himself that *if* he was ready, she would be the one.

Carlos geared up for his trek home. He kicked off his fancy loafers, stuffing them into his backpack, where they replaced his sneakers. He usually took off his tie and opened his top shirt button. Ginger would often bring him his first cup of morning coffee and make a comment about his lame ability to dress himself. She would straighten his tie and correct his collar. He figured she might not continue that practice. That simple intimate moment they shared most mornings, he would miss. With his backpack slung over his shoulder he headed down the corridor to the side exit. To his relief, Ginger must have already left. The sales reception area was deserted.

The sky had clouded up since the afternoon and it looked as if it might rain. Carlos crossed the busy street that lead to his bus stop and waited. His stomach started an internal racket that he hoped the others waiting with him would not notice. He would need to think about what he wanted to eat when he got home.

Chapter 10

The bus ride to McCarren Park took about twenty-five minutes; a little longer than usual. The afternoon traffic seemed to snarl at every corner. Carlos didn't mind the ride; he appreciated the downtime to unwind from his day. With his hoodie over his head and his dark sunglasses covering his eyes, he let his eyelids close for a few moments. His mind rebooting, clearing out the stress and guilt over the Ginger situation. He envisioned her long silky red hair floating across his chest as they lay in his bed. His hands were clasped above his head and her mounted on top of him. Then he saw her with that guy from accounting. *What was his name? Bob, that's it.* For a moment he considered that he might be a tad jealous. *Idiot, this is the perfect situation; you wanted to prevent any attachments.* He found the bus noises, the engine and exhaust, mesmerizing. Sometimes he envisioned a giant person with an undefined face taking deep breaths and exhaling with an asthmatic sound. Then, a squeal of the brakes as it made its stops. A pitter-patter chimed in against the window his head rested against. It had started raining. "Great." He mumbled to himself without opening his eyes.

The next set of squealing brakes and huff of an asthmatic exhale signaled the arrival at his destination. Carlos didn't need to count stops or look around at the street surroundings. It was an eerie sense that woke him. He never missed his bus stop.

Unlike the morning and most other days, the park was mostly absent of people and animals except for the few indigents seeking shelter from the inclement weather. His stomach growled, and he felt a twang of discomfort. Carlos' hunger got him started on thinking about dinner. "No Chicken Delight, I'm cookin' tonight." He laughed to himself; at his little rhyme.

The streetlights came on early due to the balmy, gray weather. A light mist rose off the parking lot asphalt. Carlos grabbed a shopping cart, and made his way into the Key Food entrance. His hand vibrated as the front right wheel of his cart started to wobble. *This is so annoying; they need a cart mechanic to keep these things in working order. That's an idea. A new revenue stream for Aerotech. We can create quick repair kits for shopping carts.* He started in the produce section, wobbling cart leading the way. With a slight, right-handed lean on the cart handle, the cart managed to steer straight. Carlos was good at manipulating things, even this thing. He made his way down the produce aisle picking up various salad items. *"Hmm, zucchinis, nice and fresh. Some veggie pasta sautéed in garlic and oil."* If anyone paid attention to Carlos as he shopped, they'd notice he talked to himself as he strolled down the aisles. Shopping, like the bus ride, served several purposes. It was downtime for him. His mind remained clear of business, women, loneliness, and boredom. Reading labels and comparing prices of brands made him a challenge for any woman, should a related topic come up in a conversation. He made his way past the breads and other high carb items, stopping at the fish counter. His buddy was working tonight. Most people he barely knew, who were actually nothing more than acquaintances, he considered friends. It was how his personality made him, that charismatic guy. "Hey, Joe. How's it going?" Joe, the fish guy, nodded, "Great, my friend. What can I get you?" Carlos pointed to a nice pre-cut salmon steak. "Wise choice. Got it in fresh this morning. What else?" Carlos took the wrapped piece of salmon from his *buddy*, "That'll do it. Thanks, Joe."

The salmon was delicious. Sided by a delicate portion of zucchini, spaghetti style, and a nice Caesar salad, his dinner presentation was worthy of an Instagram upload. He cooked his fish on a little propane fueled hibachi he kept on his fire escape. If one were to evaluate

Carlos Martinez's diet, they might be a bit confused. His lunch cuisine lacked in the fine dining arena along with any concept of healthy eating. But, his breakfast and dinner choices would make Dr. Atkins very proud. Amazingly, none of his neighbors complained about the grill or the pungent aroma of his cooking. After all, why would anyone make a fuss? They were his *friends*.

Chapter 11

His eyes remained closed as he took in the tropical sun's warmth. He had left New York and all the stress of his day job and night school behind for the soft sandy beaches and tranquil waters of the Bahamas. He was one of only a few African American employees in the company. Recently, he received a promotion making him the only one of his kind headed for a management career.

His peers, the ones who shared a minority status within the company, made subtle annoying remarks. They said things about his light skin color and his electric green eyes. Some of the things they said were downright cruel. He overheard them one time, call him "The token one." Even his friend and lunch buddy made comments, asking him if he wished he was born different. In truth, he did, but it had nothing to do with his skin color. He was proud of who he was. "I bet your cute girlfriend is proud of you. How about her family?" He tried to ignore their remarks. After all, he worked hard and earned his position. His stress levels hit an all-time high. He had to get away.

Emely lay beside him; he imagined her reading. No, perhaps lying face down with her mostly exposed backside tanning a deep bronze. His mind did a short rewind – She was in a seated position, her beautiful back to him. *"Would you mind?" Her hand offering him a tube of silky oil while her other hand, her long fingers, flicked the hook of her bathing suit top, releasing it. It floated in slow motion to the sand below. She slowly laid face down on the blanket. The oil glistened brightly, reflecting the tropical sun, making him squint. He felt her smooth, sensual skin as his fingers slid across her back, then down her legs. He heard her soft voice her tell him, "I want to be golden brown and beautiful, like you."*

She deserved this vacation after a long year of caring for him. The bi-weekly visits to the hospital and aftercare, while he suffered terrible pain and other side effects, took a toll on her. The doctors had been optimistic that his remission would last. They both needed this vacation to mend a broken link between the one time lovers turned patient and caregiver. Derek loved her unconditionally, and he knew she loved him back. At some point during the year Emely became more of the caregiver than the lover. He understood this and desperately wanted to renew the intimacy they shared before his illness took over their lives.

That first evening, at dinner in the hotel restaurant, Derek noticed Emely had become distracted.

They were discussing perhaps taking a scuba lesson and then going on a beginners dive. The hotel brochure they looked at showed pictures of the boat and people in their scuba gear in the water. "They look like they're having a fantastic time." Derek pointed to the picture of the people in the water. "What do you think, Emm?" Emely did not immediately respond to his enthusiasm. He tried to figure out what distracted her. Then he understood. Emely's attention became focused on a group of people at the next table. There must have been ten or twelve in the group, definitely not all couples. She seemed interested in one particular young man; definitely a surfer dude. The guy was built, dark hair and tall. Derek's stomach turned inside out. He became lightheaded. After all, he had been so ill and lost his hair and almost thirty percent of his body weight. *How could she still be attracted to him?*

"I'm sorry, sweetie. What were you saying? We could do that; it does look like fun. Are you sure you are up to it?"

They finished dinner and took a walk on the beach. Emely took his hand in hers as they dragged their feet in the still sun-warmed sand. He heard her say "I love you," but he did not feel it in her voice. Back in the room, naked in bed, she made love to him as she did so many times during the past year. He had been too weak at times to be the dominant lover, but worked hard to keep her satisfied. She did most of the work in the sexual part of their relationship during that period. Before he got sick, they had an intense and passionate sexual relationship. Outside, the palm trees swaying in the sultry breeze created moving shadows across the room's walls and ceiling. It should have been the most romantic time for both of them; but at that moment, he realized this was nothing more than a "Pity Fuck."

"Stop."

"What? Why? Are you Ok, did I hurt you?"

"No! You didn't hurt me. I'm not fragile. Not anymore!"

Her lips came down upon his; so soft and gentle. Her breath, warm and sweet. She whispered, "I love you." Derek looked into her gorgeous blue eyes, her eyes as blue as the tropical waters they swam in earlier that day. Her beautiful body faded from his mind. His heart pounded, heavy with sadness.

A beeping sound suddenly interrupted his reverie, bringing him back to reality.

"OK, Derek. You're all set." Derek opened his eyes, Emely's soft lips and brilliant blue eyes fading away abruptly along with the Bohemian tranquility. The smell of alcohol filled his nose, death seemed to be lingering all around him. The clinical technician smiled as she disconnected the IV line from the port that was permanently inserted into his chest. "See you on Wednesday; same time." He imagined the tech thinking, *"And, where's that pretty young lady of yours?"*

He and Emely had made it through that sham of a vacation week; both playing a role neither found comfortable. A few days after their return to NY, Emely confronted Derek with what he already knew. She was leaving him. They needed space; time to heal from all the stress. She swore there was no one else. He was sure that was true, but understood that there was someone else out there for her, and she needed her freedom to find him.

Besides, the return of his cancer shortly after their breakup left him even more depressed. He had no room for loving anyone. The pain and discomfort from his very aggressive treatments made life unbearable. His mind was cluttered with random thoughts of suicide. After tormenting himself for weeks, he decided that he'd had enough. With continued treatments, his stage three cancer would simply be prolonged. He would never have a pain free day again. There had to be a better way. Suicide is for cowards. The insurance company had all but stopped contributing its minimal support. His family was tapped out and could no longer help. A decision needed to be made.

Living life with dignity and enjoying it made more sense to him. He knew his family would object. Emely, had she stayed around, would tell him to never give up the fight. They all would have meant well but they could never understand what he was really going through. So many hours over the past year and then some, Derek and his fellow cancer patients would talk. In truth, they would argue "Why fight a losing battle and suffer all the way to the end?"

This treatment would be his last. Derek smiled to himself feeling a moment of peace and happiness. It's all going to be alright. Without the burden of added medical costs, Derek could afford to quit his day job and switch from night to day classes. He would finish school at the end of this year and get his degree. He should make it OK, at least until then, and hopefully have time to enjoy one last summer.

Chapter 12

When a person is raised in a small town or suburb of a city, privacy is something they know little about. The smallest, most personal details of their lives are shared with friends, neighbors, and even those whose names they may not know, but who's faces they recognize. Sometimes tensions can run high. We see brawls break out in bars and protests in schools. Looking at the glass as half full, people can care about others. They can be there for them in times of need. For example; last year, the Mid-Atlantic States were hit with a plethora of violent storms. One town in particular, in Missouri, was all but destroyed. Neighbor helped neighbor. Countless people from adjoining towns, and many from states thousands of miles away, made their way through the devastation to help rebuild – one home, one business after another.

In the big cities, it seems that people are always running to or from somewhere. Most are void of emotion, with little concern for their fellow street dwellers. Take "Mister Corporate VP" of some business, for instance. He worked hard to get to his high-stakes position. He wakes up every day with a smile. He looks at his beautiful and intelligent wife as she sleeps soundly. He has provided his family with so many wonderful adventures and things they needed and wanted. *Sounds pretty good, doesn't it?* Unfortunately, his brethren, those who have achieved similar status of some varied role in society, are not all smiling. They have all the sweet things and the prestige they worked so hard for during their adult lives. They also have an abundance of stress. For them, every day is a challenge. Yet, in the melting pot of the big city, somehow the societal classes complement each other, allowing for an even keeled community.

****

Carlos often though about his position in society. He had every opportunity to fit the big city tycoon profile. After all, growing up in Queens and hanging out in Manhattan afforded him "street smarts." His father's business, at which he is gainfully employed, is remarkably successful. Carlos, and the sales team he manages, are a major revenue producer for the company. When his father retires, he could potentially take his seat on the board of directors. *He* should be that guy who smiles every day.

The identity crisis that Carlos is going through leaves him pondering his future on a daily basis. He likes knowing that financially he is set. However, he also has a problem with high society. He does not want to be that suited up guy. That stiff who has an air about him that says, "I'm better than you and loving it."

Reality is no stranger to Carlos. In order for him to be a part of "Changing the world," money is needed. He would always make sure to stay grounded. Change takes time, and time is something he has plenty of.

Yet, with all the positives and his self-understanding of the direction he wanted to go, something was missing. At times he felt alone. Some piece of life's puzzle was missing. His coworkers respected him. He had many friends; well, perhaps close acquaintances. Dating for Carlos was steady, but each relationship seemed to be short-lived. He could not get past the wall of commitment. He pondered this from time to time. His parents had a wonderful relationship when he was younger. They seemed happy together. As a family they spent weekends at parks and ball games. His mom, a Bronx native, was a Yankee fan. This, he remembered, irritated his Queens born dad, who was a diehard Mets fan. It was fun, though, watching them jokingly rib each other when their team won. They might have been the perfect family if his dad, out of the blue, hadn't announced he was leaving his mom for another woman. Carlos, at ten years old, was devastated. His loving family, his perfect world, imploded upon him. His Dad was "*That Guy.*"

Shortly after his parents separated, Carlos' mom discovered she had stage four cancer. Aside from a few periods of tiredness and fatigue, she had no indications of anything being seriously wrong with her. His dad almost had an emotional breakdown. Carlos realized that his dad still loved his mom. His dad started helping take care of his mom as soon as they found out about her devastating illness. Soon after, he moved back into the family home to help take care of her. He broke off his relationship with the *other* woman and for the next few months they were a family again.

Carlos often wondered if his dad leaving and his mom getting sick were interrelated. For a while he blamed his dad for screwing up their lives. Later, he realized that one had nothing to do with the other. His mom left this world loved, and in peace.

Although he often considered his loneliness as his destiny, he hoped that someday he would find true love that would enable him to commit. Deep down he wanted to have a loving family of his own. He would need to get past the fear of losing someone he deeply loved and needed.

Carlos decided to get away for a while; a change from his daily routine. He was ready for an adventure. In his mind, like switching channels, he searched potential channels. Costa Rica; he could surf and explore the jungles. Africa; safari would be really cool. Perhaps the Australian Outback. He would think more about his choices tomorrow.

Maybe he could discuss it with Ginger. She always had good ideas. She was definitely adventurous.

Maybe she still wasn't talking to him.

Chapter 13

Sitting on the far side of the great campus lawn, the fortunate ones, students and faculty alike, could hear the melodies of the great, late Jim Croce. The petite blond, who many have told her, "You look so much like Hayden Panattiere," stroked her Martin acoustic guitar in perfect rhythm with her voice. Her long slender fingers moved up and down the neck of the instrument. She occasionally took a break to whisk a strand of her silky hair from in front of her eyes. Those who walked by, getting a closer view of the female artist, actually picked up on her mood as she sung the lyrics to "Time in a bottle."

If I could save time in a bottle
The first thing that I'd like to do
Is to save every day
'Til eternity passes away
Just to spend them with you

Those with a closer view would also notice the tears slowly making their way down her cheek. They would probably think she was getting deeply emotional within her singing, as any true artist should. What they did not know was that the song flowing from her lips had a personal meaning for her.

Monica's parents, John and Melony Woods, both died on September 11th 2001. They were in the first of the World Trade Center towers to fall. John Woods worked for a prestigious investment banking firm. His wife, Melony decided to ride into the city with her husband, planning for a morning of shopping on Fifth Avenue in Midtown New York City. Later, their plan was to meet for lunch at the renowned Windows on the World restaurant, located on the roof top of her husband's North Tower building. She loved the magnificent view from 107 floors above street level. Had she not rode up to her husband's office on the 103rd floor with him that morning for a cup of coffee, Monica would still have her mom.

If I had a box just for wishes
And dreams that had never come true
The box would be empty
Except for the memory
Of how they were answered by you

Monica's maternal grandparents took their beautiful six-year-old granddaughter in, to live with them. They resided in the Nassau County village of Massapequa;

a nice, middle income residential suburb of Long Island. Fortunately, her dad had a substantial life insurance policy which the grandparents used when needed for Monica's schooling and other needs. She made it clear she wanted to go to public schools. Private schools were stuffy and what she termed as totalitarian. The once popular city girl became mostly introverted. Her guitar became her best friend. She found playing sad music was like having a friend that understood her. Both her mom and dad had soothing voices and sang like seasoned artists; neither played an instrument. The songs they sang to her in her early childhood, at bedtime, and when she was upset over something, remained forever in her memory and in her heart. The guitar was a present from her grandpa on her fourteenth birthday. She picked it up for the first time while Jim Croce sang "I'll have to say I love you, in a song." She started strumming chords while singing along to the music. Her playing just evolved naturally.

Monica could afford any school, but wanted to stay close to her grandparents. She decided to apply to Brooklyn College's music program. Her plan was to get a music degree and teach music. She wanted to spread the healing potential that music had for her, to others.

Her grandparents were not happy when she told them she answered a "Roommate Wanted" ad for an apartment in Greenpoint, New York. She wanted to live off campus. The three-bedroom apartment, not far from Manhattan Avenue, became available just one day prior, and would probably been gone that same day, had she not jumped at the opportunity.

The other two girls Monica shared the apartment with were friends for several years before taking the Greenpoint apartment. The two of them did everything together, and tried to include Monica on several occasions. If she happened to say "Yes," she always backed out at the last minute by making an excuse of studying or not feeling well. After a while, and what they perceived as Monica's lack of enthusiasm to join them, they stopped asking. Monica fell into states of mild depression fairly often and preferred to keep to herself. In the beginning, her roommates enjoyed her music. But, after a while, it became depressing to them and their comments caused friction between Monica and them. That's when she started hanging out more on campus, where no one bothered her or cared if she played the music that soothed her soul.

The warmth of the early spring sun relaxed her. She put her guitar down as she lay down on the campus lawn with her eyes closed. *Maybe I'll try out for the TV show "The Voice" someday.* It was just a thought in the back of her mind. *Besides, that Adam Levine is so cute.*

Chapter 14

Carlos looked at the time on his Android phone. "Shit, 11:45." His morning was busier than usual. He had a meeting with the director of logistics to discuss inventory needs and warehousing. The director needed to update his rolling forecast for the next three months so the Finance team could plan out the next quarterly budget. Several of the administrative assistants called in sick this morning, including his; Ginger. Carlos didn't notice anything wrong with her yesterday. She did mention her date with Bob, the nerd from Accounting. His mind once again drifted back to Ginger. He envisioned her long, slender, perfectly naked body stretched out on his bed. She had no inhibitions regarding sex. She apparently enjoyed sex, and more so, enjoyed it with him. Carlos didn't really know Bob very well. He only met him a few times at company meetings. But, this guy definitely didn't strike Carlos as, *her* type. Maybe he spent the night at her place. Perhaps she called in sick to spend the day in bed; *with him*.

The switchboard was busy; it took three tries before someone answered. Carlos told the person filling in for the regular operator that he would be back around 2PM should anyone be looking for him.

The campus food trucks were busy as expected for the 12PM to 2PM lunch rush. Carlos looked around for his new friend, Nick. His stomach urged him to have a little appetizer. *"Damn, dude. You're grumbling like you smoked a FATTY spliff."* Carlos realized he was talking to himself, out loud. Or, worse; talking to his stomach like it was a live entity. Fortunately, no one heard him, or paid any attention to what he was saying, to himself.

"Dude. You're here. I kind of figured you might hang me up or something. But, here you are." He gently fist bumped Carlos. Carlos said, "That's not who I am, my friend. Are you hungry?"

They agreed on the truck labeled "Chuck Wagon", "Chuck's Best Steak Sandwiches." Carlos ordered the Philly Steak Supreme with a side of fries and vinegar. "I'll have what he's having. Damn, that looks delicious!" Nick made a somewhat goofy face and licked his lips. Carlos paid and they headed inland to Carlos' regular spot. "The tree is mine, the rest of the lawn is up for grabs." Carlos laughed; but, he was serious. He felt more comfortable with something solid behind him. Nick nodded his acceptance of his friend's declaration and sat down across from Carlos.

The day started out sunny, but clouds were moving in and the air took on a coolness not so uncommon for early spring. As they ate their meal, the mellow tunes of Don McLean's "American Pie" could be heard in the distance. Nick said, "So, no hassle from that security guy?" Carlos shrugged his shoulders, "I guess he found something better to do." Nick made a perverse hand gesture; they both laughed. "I hear that guitar playing all the time. Whoever she is; she's really good. Hang tight, I'm going to check it out. I'll be right back."

Carlos wiped his mouth with one of the tiny napkins that came with his sandwich, then reached into his backpack for a piece of gum. Nick watched him start to chew and said, "Work that gum buddy. Stinky breath from the onions?" Carlos waved him off; "Back in a flash."

The glare from the bright sun overpowered the polarizing feature of his Ray-Bans, briefly blinding Carlos' view. He closed his eyes for a few seconds and continued walking in the direction of the music. It seemed as though he only took a few steps, but it must have been more.

Carlos opened his eyes, his music source sat there, not ten feet from him. The music had just stopped.

"Hey there. That was really nice. Why'd you stop?" The petite blond, her hair in a side ponytail looked up at him; a forced smile on her face. "Thanks." She shrugged her shoulders, "I played the last verse, and the song was finished?" Carlos, in a rare moment for him, showed his awkwardness. "I hang out on campus most nice days and eat my lunch. Your music relaxes me. You're really good."

"Are you a student here?"
"No, I live close and work even closer. The campus lawn is a cool place to hang. I like watching people." *I hope that didn't sound creepy.* "Besides, I'm addicted to the food truck cuisine."
"Wow, I guess you have an iron stomach. I have to admit; I've sampled a few selections, and it's pretty good."

Carlos said, "You're always alone. My friend Nick and I are over there." Carlos pointed to where Nick sat, Buddha style. From where he and Monica were, Nick looked like a dashboard statue except his head did not appear to be bobbing at the moment. "We would be honored if you joined us." Monica smiled again, "Thanks. That's a really nice gesture. I'm usually into hanging alone when I play. It's my escape for a while that gets me through the rest of the day." The edge of her pony tail hung just a bit over her shoulder. Her dazzling green eyes sparkled in the sunlight. Carlos immediately took a liking to her. Not a sexual attraction, *which was weird for him*; a warm, I could be her friend feeling. "That's cool. If you change your mind, any time." Carlos pointed again toward Nick who now appeared to have taken Carlos's spot against the tree and was facing them.

"So, I'm guessing you found your musician, and she blew you off? Looks like I should have taken on the quest myself." Carlos looked at Nick. "Are you aware how conceited that sounds?" Carlos sat down facing Nick. "That's my spot." Nick looked back at Carlos, not smiling. "I'm just saying… Besides, she's a loner; but adorable. Kind of looks like that actress, you know, from the show 'Heroes' and that country TV show, 'Nashville'." Nick was looking over Carlos' shoulder and smiling. "What?" Carlos turned his head to find Monica standing behind him. Her guitar slung over her shoulder and her hand holding one of the straps of her backpack, which was now resting on the ground. "You really think I look like her? Thanks. I Guess."

"Monica." She extended her hand to Nick. "Nick. And this is my friend Carlos, in case he didn't properly introduce himself earlier." Monica smiled sincerely. "Thanks, Carlos; for inviting me. I hope you can forgive my rudeness. It is kind of lame hanging out alone every day. I'm not much for big groups." Carlos said, "I get it, sometimes I like my privacy. I come here to campus for the same thing. That is, until the other day when I met my boy, Nick, here. I didn't realize having people around can be a good thing. We've got a few minutes. Would you do us the honor of a song?"

Monica sat down with her legs crossed lotus style, and started strumming chords to a familiar song. She laughed, "You might be late getting back to work." She looked at Nick, "Or class. This is a long one." She began;

"A long, long time ago
I can still remember how
That music used to make me smile
And I knew if I had my chance
That I could make those people dance
And maybe they'd be happy for a while"

Her singing was enchanting. Carlos and Nick joined in for the sing-along parts.

81

"Bye, bye, Miss American Pie
Drove my Chevy to the levee but the levee was dry
And them good ole boys were drinking whisky and rye
Singin' this'll be the day that I die
This'll be the day that I die"

Don McLean would be honored.

People from around the great campus lawn were drawn to the newly formed group sitting under the old oak tree. Across the lawn to the east, sitting under her own massive oak, Randy Meyers' attention was now focused on the singing. She too, liked this song and sang along to herself. She wanted to join them, but her shyness overpowered her desire.

Change was in the air on this day, on this college campus. Confidence, friendship and adventure would come to those who longed for it.

Chapter 15

She lay in bed with her eyes wide open, staring at the pure white stucco ceiling. She could feel the heat of his body next to hers. Yet, a subtle loneliness loomed over her. After their date the evening before, she invited Bob into her apartment for a "night cap." They had enjoyed a romantic Italian meal at Vinny's in Carroll Gardens, Brooklyn. Bob proved to be the perfect gentleman. She sat and listened to his life story and then some, as they dined on Zuppa Di Mussels and Chicken Fettuccine Alfredo. The Alfredo with Chicken wasn't on the menu but the chef graciously accommodated Ginger's request. They drank a second bottle of red wine after dinner while getting to know each other better. As they left the restaurant, Bob asked her if she would like to take a walk. Ginger politely asked if he would mind taking her home as she needed to be up early for work. He agreed, as he had to do the same.

Bob walked Ginger up the one flight to her apartment door; *such a gentleman*. Out of politeness, she asked Bob if he would like to come in for a drink. She didn't expect him to accept. They talked for a little and one drink led to two. Combined with the earlier fruits of the vine and her need to self-fulfill, they ended up in bed together. She had to initiate, but not with too much effort. The sex was OK enough. But as they lay in bed afterwards, his hand holding hers, Bob said things like, "You were incredible. I think I'm falling in love." She waited for "Was it good for you?" or something like that. She wanted to vomit. Fortunately, the alcohol and sex wore them both out and sleep came quickly.

As Ginger lay in bed, the morning light casting shadows across her bedroom, she cursed herself for this situation. Her heart pounded as she fought off what she feared was the start of a panic attack. She needed a "Plan B;" *How to get Bob out of here without hurting his feelings.*

She used her legitimate migraine as an excuse, telling Bob she had a hangover. After a cup of coffee, Bob went on his way. Ginger called work to say she didn't feel well and would be taking a sick day. In truth, she actually allowed all this to happen out of anger with Carlos. Now the guilt overwhelmed her. She didn't want to see him this morning. *Why the hell do I feel guilty? He brushed me off.*

Ginger sat alone at her breakfast nook with a cold half drank cup of coffee in front of her. She looked at the empty mug Bob had left across the table from her. *I must be out of my mind. We have nothing in common. Even the sex was so... married-like.* She began to sing to herself the musical group Bush's "Loneliness is a Killer." Sadness engulfed her. *I don't see Bob getting into this music. He probably likes Christine Aguilera.*

It was the fall of 2007; Ginger's high school volley ball team had just won the state finals. The girls were ecstatic over the well-earned glory. They hugged and kissed each other in celebration as their parents cheered on. Her parents, recently divorced, were nowhere to be seen. They both promised they would be there showing their support for her, and her team. Ginger's dad traveled a lot for business. She was used to disappointment from him. Her mom had never held a full time job until the separation. She discovered a whole new world out there that seemed to not include her daughter. At barely seventeen, Ginger was on her own. Amazingly, her view of family values never wavered. Before the divorce, she and her parents had a close bond. She had fond memories of family vacations and good times spent with her mom and dad. She wanted a family of her own. She vowed to do a better job than her parents did. Her husband would never have a reason to leave her. She wondered though, if perhaps she tried too hard, and it scared men off.

Ginger thought it was different with Carlos. They became work friends first. After a year of occasional lunches, or a movie here and there – *as friends,* she began needing more from their relationship. Then one night, while they were at a bar having drinks, Carlos, out of the blue, asked if she wanted to see his new apartment. Ginger, already in the moment, and eager for the next phase, allowed herself to be impulsive when she should have been apprehensive. Evidently Carlos didn't have the same feelings. She was sure he liked her, more than liked her. Just not enough to call it something other than a friendship. *With Benefits.*

When they had sex, that one time, it was the kind of passionate wild sex of strangers in the night that ended with sincere intimacy. After that night, Carlos, the coward, could not handle their *friendship* any longer. She paused in thought. She had it all wrong. It was her who could not handle their relationship, as a friendship. He was fine with keeping things as they were.

"Bastard!"

Maybe I'll quit. He'll miss me then; and it will be too late.

Chapter 16

His Facebook page listed two hundred and sixty friends. As he perused through the communications, he could not find anything that included him. In truth, only about fifteen of those friends qualified as true friends; actually, most of them where family. The other people, he met briefly and requested "Friend" acceptance. He looked out of his third floor apartment window onto a playground below. Little kids played as their moms or nannies looked on. His few friends from Bayside High School hung out at the local shopping center. He would sometimes join them, but never connected to the group like the rest of them did with each other. Daniel brought his attention back to his computer. He realized that he thrived on what others were doing. He lived through the adventures of others on Facebook.

Daniel's mom asked him almost every day if he made any new friends. Most of the time he told her to "Leave me alone." Sometimes he would lie and say "Yes, I met someone new in my computer class." But, most irritating was when his mom asked about girls. "I know lots of girls from my classes. I love you, mom, but you are nosy and I don't tell you about them. Give me some privacy – please."

In truth, Daniel liked one girl, Randy Myers, in particular but she showed little interest in him, other than polite conversation. He thought that perhaps she might be shy; like him. Someday maybe, he would get up the nerve to ask her out. But first, he had to talk to her.

He shut down his laptop and leaned back in his chair with his eyes closed. *Tomorrow is Monday. I'll see her then.*

Daniel's second class of the day, Computer Science, ended with no embarrassing remarks from the professor. He made eye contact with Randy several times while trying to be inconspicuous. Randy seemed to avoid his attempts for attention. He suddenly became uncomfortable, thinking others in the class were aware of his awkward attempts and failures. His backpack in hand, Daniel left the Math and Sciences building to head home. He usually followed the path from the side entrance of the building, crossed parking lot A and then caught the #2 train off of Bedford. Today, fate would have him cut across the lawn to the other side of campus where he could catch the bus.

Music floating in the air drew his attention; he stopped for a moment and looked around. A small group of people, three to be exact, sat under a large oak tree. He was no expert, but he thought they were singing a bit out of tune. It really didn't matter because it looked like they were having fun. The cute girl playing the guitar had a nice voice.

"Dude! She's awesome, isn't she?" Nick waved to Daniel to come closer. "We're forming a cult, look, there's Charles Manson. We call him Carlos for short." Nick laughed. Carlos, with his hoodie over his head, joined in, followed by Monica. Carlos pulled off his hoodie noticing Daniels expression of uncertainty. "Join us. He's just messing with you. We all only met in the past few days and are hanging out for the mid-day break." This type of invite, actually any invite, was unusual for Daniel, *the nerd*.

"Hey, um; Randy!" Nick stood up abruptly waving his hands. He started walking toward her. Randy stopped, not sure who called out her name. "It's Nickolas, from history class." Randy, dressed in a pleated skirt and pastel colored blouse, waved back to Nick, still not sure if she recognized him. Nick had not previously noticed how pretty she was; until now. "Hi, Randy. Why don't you come hang out with us?" Randy smiled through her embarrassment. "Oh, of course; Nick from history. Sorry, I didn't recognize you. You know; the sun glare?" She looked up to add to her cover story and squinted. "I usually like to sit quietly and eat my lunch. I'm not big into the group thing." Nick made a sad face and pointed to his friends, "If you change your mind."

Randy turned and walked a few steps to her usual resting place. Then, she turned back toward where Nick had caught up to her; he already started trudging off, back to his friends.

"Wait!" Nick turned around to see Randy heading his way, sort of skipping. He thought her stride looked very alluring. They walked back together to the newly formed group of friends. As they approached the group, Nick put his arm around Randy and announced, "Hey, everybody. This is Randy. Randy, this is everybody." As Nick pointed and made the formal introductions, Daniel shyly waved and said, "Hey, Randy."

Daniel was overjoyed to see Randy. She did smile back when he said hello. But, Nick had his arm around her. *What did that mean*? An unusual and uneasy feeling of jealousy came over him. He thought to himself, *you are such an idiot.*

Carlos asked Monica for one more song before they all went on their way to do whatever it is each of them did on a Monday afternoon. Randy felt elated. This was new for her and it came so easy. She always found an excuse to not make the effort to mingle. Today, the mingling came to her. She looked at Nick and smiled. "Thanks for inviting me. This is awesome."

My mom will be so overjoyed.

Chapter 17

The Aerotech sales and marketing offices are located on the west side of the building. It is a quieter part of the company, situated away from the hustle and bustle of the warehouse goings on. Today seemed quieter than usual. It seemed somewhat unnatural. Carlos checked his messages and noted the time was 2:45PM. *Late again getting back from lunch*. Even though no one would call him on his tardiness, guilt shadowed him. *Seems there is plenty of that lately*. Ginger evidently did not come in to work today. Earlier, he wondered if perhaps she might just be taking a late morning. Now, he worried that she might not come back at all. Had he really pissed her off that much? He would miss her. He understood her anger; she felt like his mistress. Only, no other woman existed in his life. He wanted a best friend with benefits; she wanted a relationship. Carlos understood all this; he pondered why it bothered him so much. After all, no promises were made; no commitments. They flirted as friends for two years. They had drinks together after work on more than several occasions. That one night messed everything up.

He closed his eyes, thinking about that fateful night. The pub down the road from the factory closed at

1AM during the week. Ginger had stayed late that night to help Carlos assemble his sales forecast reports for the board meeting the next day. At around 7:30PM, Ginger announced her fatigue and need for food as she continued binding the booklets. Carlos suggested, "We're almost done. How about letting me buy you a drink to wind down the day and then something to eat?" Ginger accepted. She never told him no. Besides, he always treated her like a girlfriend when they went out. He always paid for everything and walked her home or accompanied her by taxi. He was a gentleman and a good friend; friends with everything, except the benefits.

The pub was busy and there was a short wait for one of the few tables. Carlos asked, "Want to sit at the bar? We can get food there quicker." He poked her belly gently, "Since you're really hungry." Ginger agreed and told him the bar is more fun and social anyway. They started with dirty martinis and consumed two before their burgers arrived. "Oh, my god. This is so good." Ginger looked as if heaven's doors had just opened. Two beers each with their burgers topped off the evening; both of them were mildly trashed.

Ginger's apartment was a good fifteen-minute walk, and the cool air gave Ginger a chill. Carlos put his arm around her and suggested that they take a taxi. She agreed, as it made sense, especially in their condition. In the taxi, Ginger leaned on Carlos' shoulder. "Are you ok?" he asked. "I'm fine. Really fine." Ginger kissed his cheek. "Thank you." Her hand sort of slumped downward and ended up on his thigh; he assumed, by accident. The city streets, laden with potholes made for a bumpy ride. Things were *accidently* set in motion, so he thought, until her hand made its way to the point of no return. From the moment they entered her building's outer door, their passion exploded. They made love all night and into the early morning. When Carlos awoke, sun glaring in his eyes from the curtain-free windows, she was laying there; eyes open and staring at him. She looked angelic. "Good morning, or afternoon?" She smiled, "Still morning." Carlos sat up looking around at her apartment. "So, this is where you live?" Carlos had escorted Ginger home many times but never accepted an offer to come in.

"Your place is a mess." Ginger leaned over to him and kissed his cheek. "That's mostly your fault." Carlos said, "Oh, indeed." He abruptly stood up while grabbing his pants that were by the side of the bed. "Shit. The sales meeting." Disappointment hit hard. Ginger expected, hoped, he would respond differently. She wanted more of what they had the evening before. Her body craved him to hold her; even if for just a moment before he left.

Carlos told Ginger to take her time and come into the office whenever she got up and ready. He would cover for her if anyone asked where she was. He kissed her cheek. She turned her face so their lips met. As hers brushed his, he pulled back slowly. His scent stayed with her as he turned away and left the apartment.

Her head ached from an intense hangover.

Ginger arrived an hour after Carlos with two coffees in hand and a bag of croissants. "I stopped at Starbucks. You left in such a hurry, I figured you might be hungry." Carlos thanked her and asked her to bring the sales reports into the meeting during the first fifteen-minute break scheduled for 10:30AM. He realized as she said "Sure, no problem" and immediately turned and left his office, that she was upset with him. Carlos understood he had made a big mistake letting things go as far as they did. The sexual tension between them in the past had always been kept under control. It kept their friendship exciting and safe for both of them. That one, incredible night, ruined their friendship. He knew that it was all on him. He is the older one. He is her friend. He is her boss. He knew he messed up.

Suddenly, the stress overwhelmed him. Carlos sat back in his comfortable chair and thought about getting away for a while. Maybe a week on the beach in Miami. His daydream took him to sandy white beaches lined with scantily clad young women. His mind's eye zoomed out to a picture of sardines in a can. Sporadically, one female would be in a sitting up position with a face he recognized, but could not identify. He knew people in just about every place one could imagine. *No, that's lame; I need adventure*; a road trip came to mind. *I think I will drive west as far as time will allow.* His mind changed to mountains and large open fields. Carlos envisioned the Grand Canyon with its unique rock formations and picturesque rivers. He let his mind wander back in time, adding a group of American Indians sitting around a fire, just outside of a cave. One of the tribesmen sat apart from the group. Through his imaginary character, Carlos looked around as he sat with his feet dangling off a ridge. He could feel the heat of the ancient fire behind him. A bald eagle glided a hundred feet in front of him in search of something; perhaps a meal. The prestigious bird's movements were smooth and mesmerizing. Carlos melded with his imaginary character. He now sat on the edge, looking out upon the world.

A road trip is what is needed here.

The meeting is where I need to be now.

Chapter 18

Large puffy clouds sailed across the darkening sky. The air took on a chill that made Randy shiver. Nick got up from his designated spot on the campus lawn and walked across the semi-circle of friends to where Randy sat. She wrapped her arms around herself. She appeared relentless in her effort to contain some body warmth. Nick sat next to her on her left and leaned into her. "The weather seems to be changing. Looks like we're going to get some rain." He started to remove his jacket, "Here, this will help." Randy smiled while clutching the zippered edge of his partially removed outer garment.

"No, really. I'm fine. Besides it's almost time for my next class."

"Are you sure?"

"Yes."

She squeezed Nick's arm gently with her other hand. Her smile was infectious. He found himself very much in-like with her.

Daniel could not help his feelings of jealousy. In his mind, he should be sitting next to Randy. His arm should be around her shoulders, and she should be wearing his jacket. *If he had one on to offer.* Daniel needed to man-up and tell her that he likes her. But now, in his mind, this Nick guy is making moves on her. *He is slick. His move on her, subtle. If I man-up there still might be a chance for me; with her.*

Carlos was deep in thought and not aware of the goings on of his friends. His mind had him traveling the "Main Street of America," the Historic Route 66, heading west across the old frontier.

Monica started to pack up her guitar. "You guys got to give me some suggestions for new music. Thanks to you all, since we started hanging out, I'm feeling more upbeat." Nick blurted out, "You-All? You-all want some new music? You all want to hang out and la-di-da?" His laugh that followed was obnoxious. Randy pushed his shoulder. She looked annoyed. "Cut it out; and be nice. Besides, I think it's pronounced 'y'all'." Carlos chimed in, "Yo, Nick. You all should apologize to the pretty lady who has basically brought us all together with her enchanting music."

"I was wondering." The group had all started gathering their belongings, some already standing up when Carlos caught their attention. "How cool would a road trip be over spring break?" Nick, being Nick, said, "Dude, spring break is for college students. You're the over-the-hill guy; so I think it's called a vacation." He pointed to Carlos, "Spring Break." Then he made a motion around the rest of the group with his hand; "Spring Break." Nicks poor attempt at humor caught Carlos off guard, and he didn't finish his thought. Daniel said to Nick, "Really?" And Randy told Nick he was rude. Monica walked over to Carlos, "So what's your idea for spring break. I might be interested." Daniel and Randy chimed in almost simultaneously, "Me too." Nick's face flushed a bit, "Sorry, bad manners. Let's hear it."

Carlos went on to tell them about his own melancholy and frustration. His description of a trip across the country sounded exciting. Monica thought he reminded her of Peter Pan. *And she, perhaps, could be Wendy.* She asked, "So where is this magic bus that will take us to all the magical places?" Caught off guard again, Carlos had not considered the logistics of the trip. In fact, he never anticipated the company of his new friends until just a few moments ago. "A Winnebago or something like that would work. It would be awesome." This time it was

Daniel poking holes in the fantasy. "You have an RV? Really?" Carlos shrugged his shoulders. "Well, not exactly. But, I know a guy who knows a guy. I can make it happen." Carlos took off his shades and looked at his friends with a pathetically hopeful expression. "Why don't you-all sleep on it and we can kick it around on Friday." He smiled at Monica and winked. *So, maybe I don't really know a guy, or anyone with an RV. That's a little thing, and I never sweat the little things.*

Chapter 19

Dr. Simon Maxwell DDS sighed silently as he quietly left the exam room. During the exam he said very little but made some suggestive grunts as he poked around Mary's mouth. He almost jumped out of his shoes when he gently pushed on the lower lateral incisor. He expected her to at least wince based on the swelling of the gum tissue surrounding it. Mary lay back waiting. The pain was bad, but she had gotten used to it. Her head started hurting, but she was sure it was due to the intense glare of the overhead exam light. *Dr. Maxwell could have turned it off, or at least pushed it away from her face.* The light was the last thing she should be concerned with, as her mind battled with agonizing thoughts. She realized he must have formed an opinion as to the cause of her dental issues. During the last visit to the office, she managed to convince him that she fell off her bike and hit a fence. The way he left the room today, she was sure he would make a fuss and cause more trouble for her. She considered getting up and running from the office. *Take a breath and calm down.* She reminded herself that she had to regain control before the dentist came back in. His footsteps echoed from the hallway as a panic attack creeped up on her. She reminded herself again, *OK Mary, take a breath and calm down*. A warm hand brushed her forehead. It felt warm and motherly. She turned her head slightly to her right. The young hygienist who had assisted the dentist smiled. "Do you want to talk about it?" Mary inhaled slowly through her nose. As a little girl she used to get mild anxiety attacks. Her mother always instructed her to "Inhale slowly through your nose. Now exhale slow and easy." It had always worked for her. Not so much at this moment. Mary shook her head left, then right, indicating her answer. She took a moment to reconsider her response, "There's nothing to talk about. I'm a klutz." The hygienist touched Mary's hand gently. "No one is buying that any more. Dr. Maxwell is going to call the police and file a report." The look of terror on Mary's face told the rest of the story. "I'm sorry, Mary. He is required to do so, by law. If something bad, something worse, happens to you, he would be in big trouble. You need to help yourself and get out of that poisonous relationship." Mary sat up squinting as she pushed the exam lamp out her way. "I have to go. Mail me the bill." The office was crowded and Mary bumped into several people as she wiped tears from her face and rushed out of the office.

The winds kicked up a bit in Stanton, Missouri. The early spring weather that fooled most with its warm breezes now sent a reminder that winter had barely moved on, and that spring had not yet fully arrived. Mary felt a chill across her mid-back as she drove toward her home. She thought about leaving the bastard. Throwing him out of the only home she had ever lived in would not go down easily. Her mom passed away last year, leaving her the little two-bedroom house and all the bills associated with it. She and Don had only been dating a short while before her mom's passing. In the beginning of their relationship, Don treated her like a princess. He was a year older and worked for a local automobile dealership as a mechanic. She was a senior in high school, with graduation only a few weeks away. He suggested moving in with her to help pay the bills and to take care of her. She really liked him and needed the help financially. Not losing the house to the bank was something she promised her mom in those last days. She planned on going to the local community college. She thought perhaps a degree in nursing would be a good career for her. Once Don moved in, he made it clear that she needed to contribute to their living expenses. She agreed and applied to night school. The application never got sent. Don found it and tore it up. "Don't you think you should be home in the evening? I'm not here just to help pay the bills." His entire demeanor changed overnight. Her mom told her, "You're so young to be on your own. You are beautiful and bright. Find a good man and live your life the way you want to." Don was supposed to be that *good* man. Life for Mary was a misery. Her mom promised to watch over her. She lost her faith in God, angels, and her mom. Her disappointment in them left her in a state of despair. She asked herself, "Why would they?" Those who should protect her, why would they let him treat her like he does? The blare of an oncoming car's horn brought her attention back to the road. "Shit. Damn it!" Mary swerved onto the left shoulder almost hitting the guardrail and then straightened out, regaining control of the car. She wanted to hit something so badly.

No; that is a Don move.

Chapter 20

Nick was already at the food truck called "Mr. Chow Chow." He took a bite of the oversized egg roll that he held with both hands. Grease oozed down the side of his mouth; his face said "Heaven." As Carlos approached, Nick waved, while wiping food from the corner of his mouth. Carlos laughed, "Dude, couldn't wait for me?" "Nah, sorry. I'm really hungry. Get something, I'll be over here. The super-sized egg roll is delicious."

The designated spot that amazingly, so far, had not been infiltrated by anyone else, had its first members already planted on the grass below the oak leaf laden branches. Monica had her guitar leaning against the trunk of the big oak; still in its case. Daniel had arrived a moment earlier. He was taking off his jacket when Carlos and Nick arrived.

"Happy Friday, Amigos."

Both Monica and Daniel returned the greeting.

"How was the rest of your week, Carlos? Any better since we last saw you?" Monica was very sweet; her concern seemed genuine. Carlos liked her. Her melancholy demeanor was in some ways comforting, relaxing. Despite her mood, she never brought the group down. Carlos chuckled, "Same. My co-worker is still angry with me. Work is mundane but OK..." Carlos felt the hairs on his neck prickle as he looked up from where Monica sat. "Holy...!" His instincts in control, Carlos dove over Monica, who fell backwards to avoid getting body slammed. He grabbed her guitar, and, like in a James Bond moment, went into a roll. Somehow, he managed to keep the guitar from hitting the ground or ending up underneath his body. His friends looked on in disbelief at what just went down with no comprehension as to why. The crash that followed enlightened them all. At first they saw a rogue bicycle bounce and twist as it hit the tree. Then they turned their heads in the direction it came from. About ten yards from them, a young man laid flat on his back moaning. A few feet behind him, a large brown backpack could be seen, torn open, with various items strewn across the lawn.

"Holy crap!"

Nick ran over to the young man. The others stood looking on while Monica jumped on top of Carlos and kissed his cheek. "You saved my baby! Are you OK?" Carlos looked up at her smiling face. Just inches from his. *Could his day get any better?*

"I've fallen and I can't get up." Monica, thinking his joke was directed at her said, "Oh. Sorry." Carlos grabbed her arms and held her in place. "I was kidding; just joking." Monica pushed down on him hard with her fists making his already sore shoulder hurt even more. He said, "Ouch." She got up and offered Carlos her hand for assistance.

Randy arrived as all the commotion settled down. "So, who is the spaz who nearly killed himself and almost annihilated Monica's love child?" Nick filled her and the others in on the details. "His name is Joshua. He didn't see the divot in the lawn over there." Daniel pointed. Carlos looked over at the newcomer and figured, what the hell, he appears to have the unique qualifications required to be a part of this group. "Hey, you OK? Come on over and sit down. Want some water?" Nick pulled out a package of beef Jerky and offered it around. He held it up toward Josh who politely shook his head. "No, thank you." Monica said to Nick, "That was lame. Were you brought up in a vacuum?" Nick felt silly but had no clue. "What?" Monica pointed to Joshua's head. "Yarmulke? He's Jewish." Josh smiled, "Actually, I'm Orthodox." She made a face to Nick that said *"Dummy."* Nick shrugged his shoulders, "I have Jewish friends; they eat this all the time." Monica shook her head, "Nick, he keeps Kosher." Nick wanted to ask how she knew this information but figured he had embarrassed himself enough for one day.

"All-righty. This has been an interesting start to our little group gathering. And look." Carlos pointed to Josh, then noted the bicycle by the side of the tree and shrugged his shoulders. "We made a new friend. Are you OK, buddy?" Joshua, still stunned from his fall said, "I think so, but my cousin's bike might not be." His subconscious told him otherwise. *You lose one, you break another.*

Shlimazel.

Carlos noted the disillusionment in Joshua's face. "I think the bike is fine and so are you."

"So, Josh, what are you doing for Spring Break?" Carlos ran his idea by the group.

"I always had a fascination for the history of the old Route 66. I thought we could follow that path and explore some historical places. I-78 will take us on the edge of Ohio and Illinois then we cut to I-70 leading onto I-44 and into

Stanton Missouri. That is a full day and a half of travel. We can use that time to get acclimated and better acquainted with each other; tight quarters and all." His entourage listened quietly. They seemed interested but not all that excited. Carlos became a bit unnerved. *What if they aren't interested? After all, this is my dream get-away, not theirs.* "We restock any needed supplies in Stanton and continue on. We can discuss what points of interest we want to stop at. Ideally, I would love to end up in LA. Time might prove difficult for that goal; New Mexico is more realistic. Monica chimed in. "We can play it by ear. If we are having a blast at a particular place, we could just stay there longer; if not, we move on. I'm in. My lucky guitar is ready as well." Monica looked at Carlos and smiled. Randy was frantically searching Google. "Looks like we can hit Tinker Town and the Cadillac Ranch. That would be cool. I'm in. But, it depends on how much this is going to cost us." Carlos stood. "I've got the RV covered. We can chip in for food, tolls and gas. I have to get back to work. Let's all do some research and firm things up; say, next Tuesday? What do you guys think?" Everyone agreed. Nick turned to Joshua. "Dude, I know you just met all of us, but it looks like you need this as much as we do. *Probably more.* Are you in?" Joshua looked at his mangled bicycle. "I think so. Yes." *Mama will freak.*

Carlos headed back to the office. As usual, his extended lunch ran later than expected. As he walked down the hall toward his office he heard his dad call his name. *Uh, Oh.* "Hi, Dad. What's up?" His dad motioned for him to come into his office and close the door. "How are things going, son? Your sales figures were on mark for this quarter. You should take your guys out on the town one night to show your appreciation." Carlos hated when his dad stated the obvious and didn't give him the benefit of taking care of business on his own. He made a face. *No shit Sherlock.* His dad got the message, "I'm just saying. Some appreciation; it goes a long way. And by the way, what is going on with," his dad hesitated as if he couldn't remember her name, "your assistant, Ginger?" Carlos was caught off guard. His dad was not blind, and had to have noticed the flirting over the last two years. "Nothing, Dad." "I warned you, Carlos, that getting too friendly would come back to bite you in the you know what." Carlos stood, "Everything is and will be, fine. By the way. I am on the road Monday. I am going to meet with, and hopefully close that new cargo supply company in New Jersey. If all goes well, it may be our largest account yet." His dad smiled, "The Board of Directors will be pleased." Carlos nodded, "I'm sure they will be. By the way, I'm planning to take off two weeks, next month. Actually the week after next. I'm planning to travel with some friends." Carlos Martinez Sr. stood up and put his hand out. "Great job, son. You deserve a break. Good luck tomorrow." Carlos wondered why his dad ignored his little tidbit of information about taking time off. *Was that a brush-off or maybe he simply wasn't interested.* "Make sure to send me your itinerary. There are some good deals for the Bahamas this time of year."

Ginger was on the phone, or made it appear as if she was in a conversation, as Carlos approached. He stopped for a second and waved to her, making a gesture to call him when she was free.

The phone was ringing as Carlos entered his office. He threw his backpack on one of his office chairs and answered his phone.

"Mr. Martinez? You needed something?"

"Formal today? OK. I need all the paperwork for my meeting on Monday in New Jersey. And, directions."

"I'm well aware of what is needed. I'll have it for you by the end of the day, all prepped as you requested. If that's all, I have a caller on hold."

"No; I also need you to find me a few choices for used RV's or rentals. Something late model, maybe 3-5 years old. Not a trailer. A fully drivable with room for like six or seven adults. Try not to break the bank. Thank you, Miss – Ginger." Carlos stumbled over his words and regretted trying to throw her attitude back at her.

"Will that be all males or mixed company? For the sleeping availability. Mixed will hike up the price."

"Mixed. Thank you."

"I'll see what I can find for you."

If she were Super Girl, her focused stare would have melted her phone equipment.

Ginger took a breath as her phone rang. Carlos knew she was even more upset now. Asking her to research the RV was cruel. It was him calling her back. "Yes, Mr. Martinez, how may I help you?" "I am going on a trip with friends; just friends. None are couples. Do you want to come in and talk? I think we should." Ginger told him she was too busy, with getting his requests taken care of. "Maybe later."

Chapter 21

This newly formed, unique group of friends, each had their own fantasy regarding their impending road trip. Each spent the next few days researching Carlos' suggestion for a historical excursion down the old Route 66 path. Monica had other fantasies; about Carlos, the savior of her beloved guitar. Randy wondered what Nick was like when he wasn't acting like a smart ass. Daniel wondered if he had any chance with Randy. Josh spent that evening after he met his new friends, arguing with his mom over going on a trip with people he only met that day.

Carlos stopped at the bar down the street from his home for a few beers. After winding down his day, inebriated, he made his way to his apartment. Carlos put on his headphones and played some music from the group Days of New. The track, "Shelf In The Room," was one of his favorites from the self-titled album.

"The shelf in the room has been told the truth I can't hide from the shelf in the room....."

As Carlos sang along, his mind drifted to the afternoon on the Brooklyn College campus. It was all coming together.

This trip would be epic. Monica appeared in his mind's eye. He recalled her move on him.; straddling his torso, and smiling down on him as she did earlier in the day, after he saved her guitar from certain death, by bicycle. Her sweet smile looking down on him. His vision turned sexual but faded away to something else. She wasn't teasing or seducing him. She was playful with him; as a friend. Girls as *friends* were not a normalcy for Carlos. His brain didn't work that way. He mumbled to himself, "Maybe this trip is my destiny". *Perhaps, a test from a higher power.* The realization just hit Carlos. *Ginger is my friend; we had fun. A no strings attached friendship. Yet, she considers our friendship a relationship. She can't just be friends with me.* Monica faded away and Ginger took her place in his reverie. His heart racing, Carlos flung the headphones off his head and sat up abruptly. *"Ginger is in love with me!"* His lips did not move, but it was loud and clear as if he actually said it.

Something to do; keep busy. Carlos knew this as the best way to push unsettling issues aside for a time. He picked up his phone and Googled "Route 66."

Aliased as "Main Street of America," Route 66 was one of the first highways to cut across the United States. Historically, the highway dates back to 1926. It became famous for the 1930's migration from the East Coast to the West Coast and spanned 2,448 miles from Chicago to California; with its endpoint in Santa Monica. Many of the depressed areas of the Mid-West prospered by opening supply stores and food establishments to service the travelers. In the 1980's, most of the original Route 66 roadway disappeared. Modern high-speed roadways replaced the historic pathway. Fortunately, towns from Illinois, Missouri, New Mexico and Arizona kept the nostalgic road on scenic maps. Movies and TV shows featured fictional and non-fictional events along Route 66. The sundry business boomed with souvenirs and apparel. Museums sprung up along the route, drawing tourists and adding to the economic growth of many rural areas along the route.

Each member of the group independently did their own research on cool places to stop along the way. Earlier during their campus gathering, Carlos expressed his interest for taking the southern route. Although spring started its decent on the East Coast, the Mid-West still had bouts of inclement weather.

Monica wanted a picture of her and her friends on the section of highway that had the embedded mirror imaged "Route 66" on it. To her disappointment, research found it somewhere around Amboy California. From her estimate, they would not have enough time to make it that far west. She would find another cool landmark to immortalize their trek. *The Cadillac Ranch in Amarillo would be cool.*

Joshua considered asking the group if they would be interested in visiting the Sherwin Miller Museum of Jewish Art in Tulsa. He figured it was about halfway into the trip and the group might find it interesting. The exhibit explored many areas of Jewish art forms. One major exhibit followed the historical path of the Jewish migration from Nazi Germany and also contained artifacts showing the horrendous persecution the refugees underwent. He thought about how the rest of them would react to his suggestion. Then he remembered Nick's unintentional religious ignorance. He thought to himself how he found old churches interesting. Maybe his new friends would find this tourist attraction interesting. It could be a cultural breakthrough and even perhaps, a bond of some sorts between all of them. Joshua laid back on his bed, staring at his ceiling. *Maybe not a great idea.*

Nick plotted each stopping point on a map and Googled bars and clubs. His first point of interest would be in Stanton Missouri. The 66 Sports Bar seemed cool and had good reviews. The burgers and parmesan fries sounded perfect for his group of travelers. He imagined all of them sitting around a campfire with the RV in the background. They had just returned from eating and drinking at the Sports Bar. A bottle of Jack being passed around seemed reasonable, and a joint too. His cousin would have liked to be in on this gig. He wondered if Carlos or any of the others would be cool if he brought a few bones with him.

The others all made notes for places of interest along the route west in preparation for the big discussion of what, where, and when. As they each perused the internet, their enthusiasm for the trip grew with each attraction they researched.

For most of these young people, acting out of their comfort zone was a big step. This decision to travel across America with people they hardly knew, was a bold and courageous milestone.

Chapter 22

Carlos awoke to a beautiful Tuesday morning. The sun streamed into his bedroom, suggesting a welcome warmth. Carlos' skin tingled from a slight chill in the room as he pulled the covers off and sat on the edge of his bed. He was tired but needed to go to his office early to get the ball rolling on the new account he recently landed. The previous day didn't go exactly as he had planned. His over confidence left him with his guard down and unprepared for the bullets his prospective clients shot at him. In the end, after intense negotiations, the deal was closed. Carlos had to offer hefty discounts, but in return, got not only the New Jersey business, but two other subsidiaries as well. The volume alone made up for the lower profit margin. His hoped his dad and the board would be pleased.

The Tuesday gathering came about quickly for Carlos' entourage. Amazingly, everyone seemed to have 1:30PM to at least 3PM free on Tuesdays. That is, except for Randy; she had an economics lab from 12PM until 2PM. She would be hungry, but usually packed her own lunch and ate when she met up with her friends. The group, except for Randy, was sitting together on their usual grassy place under the giant oak by the time Carlos had arrived. The spring sunshine had awakened the dormant buds lining the tree branches into deep green and red leaves. The shade they produced was a welcome evolution of the season. Nick was seated off to the side talking to some guy wearing a black "Ivy" cap, the kind cabbies sometimes wear. Carlos didn't recognize the guy and figured he was one of Nick's classmates.

"Hola, everyone." Carlos looked around, taking in a quick panorama of the campus surroundings, then back at the group. "What a beautiful day. What's up, guys?" Everyone said "Hello" back. Carlos focused on the stranger and nodded, acknowledging him. Nick took that as a good time to introduce his friend.

"Carlos, this is my friend Derek. We know each other from last semester. He and I took a night class together; Statistics. What a ball breaker that was." His friend agreed by nodding his head. Derek got up and walked over to Carlos who had already started walking toward him as well. They shook hands. "Nice to meet you, Derek." In the background, Nick blurted out, "Dude, he's like you. Olderrr." Derek laughed and said to Carlos, "I think he intended to say mature." Carlos laughed.

"Hi, guys!" Randy was a good twenty yards across the lawn when she called to her friends. She started a funny looking skip as she danced up to Carlos and kissed his cheek. "Hey, Carlos." Carlos took her hand and drew her next to him. "Randy, this is Derek; Nick's friend. Derek, meet Randy" They exchanged greetings.

"So, Derek, what's your story?" Derek was caught off guard by Randy's off the hip question. He asked Randy,

"What do you mean?"

"Well, we all have a story, most of us leaning toward sad and lonely. It's likely what drew us together."

Derek glanced at Nick, then Carlos. "Um." Randy interrupted him. "Don't look at them, especially not Carlos. We have yet to know his story. He isn't even a student here. We're all drawn to him like a magnet, and interestingly enough, he's the glue that binds this group together. Speaking for myself, I love him – like a brother. Maybe more since I've agreed to travel in such tight quarters with him; and the rest of these lovely people." All of a sudden she realized how rude and perhaps cruel her outburst was. She felt her face flush with embarrassment. Derek continued, "Um." Nick interrupted him this time. "Not everyone has a story. Not everyone's story is our business." Monica chimed in the same time as Carlos, but beat him to it. "Whoa! Easy there, guys." Derek put his hand up in a gesture to ward off Nick's attempt at protecting him. "It's OK. Mind if I cop a squat?"

"My story is complicated, but I'll make it simple for all of you." He looked at Randy and smiled, "Just remember; you asked." Nick started to interject but Derek again waved him off, signaling his comfort with discussing his situation. "I had a day job and attended night college for the past almost five years. I lived with my girlfriend since freshmen year. Three years ago, I was diagnosed with Lymphoma and have been battling it for what seems like forever. My beautiful lady took care of me, which put a strain on our love life. When I was in remission last year, we tried to rebuild the intimate part of our relationship. That didn't work out, and eventually she moved on with her life, without me. Earlier this year I found out my cancer had returned." Monica started to silently weep. The rest of the group, even Carlos fought off tears. "Anyway, the cost of the treatments and the awful side effects led me to a decision. I want to *live* the rest of my life." Monica wiped her nose thinking, *I'm cutting back on some of those Jim Croce songs*. She said, "But, you have to fight it." Derek smiled in a sad kind of way; a hopeless smile. "I have, and now it's time to accept reality, and make the best of what time I have left that I can enjoy." He held up his hands pointed outward from his body mimicking a balance scale. He raised his left arm, "Prolonged life of pain with no guarantees." Then he raised his right arm, "Or, enjoy what time is left to the fullest. I've made my choice." He smiled warmly at the group. "Now that I've thoroughly depressed all of you, what and how did you all meet?"

After the *"getting to know you"* dialog wore itself out, Carlos asked again what everyone thought about his idea. Monica was the first to say she was in, with Daniel and Joshua joining her with apparent enthusiasm for the adventure. The rest agreed as well. Nick put his arm around Derek's shoulders. "Room for one more?" He looked at Carlos who was caught off guard, and quickly tried to imagine how everyone would fit into one motorhome. "Sure. How about it, Derek?" Carlos glanced at the rest of the group for signs of yea or nay. They all nodded their approval. Nick squeezed harder on Derek's shoulders, making him visibly wince. He said, "You wanted to live life, live it with us. We'll have a blast." Derek laughed, "Well, OK then; I'm in." He paused, and asked, "What exactly are we talking about?"

Chapter 23

Monica picked up her guitar and without any hesitation, started playing Mr. Bojangles. As she strummed the opening chords she told her campus friends, "Everyone needs to sing along, we need to get this party hopping." Carlos thought, *hopping? Monica's music is hardly the hopping kind of music.* Despite his cynicism, Carlos was the first one to start singing along. The others joined in, straightaway.

"That was really cool, Monica; thank you." The rest of the group agreed. Carlos took center stage and started with, "So, I will have access to a decent RV that should handle our size group. *I hope.* There will be no place for modesty on this trip. It'll be close quarters for sure. Respect and consideration will need to be practiced at all times. We'll need to work together as one well maintained machine. We should all make a list of things we think are needed." Monica chimed in, "Like cooking utensils, food, beer, vodka. You know, the essential items." Carlos laughed, "Exactly; and other items like medicines. Only the legal kind; of course. Also, reading material. And, we need an emergency contact list in case anything happens to one of us." Josh added, "I'll bring my boombox and cool music." The group, surprised, all looked at him. "What? Being religious doesn't dictate my music choices. Don't worry, God approves of all types of music." *I hope.*

"Ok; so I figure we have ten days if we leave one week from Friday; early in the morning. Everyone needs to check their calendars to confirm this works for them." He looked around noticing most of the group were texting or utilizing some other function on their smart phones. He asked, "Has anyone driven a large vehicle or truck?" Carlos looked around, there were no yeas on this question. "Ok, then. I don't mind driving the bulk of the trip but some of you will need to spell me on the highway drive. I'll take on the local roads and parking." Carlos paused for a second before continuing. "RV's are steady on the main road but can be seriously intimidating in tight spaces and curves." Monica, who seemed to be the most inquisitive and challenging, asked, "What is the exact route we are going to take?" Carlos said, "Excellent question. As we started to discuss earlier and the other day, I need your desired stops along the old Route 66. From what I've researched, once we get off of 78 around the southern tip of Illinois, the routes heading west change names fairly often. We will hit 70 and then pick up 44 around Stanton and then route 40 toward the west coast. I'm not sure what alternate routes may be in our path. Google Maps will help with that as we reach each stopping point along the journey. Use the internet to come up with some favorite places. We need to decide on the scenic stops before we leave so I can plan our rest stops and apply for permits for overnight parking where it's needed."

Time always seemed to pass quickly when the group of friends hung out together. Carlos checked his watch and jumped up unexpectedly. "I really need to get going. See you all on Friday to wrap up everything. I'll have more details. Don't forget to give suggestions for places you want to explore. Text me or give it to me on Friday." Monica said she was going to hang out for a little while longer. Nick and Derek said they would stay too. The others started gathering their belongings. Josh, who was walking these days, ran up to Carlos. "Thanks for including me; I don't have many friends." Carlos offered him his hand. "You're one of us, man. Happy you're coming. See you on Friday."

Chapter 24

Wednesday morning, Carlos arrived early at work. Ginger hadn't arrived at her work station yet. He wondered if she called in sick again. When he got to his desk, he noticed a folder with a sticky note on it marked RV. She must have worked late yesterday or came in early this morning. As angry as she may be, she never let it affect her work. She was awesome.

Carlos made several phone calls to "RV" dealers on Ginger's list. She had pre-qualified them, making sure they had vehicles on their lots that could fit Carlos' needs. The third call seemed to be the one that had what he wanted. "I'll see you at three. Thank you."

Ginger popped her head into his office, "Did you get the information you needed?" Carlos placed his wireless headset on the desk as he looked up. Her face looked angelic this morning. "Yes, thank you, Ginger. Do you want to come in for a moment?" Ginger politely said "No. I have calls that I need to return and an early lunch appointment. Can we talk later?" Carlos said, "Sure; and thanks again." *Lunch appointment? Sure she goes out with the other girls every so often, but an appointment?*

The RV lot was located on Long Island, in the town of Ronkonkoma. Carlos borrowed his dad's car and ducked out of the office at 3:15PM. He crossed the Kosciuszko Bridge and took the Long Island Expressway exit, headed toward the I-495 east. He hadn't driven the Jaguar XJ in a while. The six cylinder performed really nice and Carlos resisted the temptation to open her up as traffic allowed. *Too bad, the 340HP rush would have been rad.* The trip took fifty-five minutes. Traffic was light, considering the start of "rush-hour." As he maneuvered through traffic, he hummed the song from the 1960's TV show "Green Acres." Driving the Jag was so awesome, Carlos almost missed the exit he needed. The large green sign for "Exit 60 Ronkonkoma ¼ Mile" came up unexpectedly. He ignored the honking horns and cut across two lanes, catching the exit ramp just in time. Google Maps directed him the rest of the way east and then south for about two miles.

The lot was huge. Long Island is so spread out compared to the city. In Brooklyn, an operation like this would need a building like a parking garage to handle these giant homes on wheels. Joe Donaldson or "Crazy Joe," as his marketing ads dubbed him, stood outside the small office talking to another salesperson when Carlos arrived. The highlighted text in the advertisement explained his nickname, "Crazy Joe, his prices are insane. He will beat any advertised competitor pricing." Carlos hated car salesmen and already started feeling anxious.

"Nice ride my friend. Looking for a trade-in?" The fifty something *old man* extended his hand in an offer to make Carlos' acquaintance. Carlos accepted his gesture and said, "Joe? I have an appointment with you." Crazy Joe smiled, a sly one; so Carlos thought. "Let's get started, my friend. As I recall, you are looking to lease, rather rent, a vehicle for two weeks. We have a one month minimum on all rentals. I have really incredible financing on a purchase deal. Leasing so short of a term is going to be expensive." Carlos began looking around at the stock on the lot and didn't bother to turn toward his host. "I have no place or need for the RV after my vacation is over." Joe replied, "Well, Ok; let's get started."

After looking at several barely acceptable RV's, Carlos spotted one across the aisle from where he and Joe stood. A thirty foot White Ford V-10 RV caught his eye. He walked over to it. "This is a beauty. May I?" He opened the door and peeked inside without waiting for Joe's reply. The pristine interior dazzled him. "How much is this one?" Joe looked a little crazy; "That one? Let me see." He had a tablet and started keying in information. "Seven people, 30 days; I'll discount where I can, based on your group only using everything for fourteen days. Let me see; what supplies do you need?" Carlos said nothing while Crazy Joe mumbled to himself. "One kitchen kit, seven personal kits, that's pillows, sheets; the works. There's mandatory insurance that we need to provide." Carlos was aware that the insurance was a rip-off; but a convenient necessity for peace of mind. Joe hit the virtual enter key with a clear gesture of his finger. "Should be around thirty-two, thirty-three hundred. I included the minimum allowance of 2100 miles. Thirty-five dollars for each 100 miles after that." Carlos stepped inside noting the kitchen had all the amenities of a full kitchen, including a microwave. There was a shower; tight space, but manageable, and plenty of comfortable seating. Carlos turned and leaned out of the RV's door, making a face; "Might be tight for my group, I need to look around at some other possibilities. I'll get back to you."

"They don't call me Crazy Joe for nothing, I'll throw in a six person sleeping tent so your group can spread out at night."

"Reduce the base to an even three thousand, all inclusive, and the over mileage to twenty-five per 100 miles."

Crazy Joe shook his head, which Carlos took as a "Not Possible." Carlos offered his hand and said, "Call me if you can work it out. I have another appointment this evening. Let me see what they have to offer." The salesman took Carlos' hand and gripped it firmly, not letting go. "You are shrewd my friend. What do you do for a living? Let me guess; Sales?" Carlos grinned. He felt empowered. "Ok, call me crazy; but OK. If we can verbally agree on the terms now, I'll work out the pricing and fax it over to your office. I'll call you tomorrow to firm up the deal."

Salesmen are bull-shitters, don't try to bullshit a salesman.

The ride back to Brooklyn took considerably longer in the rush-hour traffic. The crossover to the Brooklyn-Queens Expressway was at a standstill. Carlos' stomach started a conversation indicating its hunger. "OK, amigo. We will stop and get something delicious for dinner. I'm in the mood to cook." As he listed needed ingredients and nodded his head in agreement with himself, he imagined the other drivers looking at him. He rationalized that they would assume he was using a hands-free device and speaking on a call.

Earlier, Carlos senior asked his son to drop the car off at the factory when he returned. Carlos would park it inside the warehouse overnight. His dad needed it early in the morning. For Carlos, this meant taking the bus and crossing the park, adding to his already long day. It was still light out and the weather was perfect for a brisk walk. The regular park dwellers were not around as Carlos took his usual shortcut on his route home.

The long cash register lines at the Key Food supermarket moved along slowly. Hungry and tired, Carlos wanted to get home and eat his dinner. The Branzini, on sale, looked deliciously fresh. He picked up a helping of ready-made couscous and a side of spinach. As he waited on line he went over the other ingredients he needed. *I have plenty of garlic, olive oil...* "Lemons, I need lemons." He asked the person behind him to hold his place in line and ran over to the produce aisle. He found two nice lemons and raced back to the register just as it became his turn to pay.

When Carlos arrived at his building, his neighbor from across the hall was trying to open the outer door. Carlos reached over and opened the door for her. "Thank you, Carlos." "No problem, Mildred." Mildred was a sweet seventy something year old woman. She always signed for

Carlos' packages and sometimes waited for service men to let them in when he was at work. Sometimes she would question him about overnight visitors. He never considered her inquiries as prying. She was being motherly, and he liked it. He also enjoyed talking with her about his day, and her stories about her life growing up in the city. "Are you just getting home, Millie?" She smiled sweetly as she looked at him. Her hands shook a bit. "No, I needed a few things at the grocery and managed to get one block before I realized I forgot my wallet." Carlos helped her into the building. "Would you like me to run to the market for you? It's no problem. I just came from there myself." Again smiling, "You are such a dear. Thank you, but no. I'll eat a frozen dinner tonight and go tomorrow." Carlos mentally consulted his stomach which urged him to get moving. "No way, Millie. Have dinner with me." He held up his package. "Fresh delicious Branzini. I'll knock on your door when it's ready. Figure about an hour, if that's OK." "My, my. Is this a date? I have a nice bottle of wine I won at bingo. We can enjoy it with our dinner." Carlos laughed heartily. "It's a date then."

Carlos prepared his Branzini with garlic, lemon and drizzled it with extra virgin olive oil. He grilled the fish using his special grilling pan. The smell of the grilled fish was incredible as was the rest of the meal; and the wine.

He told his lady friend all about the impending trip he planned to take, and all the new friends he made. She told him, "Traveling with people you recently met could be interesting; or a disaster. You are a nice boy and very trusting. Look how you let me into your home. How do you know I didn't spike your wine? Maybe I'm going to take advantage of you." She winked, then smiled sweetly at him. Carlos paused in thought for a moment, then laughed. "Well Millie, this would be my lucky night." He stood up and poured more wine in both glasses. He kissed her cheek. "You are as innocent as I am, Millie." She gave him a stern look, "Listen, mister. I see who comes and goes. You're not that innocent. When are you going to find your special someone and settle down?" Carlos didn't answer. He had no idea what it meant to "settle down."

Chapter 25

Friday

"Good morning, Mr. Martinez. You asked me to remind you to send the updated sales figures to your dad for review; so I'm reminding you." Carlos noticed she was still angry with him by her terse and sarcastic attitude. *How long is she going to torture me; and that poor guy from accounting?* "There was also a message on my voicemail from Crazy Joe's RV sales." She thought to herself, *Carlos could have given his own direct number, he is taunting me. He's such an ass.* "Thanks, Ginger. Please forward the number to my email." "It's already done." Carlos also observed that her morning coffee run to Starbucks did not include him any longer. *What is it with her? Why can't she be like the other women? We had a good time. We're friends.* Carlos snapped out of his subconscious thought and returned his attention to the here, and now. Sitting in his chair, he opened the email Ginger had sent with Crazy Joe's number. He closed his eyes while the phone rang. One ring, two rings. *Crap! She's in love – with me.* Three rings, four rings. Voicemail picked up with Crazy Joe's crazy message. As Carlos was about to hang up, "Hello. Joe here." Joe got right to the point; as agreed, he would meet Carlos' price. "The faxed agreement is on its way now." They spoke for almost an hour, concluding with Carlos giving Crazy Joe his credit card information for the deposit. The RV was his for twenty-eight days. It was more time than he needed, but that was the minimum rental period. He made arrangements to pick it up the following week on Thursday morning. This gave him a day to practice driving it and inspect the accommodations. He also had to call his insurance company to send a rider over to Crazy Joe's. As he hung up the phone, his heart started pounding like a drum in a marching band. Nerves got a hold of him. At the same time, Carlos felt excitement. He had to call someone.

"Nick? Hey, it's Carlos. We're all set. I got the RV, and it's a beauty. I was thinking we might grab a drink, and perhaps lunch; talk about the trip." Nick paused before answering. Carlos caught his hesitation. "Hey, Carlos. Listen man, I got something going on at the moment. I'm going to need a rain check on that." Carlos didn't want to show his disappointment. "Oh, sorry. For sure, another time. I'll see you Friday." Ok, so Nick was getting laid and it it's not even mid-day yet. Carlos tried to imagine who. First Monica popped into his head. Randy? Definitely not Randy. Although, he thought; they all go to the same college. Then he replayed the events of the other day in his head. He had just saved Monica's guitar. She had jumped on him, playfully, but it was a turn-on, none the less. He switched back to Nick. He could be with anyone, most likely someone outside the group. After all, he only met Nick a few weeks ago. He really knew very little about him. In fact, no one in the group knew the others before the past few weeks. *This is going to be an interesting road trip.*

Loneliness hit Carlos. Had he played his cards right, Ginger would be all over him. In his mind he smelled the sweet scent of her perfume as he unbuttoned her blouse. She then turned away from him holding her hair to one side as he unzipped her skirt. He imagined it as it dropped to the floor in slow motion.

His desk phone snapped him back to reality. "Carlos here." "Ginger here. I will be going out to lunch and might be a little late. Is there anything you need before I go?" "No. I'm fine Ginger, thank you. And, thanks for the RV info. It worked out great and our trip is all set." "That's nice for you. I'm sure you'll have a wonderful time." She hung up abruptly.

This is one hell of a game we are playing; taunting each other. Why can't we just be friends?

Not two minutes went by before the phone rang again. The display indicated "Accounting Dept." Carlos picked up after the third ring. Either Ginger left already, or she simply chose to ignore the incoming call.

"Hello. This is Carlos." It was Bob, from accounting. "Hello, Mr. Martinez. Sorry to disturb you. I have a few receivables that need to be signed off by you. One of your accounts is over 120 days. Is this a good time?" Carlos did his best to be professional. "Gee, Bob. I don't know. Don't you take lunch at this time?" Bob sounded confused as he replied. "Um, no. Well actually, yes; I do have an appointment in a little while. But, I have a few moments and wanted to get this taken care of as soon as possible. Would it be OK if I run these up to you now?" "I'll come to you, Bob. Stay put."

The sign on the door said, "Bob Dick-Head, Senior Accountant." Carlos laughed to himself as his imagination transformed part of what the sign really said. He knocked firmly and walked into the office. The space was tiny as most of the offices were. Martinez Senior, contrary to most corporate theory, thought that all managers, at any level, needed privacy to be effective at their jobs. He felt that a private office created an image of prestige and authority that commanded respect. Bob was sitting behind his modest desk. Everything was in its place. Everything was in perfect order. There were plenty of stacks of folders. Several on the floor, even some on chairs. But, not a paper or folder out of place.

Everything is so neat, so "accountant-like", so "nerd-like."

"Mr. Martinez; thank you for coming down to take care of this; I know you're very busy. This will only take a few moments." Carlos offered his hand, and they shook. "We can dispense with the formalities; Carlos, please. I understand you have an appointment to get to, so let's take care of business. What do you have for me?" Bob pulled a file from a short stack, "The first two need your signature so I can deposit them. You gave aggressive discounts; I suppose for quick payment?" "Yes, I was asked to use incentives in the form of early payment, specifically Net 10 terms to help with cash flow for this past quarter." Bob smiled, but didn't even look at Carlos, he kept his eyes focused on the paperwork. "I see; OK then." *Who does this Bob think is the boss here?* Carlos did not like his attitude. Suddenly it hit him, Bob is threatened by his relationship with Ginger; whatever still remained of it. Carlos signed the two documents. "What else Bob? You mentioned that one of my accounts was late. May I see it?" Bob pulled out another file and opened the folder. Inside was a detailed accounting of the order, all the shipments and their due dates, aged by DOS column which is an acronym for Days Outstanding. Carlos studied the numbers, noticing a few payments that were promised to him during follow-up calls, did not appear. Pointing to an entry in the folder, Carlos said, "Hmm, I see. I spoke to Jim last week on this. I would assume the check is already in the mail." Carlos smiled. Bob either didn't get the joke, or had other things on his mind; like Ginger. "I'll call him right now." Bob looked at his watch trying to be discreet, but Carlos caught the nervous time-check. Carlos flicked his finger across the screen of his cell phone and then brought the device to his ear.

"Jim Alstead, please. Carlos Martinez from Aerotech. Sure, I can hold. Thank you." Carlos glanced at Bob, "He's on another call." Carlos noticed the stress in his face as Bob again checked his watch. "Sorry, Bob. He should be on any moment. We want to get this taken care of so the big guys don't get on our case. Don't you agree?" Bob nodded.

Squirm, my man. What a nerd.

It had only been five minutes; Carlos figured it seemed like hours to Bob. Jim finally picked up the line. He and Carlos talked for another five minutes. Carlos never mentioned the actual reason for his call. He asked about his weekend trip to Connecticut and how his daughter was doing at USC. Carlos briefly mentioned his planned road trip. Bob grew increasingly tense. Carlos felt the vibe. "Oh, really, sorry to hear that. I hope her recovery is quick. Let me know if you need anything. Today? That's great, we could use it. I haven't heard anything from accounting, but I'll make them aware that the check should be here today or tomorrow. Talk to you when I get back. Thanks, Jim."

"His mom had hip surgery and he was out all week. The check was mailed yesterday. I believe for the full amount." Bob smiled and looked relieved. Whether it was that a large overdue payment was coming in, or that he could get on his way to lunch, Carlos couldn't tell. But, he could guess. "Great news; thank you – Carlos." He started to stand while keying something on his computer; probably locking the computer screen. "No problem, Bob. Thanks for not dunning them and letting me take care of it. He probably fibbed, and is sending the check this afternoon. It's better to make the call and let him bring it up to me. It keeps it comfortable and friendly. The client thinks he's in control and not being pressured." Bob said, "Interesting concept; I like it." Carlos offered his hand again. They shook. "Enjoy your lunch, Bob. Sorry this got dragged out. I'm sure your appointment will understand." Carlos left the office first, with Bob right behind him.

Better to keep them waiting. Makes them eager with anticipation.

Carlos ordered take-out from Taka Sushi, a nearby Asian Fusion restaurant. He wanted to get everything in order so his contact with the office would be minimal while he was away on vacation.

He managed to take care of three calls and approve several orders before the knock came on his door. Carlos glanced at this desk clock, it had been over an hour since he called his lunch order. "Hello, Mr. Carlos. So sorry; we very busy in kitchen today. Where pretty lady who take order most times?" Carlos laughed, "Even the pretty lady gets to take a break sometimes." He mumbled, "at least lately." "Yes, yes, I see. I remember chop sticks and extra ginger; way you like. You not remember, but I do. Pretty lady always ask for them." Carlos pulled out thirty dollars and handed it to him. The delivery man started counting out change. Carlos put up his hand in gesture, "No, the rest is for you. Thanks for remembering the extras."

The three roll special came with one Rainbow roll, one Crunchy Salmon and one Crunchy Tuna. There was plenty of wasabi and ginger. *Wow, extra ginger. Ginger is in my head. Maybe she is a witch, and has a spell on me.*

The lunch was most enjoyable even if Carlos worked while he ate. He actually considered it healthier. Working while eating slows him down. Normally a fast eater, this method paced his meal, and he felt better during the day.

Bells started ringing as the PA announced a fire drill. Everyone was instructed to immediately leave the building per posted fire code policy. It was 2PM already. Ginger had the responsibility of fire captain. She should be walking around closing doors after checking that all occupants had evacuated their respective spaces. Carlos looked around, but she was not on the floor, anywhere. *Damn!* Carlos went to each cubical and office checking for occupants. He closed doors per policy and headed down the stairs and out to the street joining the other employees. Edmond Cortez, fire chief for the company, started handing out the sign-in sheets to the five captains so they could get signatures from their respective areas of responsibility. Carlos walked over to Edmond, "I'll take that for Ginger." Just as the Aerotech fire chief was about to ask where Ginger was, Carlos spotted her and Bob walking quickly up the street toward the group. "I'm headed over to her anyway."

"I checked and secured your post, all is clear. Go get your signatures." Carlos handed her the clip board and walked away. Ginger realized she could have been in big trouble, maybe even terminated from her job. Captains were privately made aware of the drill two days prior. Even management personnel were not told when a drill would occur. Carlos had covered for her.

Fifteen minutes later, everyone was back in the building with business operations back to normal. The knock was timid and unusual. Ginger never knocked on his door before entering. She leaned in, "Hey, thanks for covering for me. I lost track of the time." Carlos didn't look up. "No problem." Anger came upon her unexpectedly. She opened the door and walked in then pushed the door closed behind her. Ginger walked up to Carlos' desk, her beautiful red hair flowing over one eye. Carlos looked up at her. She looked like Breathless Mahoney played by Madonna in the Dick Tracy movie; *Angry but Hot*. He heard the words before they came out of her mouth. "What is wrong with you?" Carlos pondered for a second whether she really expected an answer. She continued before he had time to say something stupid. "You blow me off and then expect me to sit around until you come to your senses. You're an idiot!" Carlos had no idea what to do; this was a first for him. "Bob is a nice guy, and he respects me. He treats me nice. And, he's there for me." Carlos leaned forward still looking up at her now deep red face.

"I've always been there for you, always will be."
"Not in the way that counts, not the way I need someone."
"But Bob? He is a nerd with a pocket protector and a leaky pen"
"No, he isn't. He's kind and respectful and – he doesn't have a pocket protector or a leaky pen. I'm not just a one-night stand to him. You're the nerd who doesn't know when he had something good. You're the loser."
"Ginger, I'm sorry."
"Are you sorry you tried to sabotage my lunch date? That was a disgusting stunt just to piss me off!"

Carlos made a goofy, embarrassed face, "I guess it worked?" He was sorry the moment he said it. Ginger turned and walked belligerently toward the office door. "I'll stay until you get back from your trip. Then I'm asking to be transferred to another department as soon as there's an opening. It's time for me to have something good in my life." Her back to him as she disappeared into the hallway, she had one last thing to say.

"Maybe I'll just quit."

Chapter 26

The phone rang four times before Derek answered it. "Hello, Mr. Smith? This is the Ellis Clinic." Derek assured the caller that he understood the consequences of not continuing his treatments. He finally made his decision, and informed the clinic. Derek felt as if a great weight had been lifted from him. His sister had called him the night before. He lied to her when she asked how the treatments were going. Lying to his mom would be harder. Eventually he will tell them. Eventually he will have no choice. Perhaps after he gets back from the road trip with his new friends. At that point all their attempts at convincing and likely, anger with him, will be fruitless. It will be too late. All that matters at this point is that he is happy and content with life. The future had been a big unknown. Now it's cast in stone. This, he could deal with. His family needs to understand this. They would be cross at first. They will cry. After a while, they'll see it his way or be forced to accept it. This he was sure of. He typed "Route 66" into his search engine and perused the results. Today, for the first time in over a year, he felt as if he had been reborn. The effects of the poison they ran through his veins twice a week finally cleared out of his body. His immune system was getting stronger and he felt alive again. *I am aware this is only a short reprieve, but a welcome one. I can accept my fate now. I'm at peace with it.*

"What is wrong with you? We taught you better." "I love you guys; but it's time to cut the cord, grams. I'm not that timid little girl anymore. In case you haven't noticed, I don't need my meds either. I stopped taking them a few weeks ago and I'm fine. I'm actually happy. I'm alive for the first time in years. Can you pass the gravy?" Dinner at their Massapequa home usually consisted of quiet talk about Monica's day and what was happening in school. It was the same conversation topic between her and her grandparents since the first grade. Monica was withdrawn; understandably with the horrible tragedy of losing her parents on September 11th 2001. For her grandparents, her transformation over the past few weeks was perplexing. They were overjoyed that she had broken out of her depression. They were also concerned that this blessing would be temporary. That something would trigger a relapse, making her condition worse than before. "But Monica, you only met these people recently. Hanging out with them at school or at a local club is one thing. But, traveling so far away with them? That is just plain crazy." Her grandpa sat quietly for most of the dinner. Out of the blue he said, "We don't want you to go." Monica put down her fork and took a drink of water. "I'm an adult. Other kids are away at school. Their families have no idea what they do all semester or who they are with. I've never let you down, have I?" Her grandparents did not answer at first. After a moment, her grandma quietly said, "Of course not, but." Monica stood up abruptly, tears in her eyes. "I need some air; I won't be back too late."

Nickolas Caputo sat on the floor, leaning against the side of a couch, in the basement of his cousin's Richmond Hill home. "This is great stuff." He exhaled slowly. "Two hits and I'm wasted." His cousin agreed. "Indeed, it's awesome. Dude, you really tripping with people you hardly know. That's rad, but crazy. Want another beer?" Nick took the beer and chugged it down quickly. "Thanks. I needed that. My throat is parched. These people are really nice. This guy Carlos, he's the man. A little mysterious and older; not a student either." His cousin coughed a cloud of smoke. "Dude, maybe he's a psycho killer. Every day one of you is going to go missing." "No, I don't think so, Cuz." "Are there any chicks in this traveling group of hippies?" Nick laughed, "Actually, yes; there are. Two hot ones." "Dude!" Nick punched his cousin in the arm, "They're really nice girls.

We're all just friends." His cousin looked at him with a smirk. Nick continued, "OK, you never know what could happen."

"Sharmuta!" Joshua rarely used curse words; certainly, never in his house or in front of his parents. From the kitchen he heard his mother yell, "Joshua Cohen! You're not too old to be grounded. God heard you." His finger throbbed from his spastic attempt to close his over-stuffed sock drawer.

"Come down! Your supper is on the table."

The brisket smelled delicious. It was his favorite meal. Joshua asked his mom if he could help with anything before he sat down. His mother didn't respond until she joined Joshua and his dad at the table. "I hope you've given up that foolish notion for a trip with people you don't know." He explained that they are not strangers, since he knows all their names. And, that he has been hanging out with them on campus. "I'm a man, mama. I finally made friends who don't make fun of me. You don't have to worry about me anymore. This trip is something I need to do." His mother stood abruptly, "No!" She walked out of the kitchen. His dad, the calmer of the two parents, leaned back in his dining room chair.

He wiped his forehead with a napkin and leaned over to his son, patting him on the back reassuringly. "She will be fine, my boy. I will speak with her on the matter." Things rarely get to Josh. He had been awkward and a bit clumsy most of his life. He was used to ridicule. His mom could be difficult and sometimes slighting. But, she always encouraged him to be more social and meet people. *Why does she have to be so difficult? This is so important to me.*

Randy caught up to Daniel as he walked out of their afternoon computer science class. "Daniel; wait up. So, it looks like we're all making the trek across the country." Daniel looked surprised. "You are going, aren't you?" She caught him off guard. Even though they spoke a little in the group gatherings, this was a first. *Wow, she made the first move.* "Oh. Sorry, Randy. Yes; it's way cool that we are doing this. Did you pack yet? Like, what did you pack?" Embarrassment hit him. In his mind he was asking her something too personal. Like, *what are you going to wear to sleep?* He even answered in his head, back to her. *I sleep in the raw.* "Daniel? Earth to Daniel" "Oh. Sorry, Randy." She made him nervous and his mindset needed a re-wiring; fast. "I sleep in PJ's." She looked at him, "What?" *Get it together idiot, she thinks you're weird.* "I mean, we are all going to be in close quarters, what do you think the sleeping arrangements

151

will be?" Randy laughed. "You're so cute Daniel. I imagine sweats would work. At least, for me. I guess we'll find laundromats along the way so I'm packing on the lighter side." Daniel laughed, "That makes sense. I always pack way too much. I have more clean clothes when I get home than when I left." Daniel looked at his phone for the time. He knew what time it was, but did it out of anxiety, and as a distraction, for a second. "I know it's late but, do you want to grab something? Maybe a cup of java?" Randy touched his arm with her index finger; ever so gently. "Thanks, Daniel. I ate before class and I've got a study group now that I'm actually late for. I gotta run." Disappointed, but not letting it show, Daniel said goodbye. "See you Friday." "Sure, see you." He watched as she ran off down the hall toward the building exit. *That's the most we've spoken since we met in class. She is so cute.*

Carlos rested his feet on the small coffee table as he reclined back on his couch. The TV was on, but the volume was barely audible. Dan Aykroyd and Jane Curtin, as the Coneheads celebrating Halloween, were hysterical. He was scanning the TV channels when he came across reruns of Saturday Night Live from the mid-1970's. Carlos loved old sitcoms and comedy shows from the sixties and seventies. He reached over to the table without moving his feet, almost knocking over a half full glass of cabernet. He lifted the glass and drank a good amount, savoring it slowly. Earlier he had eaten leftover eggplant parmesan and spaghetti that his friend and neighbor Mildred prepared for him as a thank you for his dinner invitation earlier in the week. It had been a crazy, busy week, but he got a lot accomplished at work as well as some preparation for his road trip. His assistant and friend, perhaps ex-friend, and perhaps, ex-assistant, stressed him out. Now he needed to mellow-out. Friday the final plans would be made with the group and next week they would be on their way. Carlos smiled in anticipation of an awesome time to come.

The outside door buzzer ringing interrupted Beldar as he argued with Mother Prymaat over some ridiculous issue. Carlos muted the TV and hit the door release. The intercom hadn't worked in several months. He hoped another neighbor would call the landlord but as usual, he would eventually have to do it. He opened the door and watched as Monica made her way up the stairs. She saw the look on his face and considered that perhaps dropping in on him was a mistake.

"Hey, Carlos. I hope it's OK that I'm here without an invite. I should have called." Carlos motioned for her to come into the apartment. "It's no problem, Monica. How did you find out where I live?" "Google is amazing. I'm sorry, Carlos." She had a tear forming at the corner of her eye. "I told you it's cool; you're welcome anytime; mi casa esta su casa. What is going on? Are you alright?" Monica explained the argument with her grandparents. "Would you like a glass of wine? Did you eat?" Monica wiped her eyes, "You are so sweet. I'm not hungry, but I'll take a drink. Something a bit stronger, if you don't mind." Carlos went into his little kitchen and returned with two shot glasses and a half full bottle of Petron Silver. Monica kissed his cheek. "You're a life saver. Thank you." They talked for a while about family, and getting along with them. Until this moment Carlos said very little about his family or work situation with the group. He shared a few things but tried not to let on too much about his family's financial situation or his status at work. Out of the blue he asked her, "Wait; how did you get from Long Island to Brooklyn?" "The same way I get to campus three days a week; train and bus." Carlos attempted to offer another refill but the bottle was empty. "Oh, well. We did a good number on this one, didn't we?" Monica laughed, combined with a hiccup. They both laughed. "We sure did. I'm feeling much better now." She leaned into Carlos, her hand on his thigh; she kissed his cheek again but didn't retreat this time. He said in a sort of mumble, with his face an inch from hers, "How are we going to get you home?" She pressed her lips to his gently, pulled back and waited. Carlos stayed put. She moved in again. This time Carlos met her lips. In a repeat performance of the other day, Monica was on top of him making her move. This time it was more than gratitude. Her tongue made an assault on his mouth. They were drunk and out of control. Carlos' body didn't want to stop but his mind started screaming at him. *Here you go again, ruining another friendship.* "Wait! We can't do this." Monica had a look of shock and disappointment on her face. She asked in a panicked voice, "What?" He said, "I want to. You are..." He didn't finish his words. He stroked her hair and touched her lips with his finger. "You are amazing, and lord knows I want to; but we can't do this." "Carlos, I don't understand. If you like me, and you want to, then what's stopping you?" Before Carlos could respond, Monica continued her frantic assessment. "Wait! Oh my god. I should have realized." Carlos knew where this was going. He had no comeback ready for this. "You're gay!" She swung her leg around, dismounting off him in a rapid motion. She sat back on the couch. "Damn."

Carlos needed a moment to think, he wasn't gay and needed to assure her of that. But, doing so would likely lead to her being offended by his rejection. He would come clean if only he, himself, understood what it was that troubled him.

"Give me a moment, Monica."
"Sure, no problem, Carlos."
"I'll be right back."

Carlos made his way to the kitchen and grabbed another bottle of tequila. He had no more Patron but Cuervo would work. Monica held her head between her hands; she looked as if she was sulking. Carlos poured two more shots. "Here, this will help." Monica appeared a little stressed. "Carlos, I'm so sorry. First I invade your privacy and then I offend you." Carlos sat down next to her and put his arm around her. He felt some tension in her so he one arm hugged her, pulling her close into him. "Is this OK? I need to keep you close so I have enough courage to explain what just happened." Monica nodded and seemed to relax a bit. "I'm not gay. I am *so* not gay. I've got problems with commitment. I date lots of women. So many, it's disturbing to those who know me." Monica pulled away a little, "So, you're *that* guy? The guy who gets them drunk, sleeps with them and never calls?" Carlos, red in the face with embarrassment and intoxication continued. "Yes. I'm that guy. The truth is, I recently hurt my best friend because we mixed friendship with sex. She knew me well enough to know how it would end up afterwards. But for her, the understanding changed and it ruined our friendship." Monica tried to say something, "But." Carlos stopped her cold and continued. "You and I, we've become really close friends in a short time. I don't have very many friends and can't even remember when one of them was not a guy. I hope you can see me as a friend. Think about it; we both need that more than anything else at this time in our lives."

Monica sat on the couch facing Carlos, her legs were crossed lotus style. Her eyes staring into his soul, her mouth open, but no words came out. Carlos extended both his hands toward her. Monica still statue-like, took them in hers. Her touch was warm and electrifying. Carlos wanted her more now than he did when this all started. He knew that if she continued her lustful assault on him again, he would be rendered powerless and give in to his primal needs. Suddenly the statue came to life. She smiled and said; "OK." Carlos, still holding her hands replied with a questioning look on his face, "OK?" "Yes, OK. You are an incredibly complex human being, Mr. Martinez." *There goes that formality again; this can't be good.* She continued as Carlos' mind raced through all the possible outcomes of this evening. "You are so right on all accounts. I was vulnerable and you didn't take advantage of that. I think that alone could make me fall in love with you. That, and a few other qualities you possess. I do need a really good friend that I can trust." Carlos let go of her hands and said, "Here I am." She said, "Here we are." She leaned in close to him once again and kissed him directly on the lips. This time her mouth remained closed. She held him tight after and whispered in his ear, "Thank you."

The evening disappeared into early morning. Monica talked about her childhood and the fond memories of her parents. Carlos talked about his situation with Ginger. He also told her more about his personal situation and status at work. She promised to keep it "between friends."

"It's late; do you want to stay? I can take the couch." Monica laughed, "You really want to test this friendship thing out, don't you? My Grams will freak out." Carlos smiled and told her, "I'm calling you an Uber."

They hugged tightly again, 'See you Friday, Carlos; I love you." Carlos paid the Uber driver with his credit card then said to Monica, "Text me when you get home." He nodded to the driver who acknowledged by nodding back.

"Wait!" The driver stopped the car after only pulling out a few feet. Monica opened her window and called out to Carlos. "You don't want to admit it yet, but you're in love with her." Carlos stood there saying nothing. The car started moving again. He heard her yell, "I'm a little jealous." The end of her last sentence faded away as the car window closed and the car disappeared down the street.

Chapter 27

The capricious weather forecast called for heavy rain all day. The wind forced a pattern of raindrops against the kitchen window. The rhythmic sound made him imagine his younger cousin Miranda at her tap dancing recital, a few years ago. He didn't want to go but his parents forced him. Years later, at a family gathering, he admitted to his cousin that she was really good. Her smile of appreciation stayed with him all these years. Carlos swallowed his last spoonful of cereal as he read the New York Times. He considered taking a long weekend, but changed his mind. There was too much to do at work before his long trip at the end of next week. The text messages started coming in from his future travel companions. Carlos put together a group text message saying that everything was set to go. "Today is a washout. Next week will be crazy for me. We can communicate via text for any last minute details. Let's meet next Friday in the main campus parking lot at 6AM. You won't have any trouble finding me. Just search the lot for the cool hotel on wheels. In the meantime, let's keep in touch with each other via text messaging."

The Uber dropped him at Aerotech at 8:45AM, the rain hadn't let up yet. Taking his usual park and bus route to work would have meant getting soaked. The modish car service saved him more than half an hour. It was nice for a change; and a lot drier.

He said his usual "good mornings" to his coworkers as he made his way up to his office. Ginger was at her desk. Evidently she had kept her word, and did not quit yet. "Good morning, Ginger." She was shuffling papers, apparently trying to appear busy and did not respond to his greeting. She wore his favorite outfit; a low cut, yellow floral blouse, and a black skirt. He couldn't see her feet under the desk, but he imagined her black laced up high heels. He was pretty sure it was the outfit she wore that night they spent together. "You look very nice." *That was lame, she always looks nice.* She looked up and reminded him that he had a lunch meeting with a new prospective client. Carlos actually had forgotten his meeting and had almost taken the day off to catch up on personal things. "OK, thanks." He went into his office and closed the door so he could get his work done with as few interruptions as possible.

The morning dragged on, and even with no disturbances, very little got accomplished. Carlos' concentration was elsewhere. He opened his email and started typing.

To: Ginger O'Connell.
RE: Lunch Meeting.

Please confirm the reservation at Restaurant Verde on Smith for 1PM today. Also, please forward the restaurant's street address and my personal cell number to the prospective clients.

I am requesting that you join us for the lunch meeting today as you have been instrumental in putting the proposal together. Ask the restaurant to change the reservation from four to five. Let me know if you will ride there with me or meet us at the restaurant.

Please accept my apologies for the other day; I was out of line. *And unknowingly jealous.* While I truly want to get our friendship back in order, which is most important to me, we must keep a business professionalism about us. I need and do respect you to the utmost degree and hope you will reconsider any plan to change departments or leave the company. Either departure would be a great loss to the company as well as to me.

Carlos.

He paused for a minute, re-reading the second part of the note twice before hitting the send button. Afterward, Carlos felt a little panicked. He mixed personal and business in that email. His emotions were out of control. He wondered how she would react.

At 11:15AM an email pinged Carlos. It was from Ginger.

"Carlos, you are confirmed for 1PM at Verde on Smith. I spoke with Scott Donovan and confirmed with him as well. He and his associates will meet you at the restaurant. I suggest you take a cab, as the forecast is still threatening heavy rain for this afternoon." Carlos read it and wondered why she didn't tell him in person. They rarely used email given that her desk was ten feet from his office. *At least she dropped the formality and called me Carlos.* He figured it was his doing by sending her an email first. She mentioned nothing about his request to take part in the lunch meeting. He let it go – for now; hoping she would show up.

The meeting went well. So well, that Scott Donovan asked if Carlos had the contracts with him. "Nothing like a few martinis to get me soft and agreeable." Carlos explained that he didn't want to appear presumptuous and that his assistant would prepare the contracts and have them delivered to him first thing Monday morning. Carlos looked over at the bar and then toward the entrance for the tenth time. Ginger was not coming. He surprised himself at his disappointment. She had always been there for him. As they left the restaurant, Carlos assured his new clients that they will be very happy joining the Aerotech family.

Ginger was at her desk when Carlos returned. She looked up, but kept a serious face, "Everything go as planned?" She looked incredible, and he wanted to tell her so, but refrained from fueling the fire. Carlos shook his head in a show of disappointment. "Everything went fine, please make sure to have the contracts on Donovan's desk first thing Monday." He turned and walked toward his office. He heard her mumble, "Sure thing, Boss."

The afternoon dragged on for what felt like an eternity. At 4:30, Carlos decided to start the weekend early. He grabbed his backpack and left the office saying nothing to Ginger. He had the Uber driver let him off in front of Gino's Pizza. The sign in front said "World famous Authentic Italian Pies." They spun really good pizza, but "World Famous?" Doubtful. After an early dinner and two delicious glasses of cabernet, Carlos dozed off on his couch.

The previous day's inclement weather gave way to clear skies and lots of sunshine. Saturday in the park was like the musical group Chicago's lyrics; Carlos could hear the tune playing in his head; "People dancing, people laughing; A man selling Ice cream" *and eating ice cream*. Only, it wasn't quite July yet. Carlos hummed the tune as he headed toward the basketball courts.

All the regulars were there. The same players met every Saturday morning for the past few years. To the onlookers who were not from the neighborhood, they looked like young men of the hood playing a life and death match with sweat bands that seemed to represent gang colors. But, following the rules of the hood, respect for the colors meant not wearing what didn't belong to you. After two hours they called it quits. Carlos finished his bottle of water, bade them "adios," and headed home for a cool shower.

The rest of the weekend involved preparations for the trip, and last minute homework from the office. Sales reports needed to be finished. Normally, he would have asked Ginger to meet him at the office. They would put in a half day, do lunch, and call it a good catch up day. This time, going solo made more sense. Besides, she probably had plans. *With Bob.*

Chapter 28

Monday

Carlos had little time for anything except work. He had two appointments with clients. One in the morning that extended through lunch, and another mid-afternoon at his client's office. His workday ended at Soigne wine bar on 5th Avenue in Park Slope. The client wasn't happy with delivery times that exceeded limits designated in their contract. At around five, the client's wife, Sonia, thankfully stepped in, insisting they call it a day. Evidently, she was the designated driver. Carlos wished she had been in the meeting from the start. She was cool, calm and very easy on the eyes. The three of them ended up at the fancy bar drinking dirty martinis. Carlos asked, "How about another round? Would you guys like to order something to eat? The menu here is wonderfully eclectic, and the food is delicious." The client looked at his wife. She smiled and gave the slightest nod. "It's late, Carlos. I think it's time for Sonia and I to head home. Thank you for the drinks. You are good company." They shook hands and Carlos cheek kissed Sonia. "Oh, and Carlos, I hope the next order will be delivered on time." His wife pulled at his arm, "You are such a ball buster. Good night, Carlos."

Carlos waved, "You can count on it. Good night." Carlos thought about the menu as he reached for the freshly refilled pretzel bowl. He signaled the bartender,

"Excuse me. 'One more."

The app on his phone took a few tries before it responded. He signed into his Uber account when it finally pinged him with a connection, and ordered a car. He had just finished his drink and emptied the pretzel bowl again when his cab arrived.

"Ping," "Ping." The app signaled him to meet his driver outside.

The ride from Park Slope to Williamsburg took ten minutes. Mildred was standing in the small common area as Carlos reached his landing.

"Well, Hello Millie."
"Good evening, Carlos. Are you drunk?"
"Are you my mother?"
"No, I'm your friend. Are you OK?"
"I'm actually doing very – OK. I'm good. But I do need to go – inside, now. Good night, Mildred."
"Good night, Carlos."

Stumbling as he entered his apartment, he could feel Mildred's eyes on him as he tried to correct his gait.

"Good night, Mildred."

Carlos considered texting his friends, but had to sit down and close his eyes for just a few minutes first. His head spun, but he found his martini high amusing. He thought about the other night with Monica. He allowed himself to imagine her on top of him, kissing him. He laughed out loud; he laughed at himself and the awkwardness of that evening. He didn't let anything happen that night. He pondered; was he a fool, or a saint? The last thing he remembered of that night, was Monica calling out to him and accusing him of being in love with Ginger.

The bright Tuesday morning sunlight burned through his eyelids as they slowly opened. His body ached almost as much as his head. He was still sitting on the couch in the same position he sat in last night. Aloud, to himself, "You, idiot. All drink and no food or water." He stood up carefully, almost falling as his knees started to buckle. "First things first; aspirin." His mouth was parched and the first gulp of water hurt his throat as he swallowed.

The time on the cable box displayed 8:20AM. *He would be late to the office again; no doubt about that.*

The rest of the week, Carlos kept things in order. He made calls to clients for any last minute needs before his extended vacation. He went over some important items with Ginger, who clearly kept it professional. He did not talk about his trip except to give her a preliminary travel plan; "just in case." He wondered if she hoped that he would drive off the end of the earth. Christopher Columbus screwed that up for her when he proclaimed the earth was round. Or was it Pythagoras? *Not important.* Either way, Thursday proved to be a quiet day. At 4PM Carlos said his goodbyes to Ginger, his father, and a few others. He headed to the parking lot. Crazy Joe agreed to have the RV dropped off, fully fueled and road ready to go. Carlos signed all the paperwork after doing a methodical walk through. He was confident the RV would be safe in the parking lot with all Aerotech's tight security. He planned on picking it up in the morning and driving to meet his friends, as planned, in the campus parking lot.

With a Gino's pizza pie, (extra thin and crispy) and a bottle of Coke, Carlos started texting the group. His couch felt good, and satellite radio played in the background.

"Hi, friends. I am really excited to get on the road tomorrow. As we agreed, let's meet in the main campus parking lot at 6AM sharp. Double check your travel list for medications – (the legal kind only), booze, snacks, and any other important items. And, food. Don't forget the food you are tasked with. The RV has a large fridge and a small freezer. We can stop for supplies each day as we need them, so don't overdo it. We are going to have a blast."

Nick: "6AM, ready, set, here we go! In the morning dude."

Randy: "Awesome. See you tomorrow. Can't Wait!"

Daniel: "See you then. Thanks. Is everyone going as planned?"

Carlos: "So far as I know. Haven't heard from all yet."

Monica: "6AM, be there or be square to all. Can't wait."

Monica: "Do you want company tonight? I won't be able to sleep. How about you? Thanks for the other night."

Monica: "Oh, crap. Was that sent to the group? Listen guys, don't get the wrong idea. We just hung out – As friends."

Joshua: "Are you sure it is OK for me to come along? I am so excited. My mom is crying. She is not cool with this."

Nick: "TMI Josh, just be there for the best time ever! And leave your bike home."

Nick: "Carlos, dude. You and Monica? Really?"

Carlos: "No! And cut it out! We are not even on the road yet and we are starting to get on each other's nerves."

Monica: "No! Nick. Is being good friends too difficult for you to comprehend?" *Not that I didn't try.*

Carlos: "Good night, everyone. See you bright and early."

Derek: "Sorry for the delayed response guys (and lovely ladies) but I had to catch up on all your group texts. My phone has slow service lately. See everyone in the morning."

Derek: "Thanks again for inviting me."

Carlos: "OK. Get some good Z's. We have a long day tomorrow. Glad you are with us, Derek. We are going to have a blast!"

"Night."

"Night."

"Night."

"Nighty night."

Chapter 29

The RV was easier to handle than Carlos expected; or, so he thought. The ride was smooth. The area designated for the driver and his copilot was something like that of a fancy motor coach bus with an elaborate instrument panel. He had planned on practicing driving the RV around town before the big trip, but that never happened. Now, as he drove the large vehicle on secondary roads to the meeting place on campus, he realized there were several tough to navigate, blind spots. The navigation system did have surround view which should prove helpful. Getting use to the *space age* system might take a bit of time.

One lone car sat in the parking lot. Sunrise barely present, Carlos navigated the RV into the large open field that soon would be filled to capacity with student and faculty vehicles. Another nice feature of the RV, no road noise. With a push of a button, the front passenger door made a swish sound as the door seal released and popped open a little. Carlos opened the door the rest of the way and stepped out onto the asphalt. The lone car's passenger door opened revealing its occupant as Joshua. As Josh pulled his backpack and a duffle bag out of the car, the driver's side window slowly lowered. First a hand popped out and appeared to wave as if signaling a hello. Carlos quickly realized it was a *come here* gesture. As he approached the car, he had a troubling sense about what might come next. His mind ran a few quick scenarios; none too pleasant. "Hey, Josh." Josh looked up momentarily and waved. His face said "Run, and don't look back!" But, no words came out of his mouth. He refocused his attention on the driver. "Oh, hello Mrs. Cohen. Nice to meet you. Carlos Martinez." He extended his hand but Josh's mother did not reciprocate. *Ok, then.* "You don't look like a college student." Carlos got what was going down here; he smiled. "What do I look like, ma'am?" *A hoodlum, I suppose?* His thoughts still running amuck, he was tired and anxious. Josh finally spoke. "Mom; cut it out."

"Watch your tone young man."

Carlos figured he needed to take control. He calmly and quietly said, "I've got this, Josh." He focused on mother Cohen. "I'm sorry. Can we start over? I'm actually not a student. I am a little older than Josh. I'm a sales exec at a nearby company and enjoy eating lunch out on this open, peaceful campus. It's my downtime during the day. My friends, who all are students, met Josh only recently. He's a great kid and we enjoy his company. We were always talking about this fantastic get-away and asked him to join us." His mom replied, "But, Mr. Martinez, he doesn't really know any of you and I'm not comfortable with this." "Carlos, please; my father is Mr. Martinez. Josh is your son, I get it. I'm sure I'll be just as protective of my own son when that time comes. He's quite capable and everyone in the group will look out for each other. They're incredibly good people." Her face did not relax. His repartee was not working. He took out a pen from his shirt pocket that he used for marking up his paper map and continued. "Here is my cell number, in case you have any difficulty reaching Josh on his. Why don't you stay and meet the rest of the group? I think they will help put your mind at ease." Josh chimed in, "Mom, it's fine. I'm going to have a really excellent time. I will call you every day." Josh pointed to the trunk of his mom's car. A spoked wheel stuck out and Carlos noticed the trunk was held closed with a bungee cord. "I wasn't sure if the RV had a bike mount; but I see it does. Can we bring it? Everyone can take turns using it to run short errands, or explore locally." Carlos shrugged his shoulders, "I suppose it could be useful; and fun. Let me help you." Josh grabbed the rear wheel as Carlos lifted the bicycle out of the trunk. "My cousin won't mind. I may have forgotten to ask him though." Carlos heard what Josh said but chose to refrain from commenting. Besides, it appeared he may have been talking to himself.

Whatever clicked, Josh's mom ultimately said "Thank you" and left just as the others started arriving. Her car slowed as she eyeballed the members of the group as they walked by or exited Ubers.

Nick and Randy were in the forefront of the group. Carlos wondered, *if they arrived together, did they leave earlier, together?* As if Josh read his mind, "You think?" Carlos said, "Stop grinning; of course not."

Randy kissed Carlos on the cheek, "I'm so excited." She high-fived Josh. Nick nodded to Josh and then said to Carlos, "Dude we're really doing this. Awesome!" Carlos was thinking of the day he contracted the RV and called Nick to meet him for lunch. Nick told him he was *busy*. He looked at Randy, her face glowed. She seemed happy and excited. He looked back to Nick who said, "What?" Carlos replied, "Really?" He immediately regretted making any insinuation that the two of them, Nick and Randy, were together. Nick's face turned beet red. "Oh no; no way. You think?" Nick glanced over to where Randy was hugging Monica who had just arrived in an Uber. "Really?

I got dropped at the bagel store on Metropolitan. Randy was already there getting coffee. We walked to campus together. Geeze!" As he said that, Monica hopped over to them and kissed Nick on the cheek. "Hey, buddy." Then she leaned over and put her arms around Carlos, kissing him gently on the lips. "Hi, friend." She giggled like a little girl and skipped back to the others. Nick looked at Carlos, "How does that saying go? Those who live in glass houses shouldn't throw stones?" Carlos put his arm around Nick. "Ok, there's nothing going on between any of us. What do you say we get this thing rolling?"

The others arrived over the next ten minutes. Carlos and Nick systematically loaded duffle bags and suitcases in the under chassis storage. The girls arranged food items in cabinets and cold storage. Joshua's bicycle was securely clamped onto the mount on the rear of the RV. After each traveler took a moment to check out the RV they started to settle in. Each person picking the first of many seating positions. Nick called "Shotgun." The others made jokes and called him a child.

The engine roared to life and the great hotel on wheels eased out of the parking lot and onto the main roads. Monica started strumming "Mustang Sally" on her guitar. The others quickly picked up the tune and started singing. They laughed together as friends, good friends. Monica slowed it down and played another one that was easier for them all to stay in tune together. "Here's one from Willie Nelson. It's one of my favorites."

"On the road again
Like a band of gypsies we go down the highway
We're the best of friends
Insisting that the world be runnin' our way"

As the sun of a new day rose and traffic began to build on I-95 South, one large RV rolled down the highway. Its occupants in pursuit of some undefined form of self-fulfillment.

Part Two – On the Road

Chapter 30

[Day One, Friday]

"Dude, don't get too comfortable; we all want a turn at copiloting." Nick swiveled his seat ninety degrees, the most is would go. "We are two hours into the trip. We're not even out of Jersey yet." Daniel laughed, "Easy there; just busting your chops." Derek was seat belted on the bench seat next to Monica. He said, "Don't worry Nick, I don't want your seat; I want to drive this bad boy." "I'll take you up on that, my friend." Carlos looked in the huge panoramic rearview mirror; his passengers could see his ear to ear grin. Monica asked, "How's she handle captain?" Their eyes met in the mirror. Carlos tried focusing more on the three dimensional view of the RV's interior than her baby blues. "Smooth as silk." He caught her sweet smile as he returned his attention to the road ahead.

Daniel and Joshua made themselves comfortable at the little meal table which would become someone's bed later on. They were playing cards earlier. Randy was MIA. Carlos glanced in the mirror again. He figured she might be resting in the rear of the motorhome. Probably in the bedroom area. Clouds moved in, diffusing the sun.

This made it easier on Carlos' eyes. Earlier, even with his shades on, he had to squint when checking behind him in the side view mirrors.

Without any words, Nick got up and made his way aft to the bathroom. To his surprise, it was quite spacious. His cousin's family had a smaller camper. That one had a combination toilet and shower. *Gross.*

The next stop for Nick was the kitchen. "Anybody for a beer?" Monica and Carlos both said "No! Not while we're driving." Nick came back with, "I'm just messing around." He quietly grabbed two brews and headed back to the rear of the RV. "Hey, you OK?" The master bedroom had a full bed in it and a mini sized dresser with a mirror above it. It was actually quite nice. Nick was amazed that from the kitchen area, past the shower and toilet and into the bedroom, he could imagine being in a hotel suite. Looking around the compact but fully equipped sleeping quarters, there was a small LED TV mounted in the corner and stereo speakers played some soft pop music. "Yes, of course. Just relaxing and cherishing the quiet." Randy's eyes remained closed as she spoke. Nick laid down next to her, both of them on their backs. "Here." He touched the can to Randy's palm.

She took it. "Thanks." She turned her head toward Nick, her eyes now open, "Hey."

Welcome to Akron Ohio.

Back at the helm, Carlos took the exit that said "Rest Stop, Next Service 40 Miles." "We need gas; good opportunity to stretch our legs." The group each vocalized their approval unanimously. Carlos veered to the left, following the signs for busses and large vehicles. He rolled up to the first available fuel pump. Daniel said, "I got this one," pointing toward the fuel gauge as he made his way out of the RV. Carlos closed his eyes to rest them for a moment. As if on cue, a pair of soft and gentle hands applied pressure to the area between his neck and shoulder blades. "That feels awesome." Monica stopped for a second and gently brushed his ear with her finger; then continued Carlos' neck massage. "Do you need a break? One of the guys can spell you or even I could, if you trust me." Carlos placed his hand on hers, she stopped moving but kept them in place on the back of his neck. "I think I trust you more than anyone else, ever. But, I like being in control. I'll speak up if I feel any fatigue coming on." "Really, you like to be in control? I might question that." She started her assault on his neck again. "That feels really good. You should stop now and take a break. Go stretch, I'll follow in a minute." *That felt too good, too dangerous.*

Carlos found his friends in the general store area. "Let's get going so we can make Wilmington by dinner time." Monica paid for a magazine she had started perusing. As they made their way to the exit she asked, "Did anyone see Randy or Nick?" Derek announced, "I hit Mickey Dee's; burgers and fries for all." He looked at Josh, "Sorry, guy. I don't know what is OK for you to eat." Josh told him not to worry; and that he brought his own food. "Besides, I follow the rules but maybe not so strict for this trip." Derek laughed, "All right! Cheeseburger?" Josh stared at him for a second in contemplation. "I don't think so."

Daniel steadied himself as the pump clicked off, indicating a full tank. He knew it would be costly but he was not prepared for the one hundred and fourteen-dollar bill. *Crap, that's for a half day of driving.* He stepped into the RV and made his way to the mid-section to pick a seat. It was quiet with the engine off. Soft music came from the rear of the vehicle. Daniel made his way back. They were there, together in bed. Nick and Randy were sound asleep. Two empty beer cans lay on the bed next to them. Even though it seemed innocent enough, Daniel's heart pounded. He felt defeated.

The others returned, Carlos immediately started the RV's engine. Derek asked Daniel if he saw Nick or Randy. Daniel said, "Nope, I thought they were with you guys." *I'm not admitting anything. They would think I was creepy.* Just then, Randy approached. "Sorry guys. I passed out. I always get sleepy during car rides." "Cop a squat, sleepy head. We're on our way for another six hours. We'll be in Wilmington before you know it." With that said, Carlos made his way onto I-80 West.

"Next stop Wilmington, Illinois home of the legendary Gemini Giant." *Carlos- the tour guide.*

Chapter 31

The second half of the day's journey, all three hundred and ninety miles, seemed longer than the earlier stretch. Monica played her guitar and sang, the others joined in from time to time. After a while she took a break and joined Derek and Daniel, who were in the kitchen area playing cards. Randy had taken the copilot's seat up front, next to Carlos.

"Monica really likes you. I see how she looks at you." Carlos did not see that one coming. He kept his eyes focused on the road.

"It's not like that, Randy."

"Sure, Carlos. I'm just saying. It's cool, but you don't look at her the same way."

"We're just friends. We have an understanding. We're good."

"I get that you're hooking up as friends. I think it means more for her though; a girl can tell. You're going to hurt her without meaning to."

What is going on here? Am I that transparent?
Holy crap! I'm that guy. It just happens.

"You're right, Randy. It started to happen like that. But that's not the case now. We talked it out and we both want to be friends. The flirting, well, it's just fun for both of us. It's like therapy in reverse."

"I'm just saying…. Be careful."

Daniel tapped Randy on the shoulder. "Hey guys, what's going on? Mind if I take a turn up here?" Carlos glanced at Daniel. "You want to drive?" Daniel laughed; "I meant copiloting." Randy said, "Sure. I should check on the rest of the crew anyway." As Daniel sat down he remarked, "Maybe you should check on your strange bedfellow." Randy drew extreme color in her face. "You're an ass!" She stomped her way to the mid-section of the RV. Carlos looked at Daniel who shrugged his shoulders. Neither said anything else about the situation.

"Who's winning?" "Hey, Randy girl; we're not keeping score; but I'm killing it." "Can I join?" As Randy asked, Nick made his debut from the master bedroom. "Hey, hey. What's happening, amigos?" Monica whispered to Randy, "Is he wasted?" Randy's expression indicated that she had no idea. Derek put up his hand for a "high-five." Nick attempted to meet Derek's hand but missed. He almost fell over. Derek stood up abruptly.

"Come here, dude." He grabbed Nicks sleeve and pulled it close to his nose. "You found my stash. What's wrong with you, bro?" Nick took a step back. "Cool your jets, I took a few hits. That vaporizing pipe is rad." Monica looked really upset. She said, quietly, "Carlos is going to flip. I thought you were his friend. He asked us all to play it cool while we were in motion. What if we get pulled over?" Derek chimed in, "Don't freaking touch my shit without asking!" Monica said, "Derek, why would you bring drugs?" As she said it, his face looked really tense. She realized why. "I'm so stupid. I'm sorry Derek." Derek said quietly, "I have a medical license, I would get into more trouble than anyone if we got caught sharing. More trouble than if I had it illegally. She looked at Nick with his goofy expression, "You should be ashamed!" Nick replied, "What? Are you my mother now? I smell burgers, who's holding out?" Randy had tears in her eyes. "Only one freaking day and we're already at each other."

Daniel remarked, "Your boy Nick is acting like an idiot, Carlos."

"I heard; better to let them work it out. I'll talk to Nick, later when he's straight."

Chapter 32

She had never experienced such a depressed feeling before. Ginger was well aware of her sexual aura. At first glance, men perceived her as the dumb blond with red hair. When she was younger and naive, she welcomed the attention. Then, when she realized how demeaning her situation had become, she started weeding out the creepy, disrespectful ones. Unfortunately, that thinned the herd quite a bit. During the past two years that she and Carlos had become friends, she had no need for another man. Carlos provided the friendship, fun, and consoling when needed. She also liked her alone time. But recently, her needs changed. It wasn't due to her watching a love story, or attending a wedding that made her jealous. After a while she started thinking about her biological clock. Not that she was old, but so many of her female friends, like her, in their mid-twenties, were getting married and having babies. Some just the latter; a sign of the times.

Carlos made her feel complete. They were the best of friends. She could tell him anything. He never judged her. She couldn't be sure exactly when it happened. Their last few times "Hanging Out" before that mistake of an evening were a blur. When they were together, she would imagine them holding hands and walking in a park. Two beautiful children ran ahead of them. She realized that the happiness she felt wasn't her imagination; it was real. If she had Carlos, really had him as hers, and children, at least two like she imagined, life would be complete. She had fallen completely in love with him and wanted more from their previously platonic relationship.

Foolish girl, his dreams aren't the same as yours.

"But they could be." She said it aloud and it sounded convincing. She would not give up on Carlos. She usually got what she wanted, and she wanted her dream to come true.

The "Happy Days" ring tone startled her out of her moment of yearning. She recognized the caller ID; it was Bob. After hesitating for two rings, she answered. "Hey, Bob. No. I already had something to eat. I wasn't feeling that great earlier. Tomorrow? Umm, sure. But wait, can we meet for coffee, now? Sure; in thirty minutes, at the diner? The diner works; see you in a bit." *Bob said it; the "L" word. Why now? Why at this awful moment?*

"Where are my damn sneakers?" Ginger nearly hit her head as she looked under the ottoman. She recently purchased the floral patterned item and conveniently placed it in front of her queen sized bed. Her sneakers were hiding there, along with assorted sundry items. Normally she would never go out in public wearing sneakers and jeans. The jeans were OK, as long as four inch heels accompanied them. As she looked in the mirror hanging on her bedroom door, she sighed. *I don't look very nice. I don't feel pretty.* She muttered to herself, "Sorry, Bob. This hurts me as much as it hurts you, but it's for the best."

Ginger hesitated as she walked into the diner. Bob was seated in a booth about halfway toward the back of the room. She could see him taking a sip from his coffee cup. He looked happy and content. *And boring, in his v-neck pullover.* She pondered how she would explain that their relationship lacked substance. It was too safe and comfortable. *And boring.* The other thing, of course, was Carlos. She needed to reconcile that situation once and for all. Until then, for her, there was no moving forward. That, she would *not* share with Bob. *It's not too late – you can still not do this.*

She sat down in the booth across from him; his look said that he sensed something bad was coming.

"Hey."

Apparently, asking if they could remain friends was a mistake. She didn't really mean it, and Bob knew it. He asked her, "It's Carlos Martinez isn't it? You used me to get to him." Ginger sat there frozen, a rare moment where she had nothing; not a word. He continued. "The flirting I could understand. It happens all the time; just not to me, until now. But sleeping with me to make him jealous? That's just plain cheap and slutty." The tears were coming; she tried hard but was losing the battle. Her stomach twisted in a knot and she was sure she was about to throw up.

"It is about Carlos. But, it wasn't when I agreed to go out with you – the second time. It wasn't when we spent the night together. That was because I wanted to spend it with you." *She lied*. "But after – I had all these mixed emotions, and I knew it was wrong. All wrong. I know it wasn't fair to you." Ginger attempted to take his hand but Bob defiantly pulled away. She ended with -

"I'm Sorry. You're a good guy who deserves someone who can give themselves to you wholeheartedly."

Back in her apartment, Ginger cried until the tequila took control of her emotions and settled her nerves. She fell into a deep sleep. If dreams came to her, the morning left no trace of them.

Chapter 33

Three hundred and ninety-three miles to go on this leg of the journey. It dragged on for what seemed like, forever. Nick sat quietly on the sofa across from the dinette area, where the others took turns playing Gin Rummy for points. Monica occasionally picked up her guitar and strummed a few notes or played a song or two. In general, everyone's mood took a downturn after the earlier fiasco. Nick knew he had allowed himself to get out of control. He was sorry, but not man enough to admit it. Joshua found his way up front to the copilot's seat.

"Five hours down, about one and a half to go." Carlos then said, "Do you think we'll survive the rest of this trip?" Joshua shrugged his shoulders, not that Carlos noticed, as he kept his eyes on the road ahead. "I'm not sure, Carlos, but I can ask God for a little assistance." "Sure, Josh, if you're sure that will help us all get along, then by all means." Josh chuckled; "It couldn't hurt."

Three hours earlier, Derek convinced Carlos to let him drive for a while. "You need a break and I want a chance to drive this bad boy." Carlos took the copilot's seat and closed his eyes. His neck was sore. He imagined

Monica rubbing it again. Her fingers had magic in them. He would innocently ask, but then the others would make something more of it. Tensions today were high enough. He could only hope that today, day one, was simply the result of a much needed adjustment period. Two hours into his time at the helm, Derek announced that a gas stop was needed. "We're at the quarter tank mark." He pulled into the rest area off of I-80. The exit ramp was tight, and Derek took it a little too fast. His passengers took notice as they grabbed anything battened down within their reach to steady themselves. Derek shouted, "Sorry, guys." Carlos told him not to worry; that he had done a fine job at handling the RV. Monica announced that she would take care of the refueling. Daniel said he would pump the gas for her since he was already experienced at it. "No way, guy. I pay, I pump. Equality for all."

After a twenty-minute stretch break, Carlos resumed his position in the driver's seat. "Thanks, Derek. I needed that break." He pulled out of the service area and up the ramp that lead onto I-80 West.

Monica pointed to the navigation screen, "Exit 151A, I-57 toward Memphis 3.8 miles." "Thanks, M." She rubbed his arm gently. "How you doing?" Carlos looked at her questioningly. She continued, "With the driving. You

OK? You look tired." Carlos gave a little sigh, "I'm actually pretty good. Derek taking the helm and giving me a short break really helped. Hungry is what I am. We need a good meal tonight to celebrate our first day on the road."

First Night – Getting Acclimated

The campsite at Enchanted Gardens was less than enchanting for a four-star rated facility. There were more stationary trailer homes than visiting RV's. It wasn't the social environment Carlos had hoped it would be for their first night. The others hadn't given it much consideration earlier on, but they started Google searching soon after their arrival.

"OK, OK; not what I expected either. Maybe it'll look better in the morning." Carlos explained the "Live and Learn" theory. "It's only two nights, then we're out of here." Nick leaned over closer to Monica, "Great start; can't wait to see the next PIT stop." He chuckled, slyly. Monica frowned at him. "I thought you were Carlos' friend. Give him a break. It's not like any of us pitched in to help research and plan this trip." Nick said,

"Whatever." This pissed Monica off big-time. "You're like a little kid;" In a whiny, childlike voice, she recited, "Mommy! Daddy! I wanna ride the horsey. Can we go on the rides?" Nick got up and walked toward the back of the RV. She heard him call-out loudly, "At least there's a fresh water hook-up."

Monica and Randy prepped the steaks and hot dogs. She got Daniel to wash the potatoes and wrap them in foil. "Carlos and Nickolas, you're cooking tonight." "Roger that, Miss." Nick saluted, military style. Derek asked, "What can I do?" Randy told him, as if she read Monica's mind, "Relax." She looked at Monica and smiled. Monica returned the smile, acknowledging that she had the same idea. They both saw his disappointed face. Monica said, "Don't sweat it dude, there's still cleanup after dinner. We'll all take turns at each chore." Derek gave a thumps up, indicating his approval. "Ok, then. I'm going to take a walk and see what's around this awesome place." What he really wanted to say was, "dump". But, he, if anyone in the group, understood positive thinking.

Everyone enjoyed the delicious hot dog appetizers and steak dinner. Carlos, Master Chef, cooked them perfectly. Josh had brought a portable stove, and heated up one of his pre-prepared dinners. He had explained his kosher needs at their last gathering on campus before the trip. The girls indulged in a delicious red wine as did Carlos. The others enjoyed assorted beers. Derek handed Josh a cold beer, which he happily accepted. All was good until Nick started acting weird. Nick kept looking at Joshua and laughing. The rest of the group could tell by his face that Josh was getting pissed. Randy asked Nick, "What is wrong with you?" Nick didn't answer. He kept imagining Josh's yarmulke popping off his head like a soda cap. His laughing grew more intense as the others questioned him. Carlos stood up and walked over to Nick. "We need to talk." Nick tried to stand up while laughing and coughing like he was going to puke - from laughing so hard.

They walked around the RV for privacy. It was dark and creepy, but Carlos didn't care, and Nick wasn't all that aware of his surroundings. "Really, Nick? This isn't like you." *Not that I know you that well.* "What are you on?" Nick calmed himself down before continuing. "I smoked a little weed, and had a few too many beers, I guess. I'm just letting loose. Isn't that what we said we wanted out of this trip?" "Yes, Nick. But we agreed, no drugs. Man, we don't want to get into any trouble." Nick leaned against the RV. "Damn, it's all wet, now so am I. I'll cool it, I know it's only the first day." "And damn it, Nick, what was with you and Josh? Why would you make fun of him and make him uncomfortable?" Nick looked truly upset. "I'll apologize. Sometimes my mind does weird things to me."

Josh was talking to Derek, who went over and sat next to the newest member of the group. Nick sheepishly approached them. Derek, who knew Nick before anyone else in the group, started to say something but the words never had a chance. "Josh; buddy. I wasn't laughing at you or anyone. I'm just an ass. I had too much beer too fast." He leaned over and grabbed Joshua in a bear hug. Josh held his breath and prayed silently for a quick reprieve. "Are we good?" Nick opened his arms as if he was going for another hug. "We're good! We're good!"

Derek washed the cooking utensils and loaded the mini dishwasher with the plastic picnic plates. The girls helped. He enjoyed their company.

After dinner, Monica graced everyone with mellow strumming on her guitar. Later, she picked up the pace, and the others joined in playing drums using body parts or utensils. They all enjoyed the sing-along. A few of the surrounding campers looked on but never made any effort to be social with their modern day hippie neighbors.

Little by little, each member announced they were tired from the long day of traveling. Carlos checked the time. It was after 10PM. "Let's figure out the sleeping arrangements." No one had thought about the tent that needed to be set up.

Monica took charge. She had a pretty good idea what Nick or the other guys would suggest. "Carlos, you footed the bill, or whatever you had to do for this hotel on wheels, so, it's your say on how we do this. But, I do have a suggestion for tonight." Carlos motioned for her to continue without saying anything. He was exhausted from the long day's drive. "Alright then. Randy and I will take the bed in the rear sleeping quarters. Josh and Daniel you're on the sofa bed. Lastly, Nick and Derek..." She patted the dinette table she was seated out. "You've got to be kidding!" Nick stood up abruptly. "This should have been planned out better. Before we started this trip." Monica defiantly said, "It's just one night. We can plan better for tomorrow and raise the tent earlier in the day. Then we will all be more comfortable." Nick said, "Who put you in charge, anyway?" He looked accusingly at Carlos. "And what about your fantasy man? Where'd you stick him?" She pointed toward the front of the RV and up above the driver's seat. "Great he gets the best space. Nick kept his focus on Carlos. Or, is that for you, and her?" Monica got angry and put up her hand halting Carlos from interjecting. "First of all, Nickolas; Carlos footed the bill for the RV. He's doing most of the driving and he planned this trip for all of us. As I said before, it's just for tonight. Grow the fuck up!" Carlos reached up to an overhead storage bin that looked like what was on an airplane. He pulled down a sleeping bag and a tarp. "Nick, you're up there for tonight. I'm out of here!"

Chapter 34

5:30AM

A beautiful and bright, but frigid, sunrise awakened Carlos. He was freezing and had to pee. It took him ten minutes to conjure up enough of a will to move out of his less than spacious sleeping arrangement.

Monica was already in the kitchen area brewing coffee. As she loaded a pod into the Keurig she said, "Good morning; you look frothy. You poor, man." Her hair glistened; he had to control his imagination once again. She noticed his stare. "I figured there would be a lineup for the shower so I got an early start. Here you go." She passed her cup of piping hot Java to Carlos. "You need this more than I do. I'll make another." She looked around, "We can go in the back; Randy should be awake by now. There's plenty of room for three." She winked. "We can drink our coffee and catch the news till the others start getting up."

10:00AM

Everyone seemed calmer after a good night's sleep. Even Nick, who climbed down from the overhead sleeping bunk rubbing his eyes, seemed like a different person. "Good morning." Randy made pancakes while Josh watched in amazement. He asked, "How do you know the perfect moment to flip them?" Randy grinned. "It's a secret I learned from my dad. He's the master at making flapjacks." *If I told you, I'd have to kill you.* Derek took on the coffee. Nick directed his attention to Carlos and apologized again. He pointed up front to the bunk, "Yours for the duration. As captain of this ship you should be up there. Thanks for the offer last night, though." Carlos nodded. Nothing else needed to be said. Derek added, "Last night was last night. Today is a new day. What's the agenda for this fine day?" Monica held up a sheet of paper and dangled it in his face in a sort of teasing way. She said, "Let's get going; times a-wasting."

The minivan taxi took them to the Gemini Giant. The driver offered to wait mentioning that there was no need for more than five minutes at the historic site. Everyone took pictures and selfies of the statue that was basically situated in a small parking lot in nowhere-ville.

"Let's go into the city. I hear Chicago is awesome; there are so many famous people and places to visit. Maybe we'll see Oprah." Randy did a little jump. Everyone agreed; even the cab driver.

"Wow. It's like a mini New York. I love it." Monica had an ear-to-ear smile. Nick suggested "Let's do lunch at Michael Jordan's." Derek gazed around surveying the landscape. "Check out how the houses and brownstones are randomly positioned in between big buildings? Such an interesting mix of architecture." Josh chimed in, "Too bad we don't have tickets for the Cubs." Nick said, "We could make that happen." The girls made a face, then Monica said, "I think it will be fun. We are here, aren't we?" Carlos added his opinion. "I'm not sure baseball is the best idea." They all gave him the stink eye. He felt like the last man out. "All I'm saying is, it's not baseball season and the players are all still down south." He shrugged his shoulders and continued with a hint of sarcasm, "But, by all means... let's go."

After a long day of food, walking endlessly, and drinking at several authentic Chicago bars, everyone was exhausted. In the cab, Daniel expressed how amazing Lake Shore Drive and all the fancy hotels and apartment buildings were. "Imagine the views from the higher floors overlooking the lake." Josh added, "The lake that looks like an ocean, and is almost as deep and dangerous." Randy said, "Carlos, wasn't the Navy pier incredible." "It was." His response was terse. He had other things on his mind. The very things this trip should have distracted him from. He realized that he was missing Ginger.

"Darn it! I wanted to go to Lincoln Park." Nick threw up his hands in disgust. His friends thought him melodramatic and acting spoiled again; yet, no one said anything.

Back at the RV, raising the tent took all of twenty minutes. Nick and Derek announced they would occupy it for the night. Monica asked, "Aren't you afraid you might get mugged or something?" She just couldn't resist. Nick shot back, "Carlos survived in just a sack. I think we will be just fine. Besides, if someone wants to mess with us – that's their problem. Right, my friend?" Nick smacked Derek on the back. Derek returned a thumbs up sign.

They ate dogs with all the good fixings, cooked on the open campfire and drank beer and wine. Josh had his own supply of dinner selections that he heated in the microwave. Monica provided the music and they all sang. Everyone was in harmony again.

Chapter 35

Margaret O'Brian from Human Resources, strode down the corridor in double time. People were amazed to find out that she recently celebrated her sixty-ninth birthday. They often remarked about her age. They plainly could not imagine that she was a day over fifty. Not a wrinkle or frown-line obstructed her sweet, plain, but attractive face. She offered to take a lie detector test once, when challenged about ever having cosmetic anything done. With thirty-plus years at Aerotech she was considered one of the key players in Corporate Operations. "Good morning, Ginger." "Hi, Margaret. Good morning to you. I see that you're fast pacing again. If that's how you keep your stunning looks, I'm going to try it myself." Margaret smirked, "With your looks, honey, you should have no worries. But, it couldn't hurt. We do get older and anything we can do, should be done." She smiled at Ginger, "You should join me for a walk during lunch sometime." Ginger said, "I'd like that. Thank you, Margaret." Margaret took Gingers hand, "You're a very bright young lady. I am going to see if there's something more substantial for you. Our company needs more young management capable people." Ginger was taken by surprise. Flattery, or any type of compliments regarding work, rarely came down the pipe to her. "Thank you Margaret, that is so kind of you to say. I appreciate you looking out for me. I really like what I'm doing but I do think I'm ready for a change of pace." *From Carlos.* "Definitely keep me in mind. Thank you; see you later. I have to get back to my desk for a conference call with one of Carlos' clients." Margaret laughed, "You are something else, young lady." They each started to go their own way. Then, Margaret looked over her shoulder and said, "Oh, I almost forgot, Mr. Martinez would like to speak with you at ten, in his office." Ginger looked puzzled. "Mr. Martinez is away until next week." "No silly; Martinez Senior." Ginger got a funny, not so good vibe that started to upset her belly. *The big boss never called her to his office. He was pleasant when they passed in the hallway or when she delivered reports for Carlos. But he never directly asked her to come to his office.*

Fortunately, the call Ginger was asked to sit in on only lasted thirty minutes and was over by 9:30AM. She checked her watch. The cute little Michael Kors timepiece had been a Christmas gift from Carlos two years ago. It was barely a few months after she started working for him as his executive assistant. They hit it off, and a true friendship developed quickly. He was so easy to talk to.

Her heart pounded. She had to clear her mind. Ginger decided to make her way to the ladies room before heading over to the big boss's office on the other side of the building.

"Yes, of course. I will have my Chief Financial Officer, Ron Hicks, call you this afternoon. I appreciate you making us aware of the issue." Ginger took a deep breath to calm her nerves. She heard Martinez Senior ending his call and waited until he hung up before gently knocking on his partially open office door.

"Ginger; please, come in and have a seat." He was an older, distinguished version of Carlos. His perfectly fitted, gray pinstriped suit showed off how fit he was. Just like his son. He motioned for her to take a seat in the beautifully tufted guest chair in front of his desk. For a moment, he just looked at her saying nothing, then he slowly and smoothly stood up and made his way over to close his office door. "You seem a little nervous. There's no need. I'd like this to be an informal discussion. In fact, it may get personal and if you are uncomfortable with anything in our discussion, please do not hesitate to let me know." Ginger was appreciative of what he said, but it only made her more nervous. "How long have you been at Aerotech? Three years now?" He asked and answered his own question as he sat back down behind his hefty mahogany desk. Ginger surreptitiously drew a calming breath and said, "Well, sir; two years and seven months." The boss smiled. "You are precise. I've been told that on more than one occasion. And, how long with Carlos?" "Two years and two months; as of last week."

"Has Carlos ever mentioned his mother to you?" Ginger let her face display a sad expression as she nodded. "Ok, then you probably understand some of his shortcomings; specifically regarding his personal life. Lord knows, he's a magnet for business." *And for women*. They both probably had the same thought about Carlos, at the same time. Martinez paused for a moment allowing both he and Ginger to digest their mutual understanding regarding Carlos. Like Carlos, his father projected a strong and powerful image of himself. His perfectly crisp gray suit looked expensive adding to that authority. He continued. "I had a meeting with my Human Resource manager yesterday. Your name came up, and we discussed your previous reviews. You're a smart young lady. I think you have a lot to offer Aerotech. More than what your present position will allow. I'd like to have you meet with Margaret to discuss the creation of a new division within the HR department. It would be a management position. She will fill you in with the details."

Ginger was astonished. She should have been ecstatic that the top guy called her in to his office to tell her what should have been done by the HR people. Or, her current boss. She had no words at the moment. Except...

"Sir, please don't take this the wrong way; and of course, I am most appreciative of the compliment and offer. It's incredible. But; why am I really here?" She regretted asking such a bold question, the second the words left her mouth. The damage was done. *Oh, Oh.*

Martinez Sr. leaned back in his grand chair and let out a sigh. "You are perceptive. Perceptive, smart and beautiful. No wonder why my son is so smitten with you." She felt her body go numb. She was afraid she might vomit. "I've noticed how he looks at you, and you at him. And not just recently; since the day you started here." Ginger put up her hand indicating for him to stop. He was crossing a boundary that no boss should ever. Then again, as a father? She was confused and wanted to turn away and run. *Oh my god; where is he going with this?*

"No matter at my home or here in the office, your name always came up. It's as if you are imbedded in his soul. The past few weeks though, he has been depressed and somewhat distracted. Your name has been absent from our conversations. I'm sorry to pry but he is my son and you are a valuable asset to this company. Did something happen?"

With tears flowing, Ginger told all. She needed to vent to someone. Perhaps her boss' boss, and father, might not be the best choice, but here they were. "I love Carlos. I've loved him since we first met." She told him about their two year closely intimate but non-sexual relationship. She didn't need to tell him what happened recently between them. The current situation exposed that one on its own.

"My son is a fool to let you get away. It's not his fault though. He is damaged by his mother's unannounced departure from our family. He has trust and commitment issues. I'm partly to blame. My wife and I went through a bitter separation and eventually divorced. We didn't take into consideration how Carlos was being affected by our hostile split. Now, he is off on a trip with strangers somewhere in the Mid-West." Ginger felt bad for Carlos's dad. He looked so sad. She hesitantly took his hand in hers, "He respects you so much and loves you. You did a fine job raising him. Your son is an incredible person. Someone will mend his heart; I thought it would be me. I'm sure that idea has little promise at this point." She realized that she still had Martinez's hand in hers. She gently pulled it away. "I'm so sorry." He smiled, "No need. Thank you for coming to see me." She smiled and wiped a stray tear rom her cheek. "Thank you."

"Ginger." She stopped at the door but didn't turn back to him. "Don't give up on him; he needs you. And, I'm sure that you are the one to mend his heart." Ginger paused a second in thought before leaving the office. Her mind was twisted with confusing emotions. Too much had been tossed at her in that short time with the boss of bosses.

I love you Carlos.

Chapter 36

Sunday

With the tent taken down and packed up, Carlos started the RV's engine and announced, "Crappy parking lot – adios! Stanton here we come." Carlos pulled out of the RV Park and onto the I-55 then merged onto the I-44 to highway MO-W toward Stanton.

Monica noted the time. It was 9:45AM. She anticipated a gas stop and estimated a 2:30 to 3PM arrival at the next RV camp. Randy called out from the kitchen area, "We need supplies, mostly food. I'll start a list and pass it around."

Josh played copilot for the first hour until Monica shooed him away jokingly. Joshua jokingly agreed to vacate his seat for a good sleeping position that night. Monica winked, "We can work that out." He got up but Monica remained standing behind Carlos. "I want to drive." Carlos replied, "I'm not tired. We just started out, and it's a short sprint today." Monica gently rubbed Carlos' neck. "Please, when we stop for gas; which by my guess and that gauge over there, should be in about an hour."

"Oh Yeah; that's the spot."

"So we're good?"

"I'm good. Really good right now. Don't stop."

"If you and I were..."

Monica stopped herself. "I mean if I were your friend Ginger, you'd let me drive." Carlos pulled his body forward just enough to release his neck from Monica's fingers. "If you were Ginger, we would not still be friends."

"I didn't mean anything by that, Carlos. I'm sorry." Carlos waved his hand indicating "Whatever." Feeling uncomfortable, Monica said, "I'll tell Josh he can have his seat back at the helm." She paused and then turned to walk away.

"Wait."

Carlos turned to see her standing behind him with tears running down her cheek. "Please, come back and sit down." She did as he requested, saying nothing as she wiped her face with her sleeve. "I'm sorry, Monica. I'm at an impasse with myself. I don't want to lose her as a friend. She's embedded in my mind no matter how hard I try to focus elsewhere. I'm not good with committing to any kind of personal relationships. The other night, at my apartment, I almost did it again." Now he lowered his voice to barely a whisper. "With you." He took a breath. "You are this incredible, beautiful, and romantic person. Any guy including me would be crazy not to allow you into his heart. I'm seriously conflicted." Monica reached her hand toward him, he took it in his, keeping his left hand on the steering wheel. "I love you, Carlos, but your heart belongs to another. I know this, and keeping you close as a friend is as important to me as having you as a lover." Carlos sighed, pausing before his response. *That's what I said about Ginger.* "So, Monica. You and I can have what I wanted for me and Ginger?" Monica laughed, tears still flowing. "Well, minus the sex part. You blew that one buddy." *She had the most infectious smile; even behind tears.*

Nick approached the front of the RV singing "Hi-Ho, Hi-Ho, off to Stanton we go." He tapped Monica on the shoulder, "Would you mind if I ride up front for a while?" Monica winked at Carlos and said, "Sure. Besides, I need to start being the tour guide again for this stop. I'll be in the kitchen doing some research." Nick smirked, "I hope it's better than the cool Gemini Giant." He expected an angry comeback from Monica. He glanced over to Carlos who met his eyes with the same fear. Carlos said, "I hear you big guy; it was pretty lame. It'll be all good from now on." "What are we talking about?" Randy had just walked up behind Monica. "Come on, Randy. Let's get to work." Randy shrugged her shoulders, smiled at Nick, and followed Monica back to the kitchen.

An hour outside of Stanton, Carlos pulled into the roadside service area. Randy volunteered to "Filler up." Everyone disembarked to stretch and catch a snack at the Stop & Go convenience store. Carlos snuck up behind Monica, reaching in front of her, and dangling the keys to the RV. "You're in command of the helm." He handed her the keys and mumbled one of the few expressions he was familiar with and used often. "Estamos jodidos... *We're screwed.*" Monica's facial expression changed from sexy – surprised, to a child-like happy. She did a little dance and kissed Carlos' cheek. "Thank you. Thank you." "Su bienvenida a mi bella amiga." Monica pretended she understood what he said; it sounded nice. "I didn't know you spoke Spanish." He looked at her questioningly. "I mean aren't you, like, third generation?" Her face was so stressed from what he assumed as embarrassment that he couldn't control himself. Carlos roared with laughter. She questioned him, "What?" Then Monica joined him, hysterically laughing.

Next Stop Stanton

The first few miles were a bit rough. Everyone had a good time making fun of Monica's driving abilities. "Whoa! Wee!" they laughed, and she laughed along, making her swerve a bit more. Carlos, who manned the copilot's seat, said "Cut it out. She's doing great; for a beginner." Monica exited onto 44 as per the navigation system and Carlos' confirmation.

"OK. Three Thirty-five. You made good time missy. If you could carefully pull over on the shoulder; right there looks good, I'll take it from here." Carlos and Monica switched seats at the helm. Carlos slowly eased back on to the road, checking for fast moving cars exiting off of I-44. After a few minutes, they arrived at the RV park. Carlos pulled forward to the main entrance and paid the fee. He was handed a map with directions to their assigned campsite and a tourist booklet with attractions and other needed information.

As soon as the RV was hooked up to power and water, Carlos announced he was going to explore the area and pick up some groceries and other supplies at the local market. Monica suggested the guys build their tent while she and Randy finalized a list of cool places for the group to vote on going to on Monday. The guys moaned and groaned. Randy told them, "You guys are such whiners.

We also have to prep for dinner." Monica added, "And tonight we are cooking too." Randy laughed and said, "Yes indeed; Monica's pot-luck surprise." They both continued giggling.

"Hey, Josh. Would you mind grabbing the tent? We'll meet you on the south side to start setting it up." Josh knew he was being used. He figured, he was the "low man on the totem pole" since he joined the group last. The tent weighed sixty pounds; about half as much as Joshua. The cargo hold was low to the ground, so he dragged it to the edge and then let it drop to the floor. "Ouch! Schlamazel!" An image of his mother reciting her adoring description for him flashed in his mind. As he pulled his foot from under the large clump of canvas he mumbled, "I swore to God that I wasn't going to be that person, anymore." He bit his lip and dragged the soon to be bedroom to the designated area.

"What are you guys doing? I could have used some help." The other two burst out laughing. Nick, red faced from choking, reached out his hand, "Here, cool your jewels." Josh made a curious face. "What? Dude it's like drinking wine, but better." Nick looked at Derek. Derek coughed and with a serious face said, "Hey, it's legal for me." Nick extended his hand toward Josh.

"The only way to get rid of temptation is to yield to it."
— Oscar Wilde

Chapter 37

The walk from the campgrounds to the market took about twenty-five minutes. The air was uncomfortably humid and Carlos's jeans stuck to his skin. At that moment he envisioned Josh's cousin's bike attached to the rear of the RV. He had noticed it just this morning as he started his trek towards the Market. *Silly me*. An elderly couple nodded "hello" as he passed them on the stairs leading to the store entrance. As Carlos entered the main door, a younger couple, perhaps in their mid-twenties pushed passed him. The girl glanced his way as her male friend yanked her arm, redirecting her attention from Carlos, back to him.

The market seemed unexpectedly crowded for a Sunday afternoon. Carlos assumed that on this beautiful spring day people would be planning family barbeques. He figured most of the customers were grabbing last minute items.

As he made his way around the market, he picked up various items such as lettuce, onions, parsley, which Randy had requested, and dill. The girls planned a special dinner for one of the nights. The sign at the fish counter said "Just In." Amazingly, they had Branzini, his favorite. Carlos' imagination went crazy. He pictured everyone sitting around a roaring campfire while he twirled his fish in a grilling basket. The smell of lemon oil and garlic aroused his senses. *Back to reality and the fish counter.* He requested seven of them cleaned and scored. "They look really fresh. Surprising being we're in a landlocked region." The fishmonger basically ignored Carlos. *Hmm, probably fresh-frozen.* He then went back and picked up fresh corn, in the husk, and a bag of potatoes. He would cook dinner tonight. Carlos wondered if Joshua would eat what he cooked. Maybe a quick lesson from Josh on how to make a kosher meal would be in order.

To his surprise, there was a booze aisle. Carlos grabbed a bottle of Premium Vodka. *Hmm, need some OJ and cranberry juice too.* He figured his travel mates would enjoy a refreshing cocktail before his extraordinary dinner.

The register lines were not too long; three of the five remained open. Back in Brooklyn the store would have been much more crowded and he might have found one or two lines open. As Carlos picked a line, he realized they might need dressing for the salad. He maneuvered across the front of the store searching the signs for each aisle for "Salad Dressings." *Aisle seven, that's the one*. His cart practically drove itself. He recollected his usual experience back home with wobbling wheels.

The aisle was void of other people except one young lady standing in the middle of what looked like an avalanche of cans and bottles. She appeared upset and looked confused. *If it were me and there were no witnesses, I'd beeline out of there.* Carlos being Carlos; he had to see if she needed assistance.

"Excuse me, Miss; are you alright?"

The attractive twenty something year old, abruptly turned toward him. She seemed startled; as if she had no idea anyone else had entered the aisle. She told Carlos, "Everything is fine. I just had a rough morning. Thank you though, for asking." She tried to smile but it hurt. Carlos could tell she was in pain. As she turned away, sort of dismissing him, her knees began to buckle and she almost fell. Carlos grabbed her arm to steady her. Another shopper started down the aisle. Carlos gave her a sharp look and she immediately turned her cart and disappeared. "Here; sit down for a moment." He helped her to sit against the shelving. She said, "Oh, my god. I'm so embarrassed." Carlos sat down next to her, "Take a moment to calm yourself. You started to hyperventilate which made you dizzy." He offered his hand, "Carlos." She partially looked at him and replied, "Mary." She took his hand, and he gently responded with light, reassuring pressure that helped comfort her.

"What happened to you?" Clearly by her distress and apparent bruises, she was a victim of some sort of abuse. She made up a story, minimizing the fight with her boyfriend, which explained her distress. She also said she was rushing around and hadn't eaten anything all day. OK, that explained the dizzy, almost collapsing part of the equation. She offered no mention of hitting anything with her face. Carlos asked her, "We're in a food store, why don't we get you something to eat?" Mary thought, "Who is this guy, he is like a knight in shining armor." She said to him, "Thank you, really. I have to get home." He had to ask, being him. "My friends and I are traveling across country exploring the old route 66. We are docked in the RV park a few miles down the road. You're welcome to hang out there for a while, even join us for an awesome sea faring dinner." Mary thanked Carlos and again told him she had to go. He said, "OK; if you're sure." "I'm fine, Carlos. It was nice to meet you. And, thank you for trying to save me." Carlos nodded and waved goodbye as she started down the aisle. *That's me; the savior*. He watched her as she turned left out of the aisle and headed to the cash registers. Carlos imagined her sweet, pretty face, as the fists of a faceless man hit it. He became irritated and upset knowing that he could do nothing to help her.

Chapter 38

With the tent squared away by the three musketeers, Derek and Nick ambushed the mobile kitchen for chips, dip, and beer. Randy looked up from her travel magazine and watched them for a moment. Monica, seated across from her at the table, concentrated on her agenda planning and paid no attention to the two goof balls. The RV dipped a bit, indicating another incoming member of the tribe. Carlos, with two bulky packages, one in each arm, gasped for air as he set them on the tiny counter. Nick looked up and said, "Alright! More food." He and Derek laughed. Derek added, "Cool." "They're both wasted." Randy shook her head as she announced their feeble state of mind. Carlos grinned and then asked, "Where's Joshua? He was with you when I left earlier. What did you clowns do to him?" Clown one and Clown two looked at each other with guilty faces; then they laughed heartily. "The poor guy. After we finished pitching the tent, he passed out inside. We left him there to get some Z's."

Josh wobbled into the RV with the silliest of grins on his face. His Yarmulke hung off-center on his head. He noticed the others staring at him as he attempted to right his appearance. Monica shook her head, "You guys are idiots. Why did you let him...?" Carlos intervened before a war of the sexes began. "It's going to be dark soon and I'm getting hungry. Joshua is a big boy. He can take care of himself. Besides, he looks fine; more or less." Josh nodded in agreement with Carlos. Then exclaimed, "It's kosher, so long as you don't eat it." He looked at Nick, "We didn't eat any of it, did we?" Josh laughed whole heartedly, then closed his eyes and gave a big "Oy." Carlos took a beer from the fridge and leaned against the counter. "I met this girl at the market." He noticed Monica paying attention with what he perceived as a somewhat jealous expression. And Nick's face said what the other guys were thinking as well. "No, cut it out!" Carlos told his story of Mary and his self-loathing for not trying to do more to help her. Nick said, "Dude, you just met her. Not everyone is your responsibility." Randy looked at Monica, who seemed to have relaxed now. Then she said, "Perhaps they are. He brought us all together. Each of us seems to have some..." Randy seemed lost for words. Joshua chimed in, "Meshugas." The group all looked at Josh questioningly. Josh, with his silly grin added, "Craziness, oddities, hang-ups." Randy continued, "Meshugas." "Yes, like the messiah." Monica smiled and winked at Carlos as she said that. Nick huffed, "Or, like

Charles Manson." Derek whispered to Nick, "Un-cool association dude." Monica, who already had it in for Nick said, "What is your problem?" Nick looked sad, and apologized to Carlos.

"Can I get some help in the kitchen? Can you guys get a good fire going? Josh, can I use your pots and pans? This grilling basket is new. You stay with me and supervise. I want you to be able to eat this dinner." Carlos waved at everyone to get moving. Joshua had brought most of his own food and cooked it separately. His family kept a kosher home, and did their best to follow all the dietary rules. Josh was a bit more flexible outside of the home. Monica was still hard at work with her planning for the evening, and Monday's adventures around Stanton.

Everyone agreed that Carlos, cult leader and master chef, had prepared a delicious meal. That is, everyone except Nick, who expressed his appreciation of Carlos' talents while eating a self-cooked double hamburger.

Carlos wiped his mouth from the delicious lemon oil and looked around at his friends. With their bellies full of branzini, and smiles on their faces, cult or messiah; he did good. His inner smile told its own story. The stress from earlier in the day gone, he looked forward to a night out on the town.

"I found this cool bar for us to hang out at tonight. They have a mechanical bull, and barrels of peanuts all around the place." Monica giggled, "And live music." Carlos laughed. "Sounds great, Monica. But, who needs their music? We have you." He made her feel good. He always gave her a sense of need and satisfaction. He was a great friend. *That Ginger is a fool if she lets him get away.* Monica didn't know Ginger, but had developed a sort of loathing for her. She understood that it was her possessiveness over Carlos and not who the girl was. After all, according to Carlos, she wanted him. It was Carlos that had the issue with long-term commitment. Monica reconsidered her original thought. *That poor girl.*

Two cabs showed up at the entrance to the RV campsite. Joshua announced he was staying behind. The long day had tired him out. Nick was sure it was the weed. The group all decided that was not happening. "All or none" they chanted.

A night out – on the town

In the minivan cab, Monica announced that she found two cool places to visit on Monday. "Meramec

Caverns looks awesome." She fiddled with her iPhone and passed it around with pictures of the park and some of the caves and other activities. She continued her rhetoric. "There are, like, 40 caves to explore and we can go canoeing or stream fishing." Everyone agreed it sounded like a really great place to spend the day. Carlos thanked Monica for planning the activities. Randy said, "You're awesome, girl." She paused for a moment. "Should we tell the three musketeers when we get there?" No one replied; they all had grins on their faces that completed the joke of the moment.

Carlos said, "I guess this is the place; seems to be hopping for a Monday night."

When the group of young New Yorkers walked up to the entrance they were asked for ID showing their age. As if the NY vibe hadn't been sensed already, the driver's license confirmed it. The bouncer's attitude told it all. Josh got a second look and a head shake. Carlos and Monica both gave Nick the look of "Don't start, leave it alone." Joshua, fortunately, was either unaware or immune to it.

As Monica had earlier described the place, and showed pictures, the bar seemed familiar to them. It could be any good old beer pub in the country. The music was upbeat and loud. Groupies lined up in front of the band, dancing in place. They waved one arm high in the air and held a brewski in the other. The bar area was a large oval shape with a dozen or more mostly young female bartenders pouring drinks. Every one of them had a smile from ear to ear. Carlos thought they reminded him of pro-ball cheer leaders before the first playoff game. The patrons, young and old, paid close attention to their scantily covered upper torsos. The shelves stocked with spirits that ran across the middle of the interior bar work area, allowed one side of the drinking crowd to see the patrons on the other side. After a few drinks, some might think they were looking in a mirror, possibly wondering if that is what they looked like after a few too many. Peanut shells and dust covered the floors and every thirty feet or so, a barrel of peanuts sat next to a support column. Randy, who had strayed a bit to check out the band signaled that she had found a spot at the bar. There was just enough room for her and Derek. The others congregated behind them, placing their drink orders. Derek announced that he and Randy would take a percentage of all orders placed through them. Nick said, "I'm not paying you a cent, but maybe I would pay you." He winked and pointed to Randy. She considered smacking his smart mouth but settled for a disgusted frown. Derek started passing drinks back to his friends. "Here's your Corona, Nick." As he started to pass it back, he paused. "Oh yeah, my fee." Derek took a swig and passed on the beer to Nick. "Are you kidding?" Derek laughed and pushed Nicks shoulder. "Don't worry, friend. What I have isn't contagious. If it were, you would be doomed after our smoke-fest earlier."

Daniel drank his beer quickly and ordered another. He guzzled that one about half way when the light-headedness kicked in. Along with his beer-head came a pseudo confidence. He maneuvered his way over to Randy who seemed to be in her own world, dancing to the beat of the music. She looked beautiful. His heart pounded. *Be a man and ask her*. "Hey." She smiled, still dancing in-place. "Hey." "This place is huge, I thought I might check it out." Her gaze made him think she was not into it or too wasted to respond to his quasi invite. His paranoia and confidence weakened each second he waited for her to say something. "Guy's, what's going on here? Randy, can I get you another drink?" Nick put his arm around Randy in a sort of possessive way. She smiled at Daniel and turned to Nick. "Sure. I think maybe a Cosmo." She made like she was reaching in her pocket for money. Nick said, "No problem. I got it." Randy flashed Nick a sexy smile. "Thanks."

Daniel felt like a loser. Nick did it again. *May the best man win; it won't be me.* Randy grabbed Daniel's hand. "Come on; let's explore." Ecstatically surprised, he locked fingers with her and started moving through the crowd. "What about your drink?" "I'm not sure mixing hard booze with beer is such a good idea. Besides, it will take Nick time to get the attention of a bartender and even longer for them to make a martini. I'm sure he'll find a taker or end up drinking it himself while flirting with one of the barmaids." She motioned toward the bar and its voluptuous servers. With his confidence renewed, Daniel felt empowered.

"You look like you want to be somewhere else right now." Monica took Carlos' hand. "Why don't you call her tomorrow?" She didn't wait for him to respond. "Tonight, we are going to forget all the stuff we left back home. That's why we're all here. Come dance with me."

Derek and Josh found Nick at the bar. When Nick saw his friends he said, "Hey, dudes." Derek asked him, "Why are you drinking a pink girly drink." "It's mighty delicious, and I got stuck with it. But that's not important.

I offered it to this pretty lady here, but she refused me too. Her man hit the head eons ago and never came back. I'm keeping her safe until he returns." Derek nodded a hello. "Are you going to introduce us?" Nick looked lost. The very attractive young lady extended her hand, "Mary. Your friend here never asked me my name." "Derek; and this is Josh."

The music picked up again after a short break. Randy and Daniel made their way to the other side of the bar where there was a more or less designated dance area. "Dance with me." *Let's see what you're made of, Danny boy.*

This was not the same girl from computer class. She seemed possessed, and it was a huge turn-on. The next song was by Marshal Tucker and things slowed down. Randy nuzzled into his shoulder and asked, "Do you like me?" Daniel said, "Yes, of course. I have for a long time."

"I like you too. Why didn't you ever say anything?"
"I wanted to."
"Do you want to kiss me?"
"Yes."

"Are you going to do it anytime soon?"
"Yes."

As their lips met, all went silent. No one else existed but the two of them. Only the sound of two hearts beating echoed through that silent moment.

****

The hand on his shoulder, as it pushed him aside, had power behind it. "Sorry, buddy. That's my space you're occupying, and my woman your talk'n to." He turned to Mary, "Is this chump hitting on you?" Nick stood up as straight and as tall as he could. The guy still had a good three inches on him. "We were just making polite conversation during your..." he mumbled, "abandonment of her." Then he quickly and clearly said, "I mean absence." Red faced, and obviously jealous, the guy insolently said, "I am talking to my girl. Mind your business!" Mary's controlling boyfriend focused his attention back to her. She said, "We were just talking. No one is hitting on anyone. Why'd you leave me for so long?" "Why are you questioning me? Are you wearing the pants now? You think you're my keeper?" Suddenly, without warning he pushed her arm hard and her drink spilled all over her cute blouse. He then turned to Nick,

"You got something you wanna say?" Nick shrugged his shoulders and looked around for Josh who seemed to be MIA. *Great, just me and Cancer Boy. I'm on my own with this Jerk off.* Behind the big guy's back, Nick mumbled something. It was barely audible but Derek poked him insinuating that he should keep quiet. Mary grabbed her man's arm as she stood up. The napkin she had used in an attempt to dry herself fell to the floor. "Let's go, Don. I need to change. Besides, I've had enough of this macho crap for the night." Don's reddened face seemed a bit cooler at this point. Then he stopped and turned back to Nick and Derek. "Wait. What did you say, chump?"

Josh made his way through the crowd to find Carlos and Monica still at the bar. Both were trashed. "Hey guys. Sorry to interrupt but..." Carlos put his arm around Josh, "No worries, we're just hanging here, enjoying the music and the excellent company." He smiled and nodded at Monica who flirtatiously smiled back. Josh looked frenzied. "Are you OK?" Monica squeezed his arm. His first reaction was to pull away. Religious customs present strict rules for unmarried people of the opposite sex. As he moved away, he showed his discomfort and embarrassment. Monica realized what she had done, "I'm sorry, Josh." Josh looked like he was going to jump out of his skin. "No, guys. That's no problem, really; it's Nick. I think he is about to get his ass kicked and probably Derek too."

Nick was laying on the floor with a bloody nose while one of the other guys held Derek in a partial head lock. "You better stay down till we're gone; Jack." "Name's Nick to my friends; you can call me Nickolas." He spat a bit of blood to the floor and started to get up. "I'll say, *dick*, you sure know how to treat your woman. I bet she respects your manhood; for sure – not!" Don handed his beer to Mary who put it on the bar. "Cut it out, Don. Leave him and let's go!" Don reached behind him without looking back and shoved Mary again. She hit a bar stool and would have fallen hard to the floor, if not for a strong arm catching her. She looked up and into his eyes. Even though she had only seen him behind those dark Ray-Bans, she knew it was him. The one from the market.

"Are you OK? Mary?"

The guilt of leaving her defenseless earlier in the day all but forgotten in his sozzled state. Carlos assisted her to a bar stool. "Stay put."

While all the commotion had taken place over just a few minutes, to Nick it seemed like an all-nighter. His head was spinning, but that didn't stop his mouth. He was almost standing when Don's fist was raised again. From behind, someone grabbed his tightly clenched fist and pulled his arm behind him. "Holy Crap! What the F?" The pain of Carlos' knee in his kidney was excruciating. The nausea that followed, even worse, as Don hit the floor. One of the guys holding Derek attempted to intervene and approached Carlos. Monica stepped between them. "Are you into hitting women too?" The guy stopped and put up his hand indicating he was not. Derek looked at Carlos and nodded a thanks, then he focused on Monica and said, "What a force to reckon with in that adorable little package." Carlos couldn't agree more. At that very moment Carlos wanted her; he just wanted to hug her tight. *She's incredible.*

The bouncers threw everyone out, threatening to call the police if they tried to come back in or started anything in the parking lot. Nick was trashed as were the rest of them. "Whew. That was awesome." He pointed to Carlos. "You are the man!"

On the other side of the lot, Don's friends attempted to help him into a car. The big man pushed his friend yelling that he didn't need anyone's help. Mary told them to wait for her, she would be right back. Carlos saw her approaching and started walking toward her. Monica caught up and held his arm pulling him to a stop. "Not a good idea. Let's get out of here." "I just need a moment, Monica. That's Mary; the one I told you about from the market." Monica let go of Carlos' arm and watched as he walked up to his damsel in distress.

"I'm really sorry, Carlos. I guess you didn't expect to run into me a second time; or any of this." She motioned in the direction of Don and his friends. Carlos said, "You should stay with family or a friend tonight. Let him cool off. I know people like him. An abuser is forever an abuser. You're not safe with him." Mary told Carlos she would stay with a friend. She also said she had already made up her mind to leave him. The events of the evening just accelerated her plan. "Why don't you come with us? We have plenty of room. They are a great, fun group. You can get yourself organized and make a plan." "You're a wonderful person, Mr. Carlos; mystery man behind the cool sun glasses. In one day, you made a difference in my life. You are a savior." She put her arms around his neck and pulled him in for a long affectionate hug. Carlos waved as she smiled and turned away.

Randy and Daniel came running out of the bar. "Hey, where were you guys?" The rest of the group just looked at each other. Monica put her hand around

Randy's shoulder adding a light hug. "We can trade stories on the way back to camp."

In the cab, Monica kissed Carlos on the neck and whispered in his ear. Josh looked the other way assuming the worst, from his point of view. Derek slurred, "Get a room."

Only Carlos knew what Monica whispered. Now he had to decide how to follow his heart which at the moment was splitting in half.

Chapter 39

Intense dreams disturbed his sleep, but as the morning approached, he would remember little of them. The air in his small space above the captain's area had an unusual warmth. The scent of coconut was calming. *Wait! There's a hand on my...* His body position spooned her, and her warm body felt good. *Oh, thank God! We're both still in our clothes.* Oddly, he had sense of easiness, a comfort he welcomed.

The sun streamed in from the tiny oval window. He opened his eyes to find no one else next to him. He figured that his earlier awakening must have been a dream.

"Good morning." Her grin unsettled him. Like she had an awareness of something he didn't. Randy handed him a cup of coffee. "Umm, slept in your clothes?" Carlos, still squinting from the brightness in the RV and a wicked hangover said, "Really, Randy? Now's not a good time for questions." "Oh, cause my roomie passed out same as me last night, but when I got up to pee in the middle of the early morning, I was alone. Where do you suppose she disappeared to?" Carlos shrugged. *Crap, it wasn't a dream?* "Good morning." Daniel had the biggest grin on his face. Carlos glared at Randy, whose face suddenly went flush. He asked, "Really?" Randy handed Daniel a cup of java. "Not the same situation, Car-los." She said it using a sarcastic tone. "Whatever it is you are fantasizing, you got it wrong, Randy." "Whatever, Carlos. Not really my business." "In that, you are correct." Daniel took a sip of his coffee. "Ouch – that's hot. What are we talking about?" Randy turned away and started walking back to her sleeping quarters. Without looking back, she said, "We're not talking about anything." Daniel looked at Carlos who shook his head, indicating to leave it alone. "Wow. You must have done something." Carlos rubbed his temples in an effort to ease the pain. "No comprende Engles? Leave it be!" Randy yelled back to him, "Alright!" Daniel yelled out, "He was talking to me, Babe." Carlos took a breath, "Babe?" Daniel shrugged his shoulders and grinned. "Whatever, Daniel. Did you see Monica?" Daniel pointed to the window. "I heard her say 'What a beautiful day for a walk,' then she disappeared out the door." Carlos nodded and made his way to the front of the RV. He announced to no one specific, "I'll be back in a while; I'm going for a hike."

The park had some nice amenities. Carlos looked around while reading the wooden direction signs. "Pool,

Administration, Trails, Showers." The single hiking path soon split into two. One seemed to circle the campsite area pushing out a little then veering close to the camp. The other looked like it led to the lake area and fishing pier. The water seemed a logical choice.

"How'd you find me?" Monica looked sad; seriously sad. "I guess I know you better than myself these days. Our souls are in sync with each other." Carlos sat next to her on the edge of the small, sort of rickety, floating dock. Her feet dangled in the water, creating ripples that sparkled like diamonds. Her sneakers sat next to her. Monica looked so innocent and sweet. "About last night?" "Oh, that was some crazy stuff." Carlos tilted his head and looked confused. "No. I mean…" She pressed her soft index finger to his lips. "Nothing happened; in case your being fully dressed, didn't clue you in."

"I don't remember even getting into my bed."
"When we got back to the RV I went straight to my bed. You must have tripped or something because I heard you curse yourself. I found you at the foot ladder looking kind of lost. You were lit. I was so exhausted from helping you up and into the bunk that I needed to lay flat on my back for a second. Next thing I know its 4AM and we are – well, you know."

"Why didn't you leave when you woke up then?"

"It felt good; safe."

"I was up around that time too. And, you're always safe around me."

"I know." *That's our problem*

Carlos stroked her hair pushing it away from her eyes. "You are something else, girl." Monica's face started to twist. Carlos thought he was having a relapse of drunkenness. "The heat of your body so close to mine made me crazy. I wanted you so bad. I prayed that your arms would end up around me. That you would pull me closer so I could feel you." Carlos took her hand.

"Being just friends is going to be really hard; isn't it?"

Monica looked at Carlos with her soft eyes, her mind racing in several directions. "For sure."

The devil casts temptation on us both.

"OK, everyone; Josh! Where are you? Derek! Let's get this day in motion." Nick emerged from the tent in his tiny heart-patterned boxers. His bare chest showed his excellent muscular definition. The girls made ooh and ah sounds and made gestures indicating hot. Randy said, "You better get dressed; your outfit might be an issue at the Preserve's main entrance. "Has anyone seen Joshua?" Monica looked around; no sign of him and no answers from anyone. Derek called out from the rear of the RV. "Bikes gone; so by process of elimination, I'd say they are together." Just as Derek said that, his eyes caught the rapid movement of something approaching. He called out, "Incoming! Save the guitar!" Josh came barreling into the group's camp site, jumping off the two-wheeler while still in motion. This time, danger bypassed them. "Hey, I did some exploring. It was really nice riding along the trails. You guys should try it."

The Ozarks

Meramec Caverns consists of a 4.6 mile stretch of limestone formed caverns that formed over several million years.

The tour guide explained some of the history as they moved along the rock and dirt path. "And this is the Greatest Show on Earth." The group was truly amazed at how the lights reflected off the limestone. Randy whispered to Daniel, "I think I saw this in a move once." They next visited the "Mirror Room" and the "Ball Room" where they sometimes have concerts. "Wow, this is better than the Hollywood Bowl." Monica looked like her neck would snap as she looked up and over at the massive cavern. Randy asked her, "You've been?" Monica said, "California? Sure; twice. By plane, never by land. This is way better." Randy stated, "Too bad we won't make Santa Monica. I'd love to see the West Coast for real."

"We Should."

"For Real."

The group returned to camp late in the afternoon. The driver of the large van that transported them home recommended some good local places to eat. At about 5:30PM, as they approached the main road leading to their home base, Monica asked the driver, "Can you drop us at the place you suggested? It sounds really good." Everyone agreed that they were tired and didn't want to fuss with making dinner or cleaning up. The place had great pizza specials and salads. Josh took a cab back by himself to make his own dinner in the RV. He explained to the group earlier in the trip that he was totally fine with fending for himself for meals. He also requested that they refrain from making a big deal over it. They didn't.

When the group returned to the camp, Josh had a fire going. "How did dinner work out? I figured you might want to hang out, so I made this fire." Nick said, "You are the man, Josh." Monica pulled out her guitar, and they all sang along until sleepiness provoked them to call it a night.

"Are you sure you don't need help getting up there?"
"I think I got it."

He smiled, she smiled; everyone slept in their designated places. Daniel wondered if Randy dreamt of him. Randy dreamt that they were back on the dance floor with Daniel holding her in his arms.

As Carlos lay in bed trying to fall asleep, he thought about his time with Monica at the lake. But in his dreams, he held Ginger in his arms.

Chapter 40

"Watch your speed. Waze has postings of heavy police activity all along I-44." Derek, who drew the long straw, got to drive. Randy sat in the copilot seat. She continued, "So, we're off to another state and another adventure. I didn't realize the Chain of Rocks Bridge would have taken us a few hours out of our way. It would have made more sense to stop there first." Derek shrugged his shoulders. "Didn't seem all that interesting, anyway. Besides, didn't Monica route this trip?" "Well, yes." Randy paused a second in contemplation. "Actually, she did, but we both went over it so we both missed it. Tulsa will be great."

Joshua fell asleep sitting up in the corner of the meal table area. Nick and Monica were there too, both texting on their cell phones. Carlos joined them, "Hey guys, want some chips?" He put the bag of Sea Salted potato chips on the table and spun the bag so the opening faced Nick. "Thanks, big guy." Nick grinned. Monica said, "Hey Carlos. I had an idea I wanted to run by you guys." She lowered her voice to a whisper and pulled a color-printed sheet of paper out of her pocket. Nick said, "What's that? Let me see." He snatched it out of her hand.

Monica made a face and put her finger to her lips. "Be quiet. Don't wake Josh." Carlos asked, "What is that, Monica?" Nick answered. "Something about a Jewish Museum of Art?" Carlos' face twisted a bit showing his confusion. "Monica, why do you have that? Is that one of your preferred stops?" "No, guys. It's his." She pointed to Josh. "He must have researched places of interest last week, when Carlos suggested that we all do that." Nick said, "How is that of interest to any of us?" Monica considered how ignorant he was and looked at Carlos. "It's of interest to him. This is all new to Josh. He is open to exploring cultures outside of his comfort zone. He had difficulty with meals. We never really considered what he might like to do." Nick shook his head. *Who cares? It was his choice to come along.* Carlos bit his lip. "You're right, Mon. He must have wanted to present this as an option for a stop and then decided not to. He is trying so hard to fit in with us. We should be considerate and take an interest in a bit of his culture. I say we visit the, what is it?" Monica pulled the sheet from Nick's hand, "The Sherwin Miller Museum of Jewish Art. I'll check Google Maps and see how it fits into our itinerary for Tulsa."

Randy came traipsing back to the group. Monica took a break from her googling, "Hey, girl. Aren't you needed up front any longer?" "Sure I am, Monica, but I wanted to see what the crazy people are doing. Besides, Derek wanted me to make Carlos aware that we need to pull off at the next service area to feed the RV." Carlos stood, "I'll head up there. You guys should be seated and belted in." He got the usual dismissive looks. "Hey, what's up guys; and girls." Joshua yawned and stretched. "Good sleep?" "Yes; thank you, Randy." He stretched his neck and arched his back in one continuous motion. While Josh's sleep may have been energizing, his sleeping in a sitting position did not do as much for the rest of his body. The RV came to a slow stop. Carlos announced, "Fifteen minutes." Nick put his arm around Randy, "Buy you a Coke?" She squirmed out of his hold while noticing Daniel's stressed facial expression. She recognized his jealous tendencies over Nick's actions toward her. She figured that was taken care of the other night at the club. She also considered that perhaps Daniel needed some reassurance. "Sounds great, Nick. Get me some chips too." Nick winked, "I'll be back in a bit." Nick should have picked up on the brush-off but his ego, as usual, got in the way. Daniel asked Randy, "You want to go with them?" She took his hand. "Not particularly." *Wow, I can't believe Nick fell for it again.* Randy had no preconceptions to what or how her relationship with Daniel would progress. This whole forwardness thing was out of character for her. Daniel would come around, *she hoped*, but for now she would need to push him a little. Randy led Daniel to the bedroom area and pulled the sliding door closed.

"Does this mean we're going steady?"
"Shut Up."

"It's my turn." "No, Josh. Nick's got this one." Carlos figured Josh wouldn't stiff the group. His pal Nick, on the other hand, might.

Back on the road again, Carlos resumed the Captain's chair, and headed onward toward Tulsa. Joshua sat in as the copilot. "So Josh, if you wanna drive..." "I'll take a pass, Carlos. Haven't you seen me on a bicycle?" Carlos thought for a moment and glanced over at Joshua who had the most serious expression. They both burst out laughing.

Nick nudged Derek and motioned in the direction of the private bedroom. He mumbled, "You know what's going on in there?" Derek grinned, then whispered, "Sure do, buddy. Your dream girl is getting banged." Derek paused letting Nick see him grin. "You going to eat those chips?" Red faced, Nick shot back, "Eat-me!" loud. Everyone took notice but then went back to what they were doing. After all, it was coming from Nick. Nothing unusual there. Monica, unrelated to Nick's outburst, wondered herself what was happening behind those closed doors; in her shared sleeping quarters. Jealousy? No. Well... perhaps a little. She was happy for Randy, and for Daniel. They were both shy and from the get-go seemed into each other. Fairy tales are awesome. Monica let that one sink in for a moment before Carlos invaded her imagination once again. She daydreamed that it was her and him in that closed off bedroom. "Damn." She got up and moved onto the couch. Nick plopped down next to her. Without looking directly at Nick, Monica said, "You really are desperate." Then she looked at him with sad eyes.

"Listen, Monica. Every man wants what he can't have. It's not my style, but I can help make him jealous. He'll likely realize that what he has right in front of him is more valuable than what might or might not be waiting for him at home." Monica didn't respond, she just looked away. Nick continued. "It's clear Carlos is into you. It's that girl at home that has his head messed up. He needs someone to make him realize that; to open his eyes." Monica held her head in her hands and sobbed silently. Nick stopped talking and closed his eyes. Everyone seemed to be taking a siesta. Even Joshua fell asleep sitting up; again. Carlos cherished the quiet as miles upon miles of I-44 rolled on behind him. His mind began to wander... *Tulsa should be a little less than five hours. Stopping there was a great idea. Not only would it provide a good break for the long travel day, it was right on the route they planned on taking. The Clinton destination would add another three hours, getting us in kind of late for check-in at the next RV park.*

I-44, now three lanes, was wide open. There was nothing much to look at from a scenic standpoint. Nothing, except for the same rolling hills and distant mountains that he had seen for the past hour. Carlos was suffering from the beginnings of boredom. He looked over at Josh who seemed to be asleep. Carlos glanced at the oversized rearview mirror, which showed his entourage slumped in various positions, strewn about the motorhome. "Monica? Are you awake?" He said it softly so as not to disturb her if she was actually sleeping. There was no answer, but after a few minutes her hands rested gently on his shoulders. Their warmth aroused his senses. His nose detected the mild scent of her hand cream that he had become familiar with during some of the more intimate times they spent together. *But never that intimate.* "Hey, Carlos. What's up?" "The monotony of the drive is getting to me; it's like road hypnosis. Would you be into playing some music? Monica suggested, "How about a sing-along? That would help pass the time and keep you alert." Carlos said, "You're the best! You can wait till the rest of them are awake." She gave a little squeeze on his shoulders. *Now that's what I'm talking about*. "Sure." She said nothing more; she turned and headed back to where the others were lounging around. After a momentary pause, she knocked lightly before quietly entering the private sleeping quarters. Despite her best efforts, Monica couldn't resist and glanced at the bed. Two lumps under the covers lay motionless. She figured they were either sleeping or hiding until she was gone. In a meek whisper she said, "Sorry" and then retrieved her guitar. The shapely mounds seemed to move just a bit; Monica was certain she heard a giggle.

"Hello Darkness My Old Friend."

Monica played softly and sang in a whisper. Soon, everyone seemed to be awake. She paused her singing. "Hey, sleepy heads. Time to act like we are a party group." That caught Nick's attention. His minds-eye interpretation was not what she meant. "Carlos needs a sing-along." Monica changed-up the beat, and they all joined in. The captain smiled to himself. *Now that's how it should be*.

Tulsa

"Right on schedule!" The group seemed to have gotten over the funk they were experiencing earlier, thanks to Monica, and her guitar. Her upbeat music also helped to pass the time more quickly. For a change of pace, Nick had replaced Josh in the copilot's seat. "OK, Carlos; if we are doing this JewMu; get it? Jewish Museum. We can park in a municipal lot three blocks west of it. It says here that the lot can accommodate campers, vans and small RV's." Carlos didn't immediately respond to Nick but instead announced, "Hang on! Hair pin curve, exit ramp." The exit onto I-40 was tighter than he expected, even for the modest 30MPH he had slowed to. Everyone made the usual sarcastic comments regarding his driving and then returned to whatever they were doing. Monica's guitar almost flew off the couch. Carlos was too busy driving to save it again. She had to take matters into her own hands. "Nice save, Monica." "Thanks, Josh."

"Nick, buddy. You are a good guy, but sometimes you can be such a dick. Why do you make comments that are insulting and embarrassing?" Nick made a face indicating that he was annoyed. "I have no idea what it is you are referring to, Carlos." "Alright, come on. The remarks you make about Josh. It makes him feel bad and embarrasses the rest of us. Then you act like his friend. He's not stupid. He's trying to fit in while being the odd man out." "I'm just challenging him. Sometimes I can't help it. All he needs to do is come back at me. I can take it. Then we would have it all out in the open and the comfort level would be better." Carlos looked like he was going to pull over onto the shoulder. "Is that right, friend? How come you haven't made any Latino remarks to me? Why aren't you challenging me? What are you afraid of?" Nick squirmed; the others were listening even though they tried to look like they were doing other things. "Fuck you all if you can't take a joke!" That really did it. Carlos was red in the face. "Jokes are meant to be funny. Nothing you have to say lately is funny. If you don't cut it out, you can find your way home from Tulsa cause you'll be out of here."

Randy sat down next to Joshua and put her arm around him. He cringed, and she realized that she may have violated some religious custom. Regardless, she held tight, her hug was that of a sister. "We're all your friends, Josh; even Nick. He's just an idiot and sometimes ignorant." She released him from her loving hold and he seemed relieved. "Thanks, Randy. I'm OK." Monica asked, "Does this kind of thing happen to you often?" Joshua replied, "Not very often. But it has." Derek joined in; "You know, we brothers deal with this crap all the time. So, I get you." Everyone looked at Derek. "And this cancer thing, people think feeling sorry for me is a nice thing. They have no idea how their reactions hurt and drive my soul into deep despair." Daniel said, "I think we all have to deal with anomalous behavior and depression at times. And, things that have hurt us. Somehow we have found each other and both the good and bad are coming out. That happens in close quarters like this. We are all going to be better people because of this trip and our friendships." Daniel took Randy's hand in his. They both had the silliest grins of happiness on their faces.

After Carlos' verbal assault on him, Nick sat frozen in his seat, saying nothing. Carlos said, "Look dude, you are a cool guy. Everyone that you meet seems to like you." Nick replied, "Sure, until they get to know me." "You try too hard, Nick. Be yourself and go with the flow. Don't always go against the grain to create friction."

Changing the subject, Carlos announced, "Twenty minutes to our next stop."

Nick got up from his seat up front. "You good for a bit, Carlos?" "Sure, Nick." Nick made his way back to the rest of the group. Everyone tried to look as if they had no idea what had just transpired between him and Carlos.

"Hey, Josh. Can I talk to you?" Josh looked him straight in the eye. Nick thought he looked like the proverbial "deer caught in the headlights." To his surprise, Josh firmly said, "Not to worry, Nick. No need for a talk. We're good." He had let Nick off easy. Josh's demeanor was what it was. He never held grudges or displayed animosity. His friends who had suffered similar ridicule took a more aggressive view on those who tried to make them feel inferior or not welcome. Nick appeared contrite as he said to the group, "Ok, then. I'll say it right here; to all of you. I can be an ass sometimes." Randy said, "Sometimes?" Monica grinned and put her arm around Randy in solidarity. "Ok, often. I don't mean to hurt anyone. My dad was a tough guy, and he always made me feel like I was less than a man. You guys have been more of a family to me in this short time we know each other. Josh, Joshua; I never had a Jewish friend. And man, you are as Jewish as they come. For me it's like sticker shock. I'm sorry for my remarks. I like you and I understand if you hate me and don't want my friendship. Either way, I'm glad we are doing this stop in Tulsa for the Jewish Museum." Everyone remained silent, waiting for Joshua's response. Monica was pissed again at Nick for spoiling the surprise. Joshua Cohen stood firmly, his eyes focused on Nick. "Listen, I've had to deal with all kinds of crap being an Orthodox Jew. We stand out more than the average Jewish person out there. Possibly not as much as others of a more, different, religious conviction, but we do. I have made peace with ignorance in many ways. I don't intend to insult you by calling it ignorance but that is better than calling by other designations. Asking about a custom that seems strange or even uncomfortable may help you understand about other people's beliefs. Questioning is not rude; it's a sign of intelligence and compassion. Perhaps, if you allow me to tell you why Jewish law directs us in a certain way, you might at least understand and appreciate our beliefs even if they don't coincide with your own."

Joshua cut his rhetoric short. "Wait! Are we going to the Sherwin Miller Museum of Jewish Art? Why? How did you know about it?" Randy took the floor. "Monica found this when you were sleeping. It must have fallen out of your pocket." She handed Josh the computer printout. Josh's face lit up. "This is awesome. But you guys; if I'm the only one interested then we can skip this." Monica said, "I can't speak for the rest, but I'm stoked for this stop." Derek chimed in. "We all good brother." Nick gave Derek a light push on the shoulder. "What's with the 'Brother' crap all of a sudden?" Before anyone could say anything, Nick continued. "See, Josh? I can't help myself. I do it to everyone. But I'm going to try to not do it - so often." He extended his hand out to Joshua; and they shook. "You think you could explain things to me while we visit the museum? Maybe help with some of the ignorance?"

Carlos pulled the RV into the alternate museum parking lot. He checked the time, 2PM.

"We're here."

A giant banner hung between two poles. It shimmered in the wind boasting the celebration of the museum's "50 Year Anniversary." Josh's face lit up. "Too bad; we just missed the Purim festivities. You guys would have liked that. People dress up in all varieties of costumes and masks. There's lots of cake and other goodies too."

The lobby area was impressive. The group stuck together as they entered into the Jewish History and Culture Exhibition. "Check this out." Josh pointed to some archaeological artifacts from the early bronze age. Nick called Derek and Carlos over to where he was making faces at a figurine that appeared to be in the shape of a female. "The Hellenistic Period. I didn't know there was

Wayne Lasner

any relationship between the Greeks and the Egyptians."
"Me neither, Carlos. Thirty-Seven B.C.E. That's a long time
ago. There's a lot of history here." Carlos scratched his
head in wonder. "Sure is, Derek. This is quite fascinating."
Nick laughed, "OK, Spock."

The rest of the group found their way to the Kaiser
Holocaust Exhibition. A plaque with the history had them
all reading in silence until Randy broke the quietness. "I
took a semester of Jewish study as an elective last
semester. The course focused mainly on the Holocaust
and the atrocities in the camps." Monica looked solemn
as she said, "It was such an awful period in the history of
the world. What made you take that class, Randy?"
"Curiosity, and it was the only available elective in the
time slot I wanted. But, I'm really glad it worked out that
way. I found the stories of survival and the heroes, some
who broke into the camps and occupied territories to
smuggle people out. My heart ached for what happened
there. It's humbling and allows you to think about others
differently." Joshua had walked off on his own. He was
overjoyed to be in this place. Even more so, his elation
over the way his friends took to this place made him feel
happy and fulfilled. He was able to share in their ways as
much as his religious constraints would allow. They in
turn, now shared in his culture. They seemed fascinated

and sympathetic. What more could he ask for. *Thank you, God*. Joshua mumbled to himself, "This will make mother happy too."

"Hello, young folks. Thank you so much for visiting with us today. We are closing in fifteen minutes." Monica smiled at the sweet elderly lady as she read her name tag. "Thank you so much, Sandy. This place is incredible. We've learned so much." Carlos said, "Wow. Almost five; the hours had passed unnoticed." Even Nick seemed impressed. "This was a great idea, Joshua. Too bad you didn't share with us earlier. We almost missed out on this spectacular museum." No one could tell if his remark reeked of sincerity or sarcasm. Carlos added, "This was great Josh. Now we need to find a place for dinner and then a rest stop that allows overnight parking." Another museum employee overheard Carlos and approached the group. "I suppose the RV in our extended parking lot belongs to you? We don't have gates, but there is a night watchman that patrols every hour. We can let him know you are parking here for the night, if that helps." Carlos thought for a second. "That is really nice of you. We would like to take you up on that offer. We'll be on our way in the morning, before you open." The man grinned, "Not like the crowd is busting down the gates to get in. Any time you want to stay until is fine. It's our pleasure. And, thank you for visiting with us."

Josh pulled out his camera. "Let's take a selfie with the museum behind us." He text messaged his parents the picture of the group, all with big smiles and thumbs raised high.

Everyone agreed to walk around the town and find a place to eat. Josh said he would stay with the RV and have something to eat there. "We can try to find a Kosher deli or other restaurant. How about the Ripe Tomato? It's vegetarian. Would that work?" Monica seemed hopeful. Joshua said, "I don't think so. Don't worry. I'm fine. You all should go and enjoy a good meal." As they walked past a market, Randy suggested, "Let's get sandwiches and stuff to go and eat back at the RV." Carlos was in agreement. Nick said, "I'm down with that. We can chill tonight." Derek laughed, "What? No more bar fights for you?"

Josh was glad to see his friends return. They all ate their meals together while discussing the day's events. Everyone agreed that as much as it was exciting, every effort to avoid another bar fight would be smart. Nick had to agree, since his body aches served as a constant reminder. After dinner, Monica played guitar and they all sang. Later that evening, Monica sat on a folding chair, gazing up at the stars in the sky. Nick sat down on the ground next to her. "Beautiful night, tonight." He passed a joint to her. At first she was going to scold him but instead, took it and said, "Thanks." She took a light drag on the cannabis stick. "Mmm good." Carlos stood just outside the RV door looking in her direction. Monica passed the joint back to Nick and touched the back of his neck, then ran her fingers through his hair. She nonchalantly glanced over to where Carlos was, to make sure he saw. *Every man wants what he can't have.* She caught Nick glaring at her. "Whatever it is you're thinking; Not happening!"

Wednesday

The loud clap of thunder caused Carlos to sit up abruptly. He hit his head on the RV's canopy. The sound of the two hard materials hitting, echoed like a beat on a Jamaican steel drum. He checked his scalp for blood, only to find a slightly bruised spot.

"What was that?" Monica sat up and checked to see if she was alone or not. No one responded to her question. There appeared to be a body under the covers next to her. She poked it. Nothing. A chill came over her. *What if Randy traded places with Nick to be with Daniel in the tent? Wait, not possible. Derek would be an odd man out; Creepy.* Another crack of thunder, and the bump popped up. Monica, startled, screeched. Randy screeched back. "You freaked me out, Randy." "Sorry, Monica. Is it raining?" "I think so, Randy. The weather has been too good to us." Monica checked her phone, "It's 7:20AM. Time to make the donuts." She stretched. "Hey, Randy, if you want to be with Daniel, we could work it out somehow." Randy had a sort of shocked expression on her face. "Really, Monica? First of all; I wouldn't do that to you. Second; I hardly know him." Randy's face turned beet red from embarrassment. "OK, maybe I know him fairly well in some ways. This is all new, and I for one, do not plan on rushing into anything long term. Not yet. Unless; you need another excuse to..." She motioned to the front of the RV. "Randy! No. That's not happening. I'm over that situation." *I really am.*

On the road to Clinton...

The RV roared to life as Carlos started heading down the gravel path leading to the exit. The lot was still empty except for one car, right where the path ended and the road into town began. Its single occupant waved as they passed. Carlos waved, and mouthed, "Thank you, Sandy." Monica and Randy waved from the mid-section dining area window.

Joshua took the available copilot's seat. "Hey, so we're like three hours out?" "Sounds about right." Carlos wasn't in a talkative mood at the moment. Josh realized this and sat back with his shoeless feet on the console in front of him. The I-40, void of any other cars, seemed a bit eerie for ten in the morning. "It's like something out of a scary movie." Carlos spoke without taking his eyes from the road ahead. Josh looked around and leaned over to catch a glimpse of his side-view mirror. "I get what you mean. In a few miles the road will just end and we will drop off into oblivion." Silence prevailed for five minutes. Josh checked his messages and searched Google. "Or, according to Google Traffic, there was an accident about two miles east of where we entered I-40. I think the road was closed." Carlos said, "In my dad's time, they had CB radios; I could have asked the eastbound drivers what was going on. Cell phones are great but the driving community lost that unique communications network."

Three hours passed quickly. The group remained quiet for most of the time. Nick listened to music with head phones connected to his iPhone. Randy snuggled into Daniel on the couch while perusing her Facebook account and all the usual gossip. Daniel's eyes were closed; he looked happy. Derek sat by the window in the dinette area next to Monica, and across from Nick. He looked stressed, perhaps in some discomfort at that moment. Monica wanted to put her arm around him but decided to leave him be for now. Her heart ached with sadness as she thought about his long-term situation. Then, she smiled to herself knowing he was with friends and sharing this awesome adventure. She checked her notes for the two museums that they might want to visit. Then she searched for the campsite where they had made a reservation. She went online to confirm their stay and came across an interesting place. She said to whoever had an open ear… "This place might be a dump, but it looks really cool." Nick was in his own world, bobbing his head, likely to the beat of whatever music was playing. Derek looked her way, as did the love birds sitting across from her. "The Lucky Star Casino is right off of I-40. They have free RV parking with hook-ups and some other amenities. And a casino. I think we should check it out." "Sounds like a plan, Monica." Randy gave her approval. Daniel agreed with Randy. *Of course he did.* Derek said, "Could be fun." Nick, who apparently was eavesdropping over his music, said to Derek, "Enthusiastic, aren't we?" Monica gave him the evil eye. She put her arm around Derek's shoulder and gave him a gentle hug. "It will be fun." She wrote out the address on her pad and headed up front.

"Change of plans, Carlos." She squatted down between Carlos and Joshua, in front of the navigation console. "I'm putting in a new destination for us to call home for this leg of the trip." She programmed the new information into the GPS and stood up. "There ya go." She waited a moment, expecting the big question for why and what. It appeared Josh was doing the same, with all eyes on Carlos. He said nothing except, "OK, good. It looks about ten minutes out. Tell the others." She sensed a weird vibe from him, but let it go and headed back toward the others.

"So; I checked out the map and the casino is ten minutes off of I-40 which is also part of Historic Route 66. The Oklahoma Route 66 Museum is just past the 73 intersection; it's like fifteen minutes from what will be our home base." Monica noticed Daniel and Randy whispering. Daniel had a huge grin on his face. They were holding hands.

"Are you sure?" "Yes, I really want to." Randy kissed Daniel on the cheek. Monica tried not to invade their privacy but, they were in an RV. Randy asked Daniel to make a reservation at one of the two motels located only minutes from the casino. She told Daniel during their little private discussion, "This is nice, what we've started. I think some private time to explore where this is going is in order. Let's stay somewhere else tonight; just the two of us." Her hand lightly stroked his chest as she made her suggestion. He wanted her at that moment. The timid boy finally felt like a man.

"Is anybody listening to me?" Monica focused on Randy and Daniel. From behind her, Nick said, "Yes, we got it. Change of plans; going to a casino." Derek mumbled something like, "Oh, what fun that'll be with limited funds." "Oh, come on guys. The casino is just a time filler. A place to hang out." "A diversion." "Yes, Daniel. Welcome back." Daniel and Randy ignored the remark. Randy was about to ask their ETA, when the RV made a swift turn onto an exit ramp. From the front, Joshua called out. "We've officially arrived in Clinton." Everyone chanted a weak "Hooray!" and clapped with similar lack of enthusiasm.

"I think perhaps we need to find something exciting for us all to do." Carlos glared at Joshua who continued his thought. "I mean, when the Jewish museum is one of the highlights of the trip..." Joshua shrugged his shoulders. Carlos grinned.

"I know what you mean Josh; I know what you mean."

Chapter 41

Nick recited his monologue to Carlos about something his cousin did to piss off his girlfriend. Five minutes earlier, Joshua sat in the copilot's seat keeping conversation to a minimum. Now, motor mouth Nick was non-stop.

"Nick, buddy. Hold on a second and check this out." Carlos pointed forward and gestured with his head to look far in front of them. The tiny dots grew larger and more numerous as the RV began to overtake them. "Now that is cool. Slow down a bit Carlos."

Carlos moved into the left lane and started to pass the massive column of bikers. He didn't recognize what organization they belonged to; it didn't really matter. There must have been fifteen or more of them, all dressed in black. Some riders were females or a female riding with a male member. They looked ominous, and the roar of their motors was deafening, even inside the tightly sealed RV. Nick just stared in awe. He imagined himself riding along with them. Carlos tried to focus on the road ahead of him, being careful not to allow the RV to drift across the lane.

"Check out the biceps on that one; and that one!" Randy got so excited. She missed her man checking out his own set of muscles. Monica caught Daniel as he flexed, "Not quite the same. You would need to eat a whole cow every day and drink a gallon of beer. Then perhaps with a few curls..." Daniel grinned, then turned away as if he had no interest in her opinion. "I'm just kidding; Danny boy. You're the man. I love you; guy. Besides, this is what we needed to see on this trip. This helps complete the itinerary. What is cruising down Route 66 without seeing bikers?" The girls and guys all looked out the windows as they passed the riders. A few of the bikers caught the girls gazing and puckered their lips at them, suggestively.

The bikers became a set of black dots again as they fell further behind the speeding RV. Nick put his feet up on the dashboard in front of him. "You ever ride?" Carlos nodded, "Yes, for like two years after I turned eighteen. It was my first mode of transportation. The girls really liked it." Nick asked, "Do you still own it?" "Yes, it's stored in my dad's garage." Carlos added, "My friend and his girl were killed by a drunk driver on the Belt Parkway, near Coney Island. I haven't ridden since." Nick put his feet down, "Wow, Carlos, that sucks. I'm sorry." He paused, Carlos showed no reaction. "Ever consider selling it?" Carlos turned to Nick, his mouth open in preparation to say something. Nick jumped in with, "Bad joke buddy, I take it back. Sorry." His face showed that his lame apology was at least sincere.

Randy made her way to the front. "Hey, guys. You know what, Carlos? I could see you in black leather with your cool shades on a bike." Nick made a weird face and shook his head trying to signal her to *ixnay* the biker dude stuff. She looked at Nick, "What is wrong with you?" Something caught her eye in the road ahead of them. "Oh Crap! Look out, Carlos!" Carlos hit the brakes hard. The loud hiss of air pressure screeched, and the RV swayed and rocked. Carlos fought to keep the vehicle in control and on the road. "What is wrong with you, Randy! I could have rolled us. You could have gone through the windshield!"

"I saw a little jackrabbit in the road."

Carlos pulled over onto the dirt shoulder. He wanted to inspect the RV and make sure the tires were OK. He stood up and observed his passengers. Everyone and everything seemed to be intact, except Josh who had ended up on the floor in front of Monica. She helped him to his feet. "Everyone, just stay inside. I'll check things and we'll be on our way." It was hot on the side of the road. It felt like a hundred degrees. Carlos walked around and inspected the tires. He got under the front end making sure the tie rods had not been damaged from the excessive steering during his attempt to retain control of the RV. As Carlos stood up and started brushing off his jeans, Randy walked over to him. "I'm really sorry, Carlos. I'm so freaking stupid. You could have killed us all and it would have been my fault." Carlos's anger had already waned. It had happened, and they were all OK. The RV was OK. He put his arm around Randy pulling her close. "We're good. Shit happens. No rabbits and no people got killed on this day. Let it be written." She looked up, a tear rolled down her cheek. Carlos wiped it and kissed her forehead. "Let's get back on the road."

Chapter 42

As Carlos and Randy stepped into the RV, they heard the familiar roar of the bikers. A chill ran through Carlos. He noticed that Randy had a concerned expression on her face. "We're fine, I got this. Stay put." He stepped back onto the road and started walking toward the rear of the RV. The sun glare and the heat rising off the pavement distorted his view of the two-wheeler visitors. By the time he reached them, the last of the riders had caught up and started to dismount. They all stood there staring while what looked like the leader *of the pack* walked toward Carlos. Monica started to make her way to the front of the RV but Derek grabbed her arm. "Best if you let him handle it." She glanced at Randy who already had the look of guilt, and concern. "Whatever is happening here has nothing to do with you or us having to pull over." Monica then turned to Derek and Nick. "You think maybe he needs a little support?" She focused on Nick. "No worries, Monica. Us backing him up is like dealing with a pack of dogs. We don't want to escalate the situation by flexing any muscle. We'll be there for him if needed. Besides, there's a lot more of them." Josh added, "And not just in numbers." He gestured to the size of their bodies with his arms. Monica shook her head at them, "Whatever." *Wimps.*

"Hey, how's it going?" Carlos had no clue what else to start with. The massive group was intimidating. "Funny thing, I was just going to ask you the same thing, seeing as you're the one pulled off the side of the road." Carlos took off his shades and wiped his forehead, then put his glasses back on. "Oh, we thought we heard a strange noise and pulled over to check it out." Carlos figured that a shorter version of the story was all that was needed. "Everything checked out fine and we were about to get on our way. Appreciate you taking the time to check on us though. Thank you." The boss man asked, "Where you headed?" As he asked, Carlos realized he wasn't focused directly on him. "Clinton; how about you?" Monica answered from behind Carlos. He had no idea she was behind him. Evidently the biker dude did. She had walked up to them and he kept his cool about it. Monica added, "I came out in case my man here needed some muscle behind him." Boss Biker had a huge grin on his face that made Carlos feel more at ease. Sort of. Looking directly at Carlos and then gesturing toward Monica, the biker announced in a loud voice, "I like her! She's got moxie!" He turned to his group nodding affirmatively. His entourage nodded back, agreeing.

Carlos said, as he put his arm around Monica, "Carlos Martinez, this is Monica." Boss Biker shook hands with Carlos and bumped fists with Monica. He signaled his clan to come over and join them. It turned out that they were on a Bike-a-thon for a children's charity that ended in Clinton. Both groups exchanged names and handshakes before going on their way.

"Safe ride."

"Safe cruising."

Boss Biker called out as he mounted his bike, "You're welcome to ride with me into Clinton. I promise it'll be a thrill." Carlos waved as he took Monica's arm and escorted her back to the RV.

"You do know, Carlos, he was talking to me?" Carlos smiled,

"You sure about that?"

Chapter 43

"What a great idea, Monica. Free parking and hook-ups." Carlos seemed to be back in the game. Whatever funk had taken hold of him earlier had moved on. The sun streaked through puffy clouds and a light breeze raised some dust across the parking field. Randy jumped for joy like a little girl. "Look, there's the shuttle. Let's try to make it. I'm hungry. We can surely find something to eat in the casino." Monica added, "They have these 'Indian Tacos' that the reviews rave about." It seemed that everyone remembered about Joshua at the same time. They all turned to him with just a touch of guilt showing; except for Nick, who was already out of the RV. "Don't worry about me. I'll catch up in a bit." He was already at the freezer pulling out a pre-prepared falafel.

"Kind of small for a casino, but cozy. I imagined worse." Carlos, as usual, did his best to be positive. Randy pointed ahead, "Hey, over there; there's the restaurant." Nick said, "Of course it's on the far side from the entrance. They want you to walk through the machines to get you hooked." Derek added, "It's smart marketing." "What are you doing Monica?" "Gee, Carlos; putting quarters in the slot machines." She made a goofy face at him. Carlos shook his head and started walking toward the eatery. Was it the screech of her voice or the bells that came first? Carlos wasn't sure. Randy jumped up and down, while Monica, whose hand was still holding the slot machine's lever, stood motionless. Coins were clanging away but none really existed. The computerized sound effects created the thrill while points printed out on a paper receipt. "Not making any faces now, are you?" Even in sarcasm she shined brightly. "Very cool, Mon." Carlos looked over her shoulder to see that she had won sixty dollars. He asked, "How much?" Monica had to think for a second; Randy answered for her. "It was her fifth quarter." "Way to go, Monica." Nick chimed in, "Awesome. Lunch is on Monica." Monica laughed. "Sure, Nick. Keep dreaming."

The tacos were as delicious as the reviews had described. Josh met the group as they exited the eatery; just in time to check out the casino for more paying machines. The group split up to explore the various options for losing their money. Each of them made a donation to the casino. An hour or so later, they regrouped and headed back to the RV. "OK, so it's almost three-fifteen. Do we want to check out the museum this afternoon?" Randy put her phone down on the table. "Sounds like a possibility, Monica, but we can do that in the morning. I found a real southwest bar with square dancing. What do you guys think?" Daniel put his arm around Randy. "I think that sounds like a great idea, sweetie." Monica was the first to give Randy the stink eye. She meant to say it to herself, but it came out loud. "Sweetie?" Derek commented, "Oh man." Carlos said, "Well, sweetie, I think that sounds like fun." He looked at Monica. "Don't you?" Randy bit her lip and passed on the stink eye to Daniel. Daniel mumbled, "Were still on for later, right?" Randy didn't respond, but her face showed her embarrassment.

For dinner that night, the group enjoyed protein pasta primavera, "Carlos' Kosher Especial." He used Joshua's pots and utensils and the only two boxes of Kosher pasta Josh had brought with him. Josh supervised for his own comfort level. "This is awesome, Carlos; thank you." "No big deal, Josh, we don't seem to be able to have many meals together. I'm really glad you worked it out to join us on this adventure of ours." "Me too, Carlos." Josh had a renewed sense of self awareness. This trip and his new friends opened up a whole new world. One that he always wondered about but held back from experiencing. His fears of violating his religious customs prevented many potential interactions he could have had. This road trip forced him to live outside the walls of religious confinement. *I'm a different person today. I'm a man making my own decisions. Mama will be defiant at first, that's just who she is. But, she will be proud of me.* Joshua smiled to himself. "Are you OK, Josh? Earth to Josh." "I'm great, Carlos; your Kosher pasta meal smells delicious."

Dinner was a hit. The mini cultural revolution proved that separate ethos in close quarters could make for a successful bonding and new friendships.

Carlos took a walk after dinner and ran into one of the shuttle drivers. He asked about local clubs or places to party. "Well, sir. Tonight is your lucky night. I mean, the Lucky Star Casino has a Country Dance Jamboree. You can search all over, but anyone you ask will send you right back here." Carlos thanked the driver, agreeing to "Check it out."

"So, what do you guys think? We can drink and party and not worry about transportation. You wanted something different." Monica and Randy both said at the same time, "I'm In." they looked at each other, and said again together, "Me too." They both laughed. Nick said, "Oh, wow. They're the Bobbsey Twins." Derek added, "So, it's like square dancing?" "Yes, guys. And probably other types of dancing too." The girls disappeared into the back sleeping quarters to get changed. Carlos pulled out his trusty comb and fixed his hair. Nick made a face while addressing his boys. "I guess we'll check it out, and if it's lame we can catch a ride to one of the local bars." Derek put his arm around Joshua, "Sure, Nick. Sounds like a plan. Who you going to start a fight with tonight?" Josh laughed and said, "Maybe I can sell tickets." "Very funny. Not so funny. Putzes."

The casino ballroom was larger than they expected and there were a lot of people of all ages, mostly standing around. Most of the crowd were holding bottles of beer. The younger people, like Carlos and his friend's ages, were loud.

Without any warning, and after just a few warmup tones and drum beats, the band started playing a country rock song. People hooted and danced in place to the music. "Thank you, folks. We got a great crowd tonight. I'd like you all to form two lines, Woman on my left; men on my right. We're gonna do the Mississippi Two Step." Everyone danced with a different partner throughout the night. Even Nick got into it. Joshua stayed mostly on the sidelines. His comfort level had not stretched far enough to be dancing in mixed company. He did enjoy watching the festivities.

After their break, the band started a new set with a slow Marshall Tucker song. "Would you like to?" "Sure." Monica took Carlos's hand as he led her to the dance floor. He held her around her waist and she rested her head against his chest. "This is nice, Carlos. Thank you." Her eyes met his. He was so good looking and gentle. Carlos stood a good six inches over her. She looked up at him and time seemed to stand still. *Oh, no.* His kiss electrified her whole body. Carlos knew this moment would come back to haunt him, but there was no turning back now. Monica opened her eyes, to see his were closed. It all seemed so sincere. She wanted him; all of him. "NO!" She gently placed her hands on his chest and pushed him away. She felt the heat dissipate as their bodies separated.

"I'm sorry, Monica."

"I'm sorry too, Carlos."

"Christ! I'm so conflicted."

"That's what you needed to hear out loud to yourself. I already know that. Conflicted doesn't work for me."

"I really care for you; like real feelings."

"I have real feelings for you too, Carlos. You have no idea how much I wanted you just now. My selfish self said to let you in all the way. To let you ravish me the way I fantasized so many times. Then I could claim you as mine."

"Why didn't you? Lord knows I wanted you, Monica; want you."

"Because, I need all of you and that's not possible. Is it? She's still in your heart and I won't share. I deserve better than that. I need more of you than you can give of yourself."

"But."

Monica put her finger to his lips. "We are more than friends; just not lovers. If that ever happens, we would be lost to each other. Like this, I can look out for you and you for me. Your true love is back in Brooklyn."

Timing is everything. Just ask Carlos.... "Hey, is everything alright?" Monica wiped tears from her face. "Yes, just fine." Nick took Monica's hand while making defiant eye contact with Carlos. "I told you, Monica. I told you he would mess with your head. Damn it, Carlos. What the..." Monica stepped back, leading Nick away before something bad occurred that would ruin everything. Carlos knew Monica was right. She was the smart one in their relationship. He was not over Ginger, but in that moment that he and Monica kissed, things could have changed; if she had let it.

Carlos would get very little sleep that night. His mind roiling with guilt over the earlier situation with Monica. He tossed and turned until almost 4AM. His eyes became heavy as the shadows of his tiny nook faded to darkness. Even in sleep his mind ran amok.

Is it lust, or love? Could it be that I can't tell the difference? When I'm with Monica, I want more of her than just friendship. When I'm not with her I think of you. Would I think of her, if I were with you? I am sure I could be her friend for all eternity and be OK with that; want that. I am sure I would always need more from you. You are already my friend; that there is no doubt. We have already endured the pain that lust brings to friendship. But, that pain has opened my eyes to the truth. I need your friendship and I want to share the lust with you. But most importantly, I want your love. I want to be able to love you back.

In the morning, Carlos' revelation of love would remain hidden deep in his subconscious. Yet, some part of him knew something was different. He felt at ease. It was as if he had an unidentified problem that resolved itself.

****

"This is a room? It's a shoe box with a bed and a crappy TV." Randy held Daniel's hand. "The bed looks clean, we have privacy and I don't anticipate we'll be needing the TV." Daniel felt like an idiot. "Of course not; sorry. I'm a little nervous; how about you?" Randy said, "I'm shaking inside. I've never..." "Me neither." The admission of virginity calmed them both, placing them on equal ground with no expectations. "Kiss me." His kiss was firm yet gentle. *That boy from computer class has been transformed into a man and he is; Oh my...*

Chapter 44

"Good morning. This is Ginger; how may I help you?" She listened to the caller's request for Carlos' attention to a matter that could easily wait for his return. "Mr. Martinez is out of town until next week. No, I'm sorry; he's not reachable. I can have him call you as soon as he returns." Some fifty messages like this already plagued her. She didn't realize how many calls he must have taken on his own. Every time a caller mentioned his name, or she opened his mail, loneliness overcame her. She missed her friend. *Maybe I should call him.*

Carlos had left instructions for everything that had to be taken care of while he was away. What Carlos didn't leave, was his final itinerary. She remembered him mentioning when she asked, that they would be "winging it." Ginger's heart ached for him. Breaking up with Bob proved to her that she still had deep-seated feelings for Carlos. Much deserved guilt plagued Ginger. Bob didn't deserve to be hurt. He accused her of using him, and he was right. She also knew that she hurt herself as much as him.

Carlos had issues; even his dad admitted that. She knew it long before their friendship advanced to that disastrous next level. There were lots of girls. For the most part, one-night stands. Carlos intimately talked about them with her. She was his friend and confidante. She understood him better than he did himself. She should have been more guarded. None of that knowledge can change what happened between them. Now, she needed him to love her; and only her. She was broken and no one else could mend her. *I have to call him.*

After three rings, Ginger's nerves were frazzled; she almost hung up. Then there was that familiar blip sound indicating the phone had been answered. "Hello?" *Oh my, a female answering his phone.* "Hi, I'm trying to reach Carlos Martinez." Randy considered she might have made a mistake answering Carlos's cell phone. He had left it on the driver's console where she was seated, reading a magazine. She asked the caller, "Who's calling?" "Ginger; from his office. Who is this?" Randy almost dropped the phone, she jumped up and down in her seat. "Hold on." She covered the phone and squealed, "Monica, come here; quick." Monica had just come back from a walk to the casino. "Hey, Randy. When did you guys get back?" Monica made a girly face and said, "I want details!" Randy, still frantic said, "Ok, OK – later. She's on the phone!"

"Who's on the phone?"
"Her; Carlos' her."
"Ginger?"
"Yes."

Monica took the phone from Randy and quietly asked her, "Where is he?" Randy pointed to the back of the RV.

"Hi, this is Monica." Monica took the cell phone and walked outside and behind the mobile home. The two loves of Carlos Martinez Jr. spoke for almost twenty minutes. After she ended the call, Monica felt like a huge weight had been lifted off her shoulders. She actually smiled. Carlos stepped out of the tiny shower in his robe. His hair looked even sexier wet. Randy tried to hide behind her magazine as he headed into what was her designated room, to change into proper clothing. She prayed he didn't ask where his phone was.

"So?" "Shh." "Come on Monica, what did you tell her?" "I told her how much he really missed her. That he didn't exactly admit it, but it showed in his moodiness every day. I told her that he confided in me about her and that he missed her." Randy was turning blue from not breathing. "And?" "I also told her that if she didn't come claim her man quick, I was going to make a play for him. She had no idea how serious I was." Randy looked like a little kid waiting for the ice cream man. "And?" "I told her we would be in Amarillo on Friday. I have her phone number so I can text her when we know when, and where."

"What? When and where? What are we talking about?" Randy bit her lip, her face twisted and her eyes got really big. Freaked out, Monica jumped. "Hey, don't sneak up on me like that!" "Sorry." Carlos took her hand, "Are we OK?" She pulled it away slow and easy. "Of course we are." "Great, I'm going to the casino." He looked around, "Any takers?" Josh was the only one who answered. "I'll take a walk." "Is that my phone?" Monica, again startled, "Oh, yes; I saw it laying on the floor and picked it up. Here you go." As soon as they left. Randy started asking more questions. "Why don't you fight for him? I get that you want him to work it out with her first, but you obviously love him. Why help her?" Monica leaned against the counter and in a whisper, "I think a lot of women loved him but he didn't have the same feelings back for them." Randy said in a low voice, "Except for you; and her." "Yes, I'm sure he loves us both, but he has history with her and I think he is attached in a way we are not. He and I do have something special, just not on the same wavelength. Either way, after tomorrow the story's ending will be written."

Nick, Daniel and Derek were playing cards. They tried but failed at their attempt to eavesdrop on the girls. Randy asked, "Hey, can we play?" Nick, the wise guy said, "What do you have in mind?" Randy shook her head in disgust, then smiled at Daniel. Monica said, "Cards; you fool." Nick reached across the table and nudged Derek, "I think she likes me." Randy pulled a folding chair to the end of the table and Monica sat next to Derek. She leaned against his shoulder. "So; what are we playing?"

****

Ginger made a few quick calls, and then one more to Human Resources to tell them something had come up and she needed a few days off as personal time. She forwarded her calls to the front receptionist and headed for the door. Her heart pounded as she wondered if this was the right way to get what she wanted.

"Are you OK? Where's the fire?" Ginger stopped short, she recognized the voice. Embarrassed she turned to face the big boss. "Hello, Mr. Martinez." He asked, "Anything I can do to assist? Our insurance won't cover a broken ankle due to high heels. At least I don't think they will." "Oh, not to worry sir. I just have urgent personal business that needs my attention; at home." Mr. Martinez grinned, "I see; well then you had better get on with it." Ginger turned and fought to maintain control so as not to start running again. From behind her, she heard him call out, "Say hello to my son."

A blanket of grey clouds rolled in, and a chill in the air made her shiver as she waited for the bus. Something across the avenue caught her attention. *Oh, no! Oh, no!* He looked so much like Carlos, it was unnerving. She couldn't get control of her breathing. He held his hat as he fast paced across the avenue toward her. He started speaking before he made it all the way to her. The bus had just pulled up. Martinez Sr. told her, "Let it go. Come back to the office with me now." His tone was authoritative, more like a strict father than a boss. She said nothing as he took her arm in his and led her back across the traffic riddled avenue.

His secretary brought them both coffee. "Tell me what's going on and where you were rushing off too." At first she was shocked that for the second time this week, the president of her company pushed boundaries in such a way. He was out of place minding her business. Then she recalled their conversation earlier that week, and realized his fondness for her was related to his son. Ginger calmed herself down and explained her plan to head Carlos off in Amarillo, Texas. She professed her love for him. Ginger also explained that this was her last attempt to make him realize how much he cared for her and how much he could trust her.

"How did you know where I was going?" Martinez smiled warmly, "I'm very good at reading people. I saw it in your face. You had a similar look when we last spoke. Did you call him?" "Yes, but one of his friends, one of the girls he is tight with; I mean close with, answered. She told me when they plan to be in Amarillo. I spoke to her for almost twenty minutes. She seemed to want to help me square things with Carlos. But..." "But what, Ginger?" "I got the odd sense that she pushed too hard. I'm afraid she and Carlos have more than a friendship. Part of me senses she may be standing in the way of me and Carlos." She paused as a tear formed in the corner of her eye. "Part of me has the sick feeling that *I* might be the one standing between *them*." Martinez Sr. told her to be strong and fight for what she wants. "Show him what he already knows. He'll ultimately make the right or wrong decision and then you can get on with your life; whichever way that leads." The big boss called his administrative assistant and asked her to come into his office. Please book a late morning flight for tomorrow for Miss O'Connell, out of Kennedy to Rick Husband Amarillo International Airport. "God willing, you'll only need half the ticket. My son is no fool. Everything will work out." Ginger wrapped her arms around her boss and kissed his cheek. "Thank you. Thank you." She wiped her tears from his face gently with her hand. "I'm so sorry." Martinez took her by the shoulders and marched her to the door. "Go get our boy."

Chapter 45

Monica awoke feeling elated. With an inner smile, she thought to herself, *a new day, a better attitude*. "It's a gorgeous Thursday and half the day is gone already! Let's get moving everyone!" Spoken with authority, her friends needed to take heed. Randy was the first to show up with her mini backpack slung over her shoulder. Daniel was right behind her. "Hey Monica, what's the agenda for today?" Something seemed different with her girl. Randy then said, "Oh, my; are you OK?" Monica made a questioning face that turned to more of a frown. "I'm fine, and it is what it is." She lowered her voice; "Besides, Carlos is too old for me. My grandma would have a heart attack." Randy smiled, "Yes, but he is so cool and handsome, and has a real career." Monica smiled back as if she was going to agree on that note. "Nope. Not going there anymore. I've smelled the roses and I'm awake now." She called out, "Let's get the show on the road, folks!" Daniel, from behind, put his arms around Randy's waist and kissed the back of her neck. Randy flushed with embarrassment as she placed her hand on his, and affectionately said to him, "Hey, you." Monica gave a little giggle, "You are so cute together, I'm so happy for you guys." She genuinely meant it.

The screech of his hand brakes startled the girls. Joshua dismounted his bike while still in motion, like a pro. Monica thought how far he had come, maturing so much in less than a week on the road. "Hello, girls. I rode to the casino to look for Derek. He's on the shuttle. I think he won like fifty bucks on the slots. It's amazing that no one stole my bicycle." Randy asked, "Didn't you lock it up?" Joshua laughed, "I forgot the bike lock." *Imagine that.* Nick chimed in, "Imagine that." Carlos added, "Who would steel a bike out here? Where would they go with it?" From behind them the voice of authority called out. "Ok; enough. I want to get going!" Monica seemed a bit agitated.

Fortunately, things were quiet at the casino. The shuttle driver, a friendly sort, made the group an offer to lend them one of their concierge vans. He had already asked his boss who apprehensively agreed. "Just bring it back in one piece, or my boss will have my head." Monica and Randy mapped out the travel plan for the day.

"First stop, Oklahoma Route 66 Museum!" Monica shouted it out loud with great enthusiasm. Joshua said, "I checked it out online. The museum has several awesome exhibits showcasing the history of Route 66, and great music from the Eagles and Woody Guthrie playing."

The museum was really interesting, but only took a little over an hour and a half to tour. "My belly hurts from hunger." Derek laughed, "You're always hungry, Nick." Carlos agreed, "Nick and I have that in common. Lunch is our favorite activity. What do you guys say we find a fun place to chow down?" Monica was already on her phone. "Let me see... This looks good, Lucille's Roadhouse Diner. We have to get to Weatherford. It says here, this place replicates the original Lucille's Service Station and Roadhouse. It looks like a real 1950's diner with great burgers and my favorite, chicken fried steak." Carlos searched Google Maps on his phone. "It's a bit of a ride, looks like about forty-five minutes to an hour back on I-40." Nick made the point, "So, what else is there to do, let's go." Everyone piled into the less than fancy Ford van. "I'll drive." Everyone shared *that* look of fear. Carlos said, OK, Nick. You drive." Nickolas dealt fairly well with the remarks about his driving as he headed east.

Lucille's Diner turned out exactly as described. Nick proclaimed, "This is the best burger ever!" Monica asked, "Better than the campus food trucks?" Carlos laughed. "Must be; I don't remember him making goo-goo faces over food back home." Randy handed Nick a napkin. "Your eating manners are less than desirable, my friend." She tapped her index finger to the side of her mouth indicating where he should wipe his. She turned to Daniel who was seated in the booth behind her, and playfully pulled his hair. "How's your chicken fried steak?" Daniel picked up a fork full of meat dripping in gravy and fed it to his girl. She made a face as if she was in heaven. "That is yummy!" She leaned over and kissed his cheek. Monica laughed, "Now *you* need a napkin, Dan The Man." Nick shared his opinion as well. "Why don't you two get a room? Oh, wait. You did that already." No one responded and Nick kept quiet for the rest of their time at lunch. Josh tapped his can of Coke as he finished his sandwich that he had prepared earlier in the RV. "What's our next stop for today?" Monica was already doing her thing on her phone, "I suggest we head back toward Clinton. There are a few interesting places we can check out. Let's see, the Cherokee Trading Post and Boot Outlet." Randy said, "Ooh, I could use a new pair of boots. Maybe knee highs?" She glanced over her shoulder at Daniel who looked as if he already started a fantasy in his head. She said softly, "Hold that idea for later." Monica poked Randy's shoulder, "Girl, who are you, and what did you do with

Randy?" Randy's face flushed a soft shade of crimson while the others laughed at Monica's remark.

"Ok, after that, we can try the Mohawk Lodge Indian Store. It says here it opened in 1892 and they still trade genuine artifacts." Randy, on her own phone said, "And, they have real blankets. I want one. We can get genuine beaded bracelets. I need some souvenirs; this might be a perfect place to find them." Carlos and the others agreed. They paid the bill and headed out to the van.

"Hello, officer. Is something wrong?" "Is this here your vehicle, sir?" Carlos hesitated, not sure what was happening at the moment. "Yes, officer. Well, actually no. It's borrowed." Carlos pointed to the advertising logo on the side of the van. "I can see that son. Kindy remove your sunglasses while you-all are speaking with me." Carlos did as the officer requested. "I'll need to see your driver's license and the vehicle's registration." Monica walked over next to Carlos and took his hand. "We were just heading back to the casino. The management office loaned us the vehicle for the day to do some sightseeing." The officer ignored Monica and continued looking at Carlos' license. "From NY? Been there once. Too crowded for my liking, and not all that friendly." Nick murmured,

"Kind of like here?" The officer looked up at the group. "You all step back, over there; except Mr. Martin-ez." He motioned for them all to move away. Then he asked Carlos, "Any drugs or alcohol in that vehicle or in your possession?" Carlos felt a bit unnerved. He had nothing, but Nick most likely did, based on past experiences. Derek too. At least Derek had an excuse and a license; albeit, not from this state. "No, sir. Of course not. We're all on holiday break and enjoying traveling your beautiful state." The officer started to hand Carlos' license back to him but pulled it back just as he was about to take it from the officer. "Do I have your permission to search the vehicle?" Their eyes met. Carlos kept his cool dark eyes focused without blinking. Nick started to twitch. Monica leaned against him and took his hand, squeezing it. Her firm hold seemed to calm him. "No problem, officer. Go right ahead." Carlos held out the keys. The officer ignored the gesture and again started to hand him back his driver's license. "That won't be necessary after all. I'm sorry to have troubled you folks. Behave, and enjoy your visit." Carlos walked over to the group who all showed their relief. "Let's get on with our travels." He looked at Monica holding Nick's hand. She pulled it away quickly and said, "Yes, let's get going."

The drive to the Mohawk Lodge Indian Store took another hour and forty minutes. Traffic moved slower on I-40 than the outbound trip earlier. Daniel and Randy took the third row seat for two. Randy snuggled into him. "This feels good." Daniel said, "It does. I can't believe it took me so long to ask you out." "You didn't actually ask me out, Daniel. I'm certain it was me who asked you to dance first." Daniel put his arm around her and hugged her tight.

"And, I am a lucky man that you did. So?"
"So what?"
"Are we officially dating, like steady? What happens when we get home?"
"What do you want to happen?"
"I think I love you. I can't imagine not holding you in my arms."

Randy didn't expect Daniel, the shy, daydreaming guy from computer class, to be this guy holding her now.

"I love you, too."

The guys looked around the store for a few minutes and then regrouped outside while the girls shopped. "That was close back in Weatherford. I thought for sure we were going to be set up or something." Carlos looked at Nick, "Lucky for all of us that he wasn't interrogating you. Was there anything in the van?" Nick swore there wasn't, but didn't indicate if he had anything on his person. Carlos glanced at Derek who shrugged his shoulders, "Don't look at me. I have no idea about my boy here, and my stuff is safely stashed back at the RV." Carlos put up his hand, "You know what? We didn't talk about it the whole way here, let's not now either." Joshua mumbled, "God was watching over us." Carlos replied with "Amen."

Monica and Randy came marching out, both with huge smiles and bags in each hand. Daniel took the bags from Randy as a gentleman should. "Thanks, D. I got you the cutest moccasins. They have blue and green beads on top and the leather is so soft. I hope they fit." The rest of the group again made little fun remarks about the two of them.

That evening, the guys took care of dinner. Carlos made tacos while Derek and Daniel made a concoction of rice medley. Nick made a salad, and opened a jar of salsa. Joshua used his last pre-prepared frozen dinner plate. "I'm going to need to find a Kosher market tomorrow." Nick remarked, "Good luck with that, my friend. Have you not noticed where you are? Starvation can be horribly uncomfortable. What do you think, Carlos?" "I think, Nick, we will find a Kosher market for Josh." Josh prayed silently, asking God to understand why he traveled on the Sabbath. He promised that this trip would be the one and only exception. He asked for forgiveness while he finds his way in the world. *"And God, please help mother to understand why I needed to do this."*

Monica pulled out her guitar and started strumming some chords. Carlos noticed her face go all scrunchy, but said nothing. She adjusted the keys a bit and ran through a few more chords. "Ah, that's better." Josh called out, "How about some CSNY?" Derek, from his seat up front at the helm said, "Good call, Josh." Monica started strumming chords to "Our House," then after just a few, she switched to "Teach Your Children" and back and forth a few times, while laughing and singing along. The others joined in, trying their best to keep up with the alternating lyrics.

Carlos admired Monica. She had a tough time when she was younger. In the past few months she had blossomed. Her inner beauty found its way out to sit alongside her undeniable outer beauty. She had the whole package. He sat back in his tiny space, shared with Randy and Daniel on the mini couch, and closed his eyes. The music melted into the background in this new dimension he allowed himself to glide into for a brief moment. *Ginger would like Monica. They could be friends.* He opened his eyes, realizing that perhaps they would be rivals. Then he also recognized the reality that Ginger was no longer in the picture. He ruined what they had. He betrayed her trust by hurting her feelings. He ignored her when she made a plea for him to show he cared. If she originally used Bob as a means to make him jealous, a sort of test; then he failed. Bob from accounting treated her in a way she deserved to be treated. He placed her on a pedestal. To Bob, Ginger was his queen. Carlos looked at Monica and a warm feeling came over him. He loved her as a friend, more like a sister. He never wanted to lose that. He wanted her in his life from now to eternity. But Ginger, she is the one he wanted to spend every moment with. He suddenly shouted, "I've got to go home!" The music stopped. Silence filled the RV. "What? Carlos?" He ignored Monica's question. "Sorry, guys. I need some air." They watched as he quickly strode out of the RV.

She wanted to go after him. Nick could sense her concern. He nudged Derek out of his seat. "Hey, Monica." "Hi, Nick. I know what you're going to say. I'm well aware of the situation. He needs his space." Nick took her hand, 'Forget Carlos for a moment. You always make it about him." Monica's eyes glistened like diamonds as tears began to form. "He seems to mostly make it about us; don't you think?" "I think you are incredible, and deserve better than chasing after something you can't have. Besides; he doesn't deserve someone like you. He's too numb to intimate relationships. I know I've been an ass at times, but when I'm around you I want to be a better person." He could see her mind was working. She was uneasy at where she thought he was taking this conversation. She held up her hands in a gesture to stop him from continuing. "Nick…" "Let me finish Monica; please. I never had my heart skip a beat like it does when you're around me. You're in my head, even when you're out of sight. I'm jealous when you're with him." "But, he's your friend. And, he and I are just really good friends. We both have that understanding. It took me a little longer to accept the reality." She paused and put her other hand over his. "You and me?" The conversation between Nick and Monica carried on as if no one else existed in the tight quarters of the RV. They all paid rapt attention, as if they were seated at a live Broadway play.

"This is a lot to handle right now, Nick. Can we just leave it alone for tonight?" Nick said, "Sure. I get it." He started to get up. "Wait." She latched onto his arm resulting in him almost falling back onto her. "I could use a hug, and a friend right now." He sat back down and

Monica snuggled against his chest while pulling his arm around her shoulder. She whispered in his ear, "They're all staring." Nick reinforced his hold around her. "Good. Let them." *Is this really the same guy we left Brooklyn with?*

Exhausted from a long day of sightseeing, everyone found a spot to crash. With no place for a tent, the group had to improvise. Daniel and Randy made a last minute decision to head back to the motel for one more night. Monica took the Captain's nook above the driver's area. She figured that when or if Carlos returned, he would be OK with it, considering it was the smallest private area and she was the only female in the RV. Carlos returned around 11:30 to find them all sleeping. He climbed up the little ladder to find his space occupied. Monica looked angelic and *snug as a bug in a rug*; he had to smile. Josh was on the mini couch, and Derek across from him on the converted dining table. Carlos made his way back to the rear bedroom area, expecting to find the two love birds. Instead, he found Nick snoring away. Carlos figured Nick had high hopes for a visitor. *Well, that's not happening and it certainly isn't going to be me, either.* Sleeping bag and a pillow, which he carefully snatched without waking Nick, Carlos found a tight spot on the floor between the galley and the shower. He hoped that no one would step on him in the middle of the night.

Chapter 46

"Oh, man; this is too close for comfort. Someone, open a window!"

Either the sun sneaking through the little window above the dining table that doubled as a bed, or the variety of feet tripping over his body, awakened Carlos. Fair is fair, but he was reclaiming his sleeping quarters; his body ached. The reedy padding of the sleeping bag did little to buffer him from the hard floor beneath. Carlos lay flat on his back, stretching his aching muscles. His first thoughts were of Ginger. He wondered what she was doing at this moment. He imagined her getting dressed. He could imagine her pulling on her skintight blue jeans, slowly inching them up toward her waist. Wait; today is Friday. She would be wearing one of her silky pleated skirts and a button blouse. And, those crazy high heels she seemed to navigate with, flawlessly. Then, there's Bob. *Why the hell does he have to be in my head?* Could she be happy with him? Carlos considered the possibility, but decided that It didn't matter because he was going to end this trip after Texas, and head home to tell her; no, to *beg* her to be his one and only. At that moment, Carlos realized that he loved her. "I'm in love with you, Ginger."

He said it aloud but under his breath so that no one actually picked up on what he said. He sat up just as Josh tripped over the edge of his portable bedding and nearly landed in Carlos's lap. "Easy there, Josh. You OK?" "Sorry, Carlos. I'm fine. Why are you in the middle of the floor?" Carlos started to maneuver out of the sleeping bag. From behind him, Monica said, "It's my fault. I was so tired, and there was no place for me, the only female." Carlos stood facing Monica and grinned. "No problem, Monica. I guess the lovers took a room last night." "I guess so." She smiled shyly; her face making a silly expression. Carlos realized he was wearing only his boxers. Josh felt out of place and continued his trek to the bathroom, which was occupied by someone already. "Carlos, you should have woken me. Or, we could have shared. We're buddies; right?" "Buddies, yes. I don't know about the sharing bit, that's asking a lot, Monica." Carlos winked. They both laughed. "What's asking a lot?" Nick walked toward them rubbing his eyes. He was jealous and had no idea why, or what his two flirtatious friends were talking about at that moment. "Just goofing around, Nicky boy. Time to make the donuts and get this show on the road. Somebody should make the wake-up call to Randy and Daniel." He looked at Monica. She said, "I guess that would mean me." Nick suggested to Carlos that he get dressed. Carlos looked down at his boxers, "Probably a good idea."

The RV looked as if a family of hoarders had invaded its space. Various articles of clothing and food wrappers cluttered the cramped living space. Monica pleaded with everyone to pitch-in and do a good cleanup and reorganizing before embarking on the next leg of their trip. With everything battened down and packed up by 8:45AM, they were ready to hit the *dusty trail*. The love birds made it back to home base in time to leave, and after all the chores had been finished. Carlos thanked the concierge and his shuttle friend for their gracious accommodations; slipping each a generous gratuity. The RV pulled out of the parking field and made its way back onto I-40. "You OK to drive this morning, Carlos?" In rare form, Nick seemed genuinely concerned. "Yes, I think I'm fine." "If you say so, buddy. You're kind of looking bent out of shape." Carlos shook his head. "You try sleeping on that floor all night without an air-mattress." "I heard Monica say that you had options." "Be cool, Nick. Besides, who are you kidding? I see how you are around her lately. You're totally into her." "No way, man." "Way, Nick. She needs a no-bullshit guy. She deserves someone who can offer stability and someone who can make her feel safe." Nick sat in the copilot's seat facing Carlos. "Oh, and that most certainly is not me; right?" Carlos answered with, "Or me." Nicks face drew deep color. "Well, for sure not you. Your heart and soul are somewhere else that no woman seems to be able to tame. Me? I may be a little crude and out of control, but everyone knows what I'm about; no bullshit here. If she likes me, it's really me that she finds interesting. I *can* make her feel safe. I want to take care of her." There it was. Nick had said it out loud, surprising even himself. Joshua walked up to the two of them. "You guys do know that we all can hear you. Monica locked herself in the rear sleeping area." Carlos said, without turning, "You should be seated while we're moving." Josh frowned and returned to his seat. After five minutes of silence, Carlos said to Nick, "You're right about me; partly. I can love; I have loved. I just can't follow through with any commitment. This way, I can't be hurt. Monica has become incredibly special to me. I love her sincerely – as a friend or, more like a sister. Sure, we flirt. It's what we do, but that's all. And you, my friend; you are a good guy. She could do a lot worse than you." Nick grinned. "Well, then; we understand each other." "We do." Carlos said the words to Nick, but in truth, doubted Nick believed him. He wasn't sure he believed himself about his true feelings toward Monica.

An hour into the trip, Carlos pulled off the highway for a gas stop. At first, only Derek stepped out of the RV to stretch his legs. Carlos allowed a moment of privacy before following him out. As Carlos swiped his credit card to activate the gas pump, Monica hip bumped him. "Hey!" Carlos asked, "Are you stalking me again?" In a cute voice, she replied,

"Maybe."
"You are such a tease."

They paused their conversation, saying nothing for a moment. Then, Monica added,

"Derek's not looking so good."
"Yes, I noticed yesterday that he looked really tired. I'm worried about him."

They both watched as Derek leaned against the RV looking melancholy. He had no sense of his audience of two. Neither commented any further, but both had the same thought; perhaps he regretted his decision not to fight the cancer. After another minute, Monica touched Carlos' arm gently. "He's a really good guy underneath his bullshit, tough guy façade." Carlos made a questioning face. Monica quietly expounded on her statement. "Nick.

I'm talking about Nick. I think I like him." Carlos looked up toward the heavens, and then back to her. "I think he likes you too." Monica looked away for a second to compose herself. "Are you OK with that?" Carlos said, "If I wasn't OK with you and him, would it matter?" "Yes, of course. You and I have this special relationship that I never want to lose. But I need someone to be close with intimately. Someone who wants me, and only me. I don't know if that is Nickolas, but if that starts to happen, could you be happy for me?" "He's my friend and you're my.... But I'd crush him if he messed with you." Monica kissed Carlos on the cheek. "I do love you. You're the best." She caught a glimpse of Nick peering at her from the RV's window. She didn't acknowledge him at that moment. "See you on board, Captain." As Carlos returned the fuel hose to its holster on the fuel pump, he watched Monica as she stepped into the RV. His mind still messed with him. *Look away Carlos; take a breath.* Carlos looked for Derek, but he was nowhere to be seen. He figured his conversation with Monica went so deep, neither noticed Derek slip pass them.

"I saw you. You looked upset; jealous perhaps?" Nick had no words. Monica caught him off guard. She sat down next to him. "I'm cold." It took him a few seconds before he woke up and put his arm around her shoulders.

She said, "That's much better. I'm warmer now. Your arm around me, it's nice" He held her a little tighter and turned facing her. Their eyes met. "So mister; now what?" Nick's lips met hers gently, almost shyly. He pulled away unexpectedly. "What about…" "I told you. We are just really close friends." She paused for a second. "I treasure Carlos' friendship. You have to be OK with that." Nick said, "OK" and kissed her again. *Well; not really OK with that.*

Signs for Amarillo became more frequent as they drew closer to their next destination. "Almost there!" Carlos made his announcement as he approached the exit for US-60 East. The road merged into US-287 North. The sign read "Downtown". At the end of the road the sign read, "Old Route 66," Tucumcari to the left, and Amarillo to the right. Carlos made the right turn and soon after, followed the signs to the Amarillo Ranch RV Park.

"Wow. Look at this beautiful scenery." Randy gazed out the window in awe. "It reminds me of Arizona and Red Rock Canyon. My parents took me there on a vacation a few years ago." Randy got up from her seat motioning Joshua to swap places with her. By now the group was on board with hers and Daniel's blooming relationship. Randy snuggled in close to Daniel. "You'll like my parents; they're great." Daniel smirked as if holding back a laugh. She questioningly said, "You do want to meet them?" Daniel let loose and burst out laughing and coughing. "Yes, of course." "Then what?" His emotions now under control, Daniel pulled Randy in closer. He quietly told her, "If you had elongated the 're' in 'they're', you would have sounded like Tony the Tiger." She looked at him, puzzled. "You know? Like in Frosted Flakes. They're Grrreat!" His growling voice surprised her and the rest of the group as well. She stared at him as if she was shocked at his outburst, then she broke out hysterically laughing. Everyone laughed.

After Carlos checked in at the RV park office, they proceeded to the assigned slot. Unlike at the other stops, here the campers and RV's parked alongside each other. While checking in, Carlos had seen a sign for rental cars. He inquired at the desk. "Yes, sir. We have mini vans, compact cars, and scooters. How many are there in your group?" Carlos told him seven. "I guess you'll be needing the minivan then; Sixty-six dollars for the day. That be 7AM to 7PM. Being as half the day is gone, I'll knock off ten bucks." Carlos laughed, "That's a good deal, my friend, but we need it for getting around this evening. How about regular price till midnight?" The clerk made a face. Carlos said, "Hey, no problem. Is there an Enterprise in Amarillo?" The clerk waved him off, "I don't know; Pay me cash and you can have the van until whenever. Just have it back in the lot by 6AM. That's when my boss comes in to work." "Deal – thank you."

"OK. Cadillac Ranch should be very cool. This is what we're here for, right?" Nick put his arm around Monica, "You all heard my girl here. Let's get going." Nick paused, taking a breath, "Wait. What about lunch?" Monica, slightly uncomfortable, noticing Carlos' reaction to her being embraced by Nick, said, "You're always worried about your stomach. I thought perhaps we should try Blue Sky. It's on the way." Randy got all excited. "Yes, yes. I read about that place. It looked awesome. They're supposed to have scrumptious burgers!" She knew it was coming. She looked at Daniel but wasn't quick enough to stop him. "They're… Grrreat!" She said, "Oh My God. You're out of control." Nick looked up as if that remark was reserved for him.

Derek elected to stay behind and eat whatever was in the kitchen fridge. "No way, dude; go smoke a bone. You're coming with us." Nick paused a second and continued, "You came on this trip to have fun and put that F'n cancer out of your mind. Don't get all depressed on me now!" In reality, Nick, the tough guy, was hurting inside for his friend. Randy said, "Leave him alone. Can't you see he's having a bad day?" Derek waved his hands. "My boy Nick here is right. When I push myself, I do feel better. Give me ten and I'll be ready to go." Nick clapped his hands together, "That's my boy!"

Lunch was incredibly good. The burgers with jalapenos, cheese and salsa must have been delicious based on the juicy residue dripping off the chins of those who indulged. Carlos had the chicken fried steak and exclaimed it to be the best he ever had. Randy spent half of the lunch time on her phone trying to make a reservation at the Baymont Inn. Daniel handed her his credit card; his dad's card. "You got Clinton; I got this." He would deal with his family's questions when he got home. "What?" Daniel was annoyed at the grins on his friends faces. "It's not like there's room for all of us in the RV, and the tent situation has pretty much expired since Clinton. You guys should be thanking us." In harmony, they all chanted, "Thank you, Randy and Daniel."

After lunch, Derek seemed better. Maybe distraction is what he needed; maybe the weed, or likely both. They all piled in to the ancient Volkswagen van and headed onward to the first attraction of the day. Josh remarked, "This is a cool form of transportation. We could paint flowers on the outside and make like we are hippies from the sixties or seventies." Nick was like, "Or Scooby Doo!" He pointed to Monica, "Daphne; I'm definitely Fred Jones and Daniel can be Shaggy. Randy you're Velma." He looked at Carlos and Joshua, "Which one of you want to be Scooby?" He paused his rhetoric for a moment. "Josh, you can be Scrappy Doo. I guess that leaves the best part, Scooby Doo, for you, Carlos."

There they were, at Cadillac Ranch. "There's a bunch of cars half stuck in the ground with their ass's pointing to the sky." Monica pinched Nick's arm gently. "It's a famous landmark of Route 66. You're supposed to make your mark." Carlos took off his backpack and pulled out a can of gold spray paint. "Here, Monica, as you suggested." He handed the spray can to her. "You first. Pick a car." Nick shook his head, "Way to go, Carlos. Seems kind of natural; you holding a spray can ready for some graffiti." "Nick!" Monica looked angry. "It's just a joke, Monica. Right, Carlos? We're buds. I'm just joking around." "Sure, Nick. But you're still an ass." "That I am; someone has to be the life of this party." For his turn, he wrote something like, "Nick was here and now he's gone, but he found love and lots of fun." He handed the can to Josh, who declined, and told Nick to give it to Derek.

They walked around the ranch of sorts, and then piled back into the van. As they were driving, Derek said, "Check out the amusement park!" Randy got all excited, "Let's stop." Carlos swerved; the crappy van felt as if it was going to flip. Monica called out, "Easy, cowboy; tight quarters back here."

The sign read "Wonderland Amusement Park." Nick and Carlos seemed to need help with relieving the tension between them; the bumper cars took care of that. The girls and Joshua went on the roller coaster together. The guys drank beer and looked on as they roared by and screamed. "They all sound the same; high-pitched squeals." "I suppose, Nick. None of us are brave enough to ride it." Nick said, "Sorry about the joke in bad taste earlier." "No problem, Nick." "Really, dude. I mean it." "We're cool. Drop it." Derek and Daniel took a walk over to the water balloon booth. Nick asked, "You think Derek is going to be OK?" Carlos shrugged his shoulders. "Without treatment, probably not. He made his choice." "If he gets much worse, I'll take the train home with him." Carlos looked at Nick and nodded. He put his arm around Nick, "You better treat *our* girl right. She's definitely into you." He paused, then said, "Go figure."

The RV looked really good to everyone. They were all tired. Monica announced her idea to head to 6th street. "We can get pizza or something fast food for eats tonight. There's cool music and booze stations. It's supposed to be a wild, fun time." Randy and Daniel declined, saying they were really tired. Nick called them wimps and insisted the group hang together. "All or none. Who wants to ruin the evening by forcing us all to miss a great night on the town?" Monica added, "I'm with Nick on this. We should all try to take a nap before going out tonight to recharge our batteries." Randy took Daniel's hand, "Alright, we're in; at least for part of the night. We already have a room booked. We'll go there for our *nap* and meet you on 6th street later. Everyone else agreed. Nick said, "Great. Besides, we can sleep late tomorrow morning." Monica quietly made her way to the rear sleeping quarters. She replied to an earlier text from Ginger saying she had arrived in Amarillo and was staying at the Baymont Inn. *What a coincidence that's where the other love birds are going to stay tonight.* Weird thoughts ran through her head. *Cut it out, you have Nick and he's into you.* Monica replied that she would text Ginger with their location when they got to 6th street later.

Her mind raced with controversy. Yet, she got satisfaction from knowing that Carlos would get the opportunity to confront his true feelings for Ginger. Even though her body was exhausted, napping seemed unlikely. Monica strummed some tunes for a little while; then like the rest, she dozed off to a peaceful slumber.

Chapter 47

Three outfits were strategically laid out on the queen sized bed. On the floor, in line with each one, sat a pair of high heel shoes that had been carefully matched by their owner. Her nerves on edge, she paced back and forth, pondering her choices. Her hair and makeup done to perfection, she stared at her reflection in the vanity mirror before returning to the ensemble of clothing choices.

"Which one?"
"Which one?"
"Which one?"

"You; you're the perfect one for him."

Finally, after thirty minutes, Ginger made her decision. Earlier that day she found her way to the Westgate mall. As she walked the aisles in Victoria's Secret, she imagined what Carlos' reaction would be to seeing her. Or, what she hoped he would say. First, he would quietly walk up to her. He would take her in his arms and hold her. Her mind quickly placed them in a bedroom, any bedroom. He slowly removed her sheer blouse, the one in the middle of the three she had to choose from. His eyes would light up showing his excitement at what would be revealed under her outer garments.

"May I help you with anything?"

"Oh, no; I'm just trying to decide which one I want." The attractive, young salesgirl smiled. "There's not much you can go wrong with in this store. Let me know if you want to try anything on." Ginger ran her fingers across the Chantilly lace of the Ink Blot blue bustier. *This is perfect.*

Now, back in her hotel room, she wondered if it was too much. Carlos and his friends traveled across the country sort of roughing it. She doubted he had anything other than jeans with him. She did note that even his jeans were designer. He always dressed fashionably, even when in grunge mode. She considered stepping her fashion plan down a little then stifled that idea. She was going for all, or none. Ginger paired the black and white Daisy Lace skirt she found at Neiman Marcus with her black stilettos. She added a very sheer white blouse. Her outfit could be considered middle ground between dressy and casual, but most definitely sexy. She imagined herself standing next to Carlos; she in her outfit and he in his dark jeans and sleek Cole Haan Oxfords.

The nausea came on quickly. Her nerves got the better of her. She was afraid that if her heart pounded any harder it would burst. *Breathe; in through the nose, out through the mouth. Breathe.* She calmed herself after a few moments, checked her makeup and went back into the bedroom. The clock on the dresser showed 7:20PM. She considered calling the airlines and going home; now. *What if he doesn't want me here? What if he really wants her?* "No; I'm positive he loves me!" She said it out loud, with conviction.

Ginger took one final look in the full-length mirror that the hotel conveniently hung on the wall near the bathroom. She turned sideways and checked from her heels to her neck. Everything was in place and no wrinkles. *Perfume; I almost forgot.* She tapped on a touch of his favorite scent. He told her that night they spent together that it was her natural scent combined with her perfume that drove him crazy. He told her that no one ever affected him the way she does. She supposed, in that moment, he believed what he said. She was angry at how he acted after that night. She should still be angry. Tonight would determine the fate of their love; and their friendship. Both enigmas so tightly entwined that neither could stand alone.

The hotel bar was less than happening; but then again, this was Amarillo, Texas. Ginger sat down at one of the few available stools and ordered a Vodka Martini. She was well aware of interested stares from several of the male patrons. In this moment, and half way through her drink, she welcomed the attention. She signaled the bartender, a worn-out forty something woman, and ordered another round. "Please, allow me." The well-dressed middle aged man took the last available seat which happened to be next to her. He asked, "Are you here on business too?" Ginger smiled. "No, not exactly." The bartender placed her drink in front of her and removed her old glass. Repeating his request one more time, the man all but begged, "Please; allow me." Ginger quickly pushed a twenty she already had on the bar toward the server. "Thank you; you're so kind to offer, but I prefer to pay my own way." He chuckled, "Independent, *and* sassy." Ginger took a sip of her neat martini, "Is your wife aware of your flirting when you're away on business?" He grinned, "What makes you think I'm married?" "It's written all over your face. If you were single you would be more reserved. Married men are more outspoken, bolder. They have nothing to lose if rejected. If I were a married woman looking to step out... You would be an ideal candidate." "Really, and how's that?" "You're good looking; exceptionally handsome, in fact. You're well dressed and you appear to be financially comfortable. If I were looking for a one-night stand, you'd be my guy." His expression said, *Wow, she's got my number all right.* The gentleman started to say, "Well..." But she interrupted him; "Ginger." He continued, "Tom; nice to meet you." Tom extended his hand which Ginger dismissed with a smile. "Well, Ginger; what if I told you that your assumption is slightly off and that I was married, but now I'm separated?" Ginger's phone beeped. She glanced down at it. The text was from Monica with the name and address of the bar they were all heading to. "Well, Tom; I'd say you're full of it." She stood up, "It was nice talking with you, Tom; and good luck. You might try being honest and saying what's really on your mind. There are plenty of lonely people in this world." She winked at him, ending their short conversation. She left the hotel bar with the eyes of every male patron following her, and the envy of every woman.

"Miss; You look lovely tonight. Would you like me to flag a cab for you?" "Yes. Please." She gave the concierge a five. "Thank you, Miss. Have a wonderful evening." The cab driver asked, "Where to?" Ginger pulled out her phone and recited her destination's address to him.

Chapter 48

The vibrancy of 6th street lived up to its reputation. Music of many differing genres blended together in the night air, emanating from the many bars and restaurants that lined both sides of the storied thoroughfare. Joshua's face showed how overwhelming this new world was that his friends introduced him to. He was happy, but felt slightly out of his element. Back home, his world consisted of many restrictions. He felt not only the eyes of God on him but those of his peers and family. Especially mother Cohen's. Here, in this wild Southwestern town, only God had knowledge of his antics. He relied on his faith in God and hoped God approved of his mingling of cultures. Joshua had confidence that God knew of his devotion and that he kept true to the pure cultural requirements. OK, perhaps there may have been some slight deviations regarding strict use of Kosher utensils, but he did do his best. Josh believed his good intentions to be worthy of some points. Besides, exposing the *gentiles* to Jewish history and educating them regarding tolerance, had to be worth even more points. These were his only non-Jewish friends, and he liked them. They made him a better man. *God, they made me a better Jew. I understand more about myself now than before I met all of them.*

Dinner consisted of pizza and burgers. Josh found a falafel cart run by the local Chabad. He found it sad that there were few, if no actual, Kosher restaurants locally. The one catering establishment he had found online, closed over a year ago. Josh had eaten back at the RV before they left for town, in anticipation of difficulties finding food he could eat. He wanted to meet the Rabbis and speak with them while donating to the Chabad. Purchasing a sandwich was his "Ice Breaker."

"Wow, Josh. That looks delicious." Joshua wiped his mouth with a napkin, "It is, Randy. You should try one." "OK." She leaned in as if attempting to take a bite of his sandwich. He pulled back in a pre-programmed reaction. "I'm sorry, Randy. That would be considered a little too familiar." He looked embarrassed as he glanced in the direction of the Chabad food stand. Randy doubled over hysterically laughing. Daniel walked up to them. "What's so funny?" Josh looked away. Randy calmed down a bit and said, "Nothing really, Daniel." She said to Josh, "I was just teasing you. I would never try to eat your sandwich." Josh laughed too, "I know; I know this. I was kidding too." *Not really.*

Monica checked her phone for messages and noted the time. "Hey, guys. What do you say we head over to that club, Midnight Rodeo?" Nick, clearly inebriated, and with his arm around Derek who followed suit, said, "I think we should hang out here. This place is rocking." He released Derek, "You OK, bud?" Derek grinned and nodded affirmatively. "Monica, we found a little place with a cool country rock band playing." He extended his arm for her to take hold of. She had to carefully persuade them, or at least Carlos, to check out the night club. *I've got to get Carlos over there before Ginger arrives*. She latched on to Nick, but as he gently pulled her in the direction of his desired establishment, she pulled back almost spinning him of balance. "No, stud. I want to check this place out. We can come back here later." Carlos agreed with Nick, "I'm good with hanging here for a little while longer. I think I might try one of those chickpea thingies that Josh is eating." Monica made her pouting face. She had every expectation that Carlos could be suckered by her display of emotional weakness. "OK. OK, Monica. You're the activities director. Come on guys, onward to the next place of the night."

Monica breathed a sigh of relief.

Whew! That was close.

Chapter 49

"ID please, Miss." She paid the six-dollar cover charge and entered the club. Like most bars and clubs, it was dark and noisy and smelled like beer. The crowd seemed young; *but then again we're not in Brooklyn anymore.* "Excuse me, miss." *That was the second time someone called me miss!* A pretty girl with a five spot asked if she wouldn't mind getting her a Bud. Ginger looked around making sure none of them, the unknown people she was supposed to meet with, were around, especially Carlos. "How old are you?" "Twenty-one, last week; I forgot my license. The guy at the door let me in as long as I wore a stupid bracelet." She saw that Ginger had a doubtful look on her face. "For real. I swear." Ginger shook her head. "OK, Sure. Now tell me how old you really are. Where's your bracelet?" The girl looked embarrassed. She pulled up her sleeve revealing the color coded nylon. "I'm nineteen. Please...." Ginger recalled pulling the same crap a few times back in the day. She was taller than average for her age and incredibly hot looking, so the bouncers usually let her slide. She took the girl's money. Stay here, they have cameras. I'll put it down and walk away. You can pick it up only after I leave. If you get caught, I'll tell them you swiped my beer." The girl did a little happy dance and agreed to the terms.

The bar crowd became excessively loud all of a sudden. The lights flashed and the DJ controlled music quieted down. Someone made a muffled announcement, and the crowd started cheering. There it was; live music. The band came on with some hardcore country rock. The floor vibrated from all the stomping and dancing. It took Ginger almost ten minutes to fetch herself a Fireball Whisky, the special of the night, and a beer for the underage brat. She took a few sips of her whisky and one of the beer, making it easier to carry them without spilling any.

"That'll be six dollars for you, and ten dollars for you darling." "Wait! What? Why is mine more than his?" The bouncer grinned at Randy, "Cause your fake ID looks fake. Next!" "I told you, Randy, to let me get it for you. My guy does great work for only fifty." "My guy only charged twenty. I thought it looked pretty good." "Obviously, not good enough." Monica put her arm around Randy. "Don't sweat it; between all of us, we got you covered." Nick nudged Derek playfully, "You good big D? I'm going to ask Monica to hit the dance floor while the music is still hopping." Derik shrugged his shoulders, "Good luck with that." Then Derek sort of smiled, "I'm cool; actually doing fine right now. Me and Josh will check out the place." Joshua high-fived Derek. "Let's go." Randy and Daniel followed Nick and Monica to the dance floor. Derek and Josh started moving into the bouncing crowd. Derek looked back at Carlos, who looked like a lost soul. "Coming, Carlos?" Carlos waved to Derek and Joshua, "I'll catch up after I get a drink."

Carlos moved across the floor toward the bar. The crowd was three deep so he decided to backpedal and reroute around to the other side, where it appeared to have easier access.

The crowd seemed to thicken, making Ginger's return to where she left the girl, a little more difficult. "Hey; over here!" Ginger put the beer down on the side table. "I thought I told you to be cool!" "Sorry."

"Ginger?"

She froze, unable to take a breath. Her hand started to shake, splashing some of her drink out of the plastic cocktail glass. "What" How? What are you doing here? How did you find me?" Still no words came out of her mouth. She suddenly felt faint. The whisky slipped from her hand but Carlos, the savior, caught it without losing much of its contents. He placed it on the counter.

No words were needed. As he held her firmly in his arms, she thought she would melt. Ginger pulled back from his hold so she could look into his eyes. "I'm sorry, Carlos. I had to come see you. I would have died if I waited one more day; one more hour. I..." Carlos cut her off, "This trip was supposed to help me clear my head and get our relationship in perspective. All it did was make me miss you more every day. I hurt you and that is the last thing I would ever want to do. I was a fool. I'm crazy about you. I want to spend every moment with you. I love you, Ginger." Carlos kissed her long and hard. As if they were transported into another dimension, the room with all its commotion no longer existed for the two of them. The music faded into the background.

The young girl took her beer, "Thanks for the brewsky; keep the change." Her words fell on deaf ears.

Monica seemed distracted. "What are you looking for? I'm right here in front of you." "I'm sorry, Nick. I was just looking..." "For him! Damn it, Monica." Nick started to walk away; Monica grabbed his arm firmly. "Wait. Yes; I am looking for Carlos. The other day I answered his phone and it was *her*." "The other woman?" "Yes; Ginger." I've been texting with her ever since that day. She's supposed to be here at this club tonight; for Carlos. I helped arrange it." "Wait a minute. You conspired to set up Carlos with the girl he left behind?" Monica sighed. "Yes. She is madly in love with him and he is apparently, un-admittedly, with her. One of them had to take the bold step and she came through." Nick grinned, "I'll say; like a thousand miles." Nick pointed. "Like, Wow. I guess that's Ginger." Monica's heart fluttered, she felt weird as she watched her plan coming to fruition. She couldn't tell if disappointment or happiness overwhelmed her. They both peered through the crowd looking on as Carlos and Ginger reacquainted themselves. Nick took her hand and squeezed it gently. "They look good together." Monica squeezed Nick's hand back, sending him the positive vibe he hoped for. She said, "Yes, they appear to be the perfect couple." Nick started to lead her toward the dance floor area that now seemed to include the entire club floor. "Forget Barbie and Ken; let's dance."

As the hours slipped by, the single guys drank and checked out woman; neither of them brave enough, or in the mood to approach anyone. Josh talked with Derek, asking what he would do once he got home. Derek admitted that he needed to come clean with his family.

Josh consoled him, and as their conversation started to wind down, Derek told Josh, "You know, Josh? You would make a really good clergyman. I mean, Rabbi. I'm feeling much better just from speaking with you. Thanks, buddy." Joshua considered Derek's statement, and as if God had planted the idea in his head he said, "Perhaps I might be a good Rabbi. I *am* a good listener." *Yes, that could be my calling. Mother would be happy; papa would be proud. Wait; then I'd have to leave Brooklyn College and my friends to attend Yeshiva. Hmm...*

Chapter 50

As Saturday began with the sun rising over Amarillo, Texas, the red rock hills began to glow among the low lying greenery. The deep blue sky, iridescent and scattered with soft layers of puffy clouds, lit up the historical two lane Route 66; the quiet road, so many travel for nostalgia. The path seven young people followed for an adventure. The adventure that lead them out of loneliness and boredom and into maturity and solace.

"We didn't engage in sex last night." "I know. It may have been one of the toughest things I ever had to endure. *Certainly the most noble.* I wanted to hold you close to reassure you that I'll never let go." Ginger wriggled herself even tighter into his embrace. Carlos' arms were strong; she felt safe and secure. "You know, Carlos? We've got a lot to discuss. I wasn't sure about my coming here; you broke my heart. I disregarded the fact that you have issues committing. I guess, in my head, that didn't apply to me." Carlos kissed her beautifully naked shoulder. "It doesn't. It never did. Idiot me just didn't realize it. I wasn't with, didn't want to be, with anyone else since that night." Carlos saw no need to complicate their renewed situation by explaining his and Monica's relationship. At least not at this moment. "You were in all my dreams. Every day on this trip, you were with me in my heart. I wouldn't have made it past today before calling my part of this trip over, and racing home to tell you." Ginger asked, "Tell me what?" Carlos' face twisted, he bit his lip. "What a fool I am and how much I need you in my life." They lay together in silence for a few moments.

"You're going to need to find a new assistant."
"You quit Aerotech?"
"No; well sort of. Consider this my two weeks, notice."
"Ginger, you can't..." Carlos had to recognize that for once he was not the one in control. "Well, I guess after everything; I can understand. Whatever is best for you; that's what I want."
"Thank you for understanding."
"I don't understand, not really. But I suppose if we're going to get married, we shouldn't work together."

Ginger froze. She tried to take in a breath, but her body and all its parts remained motionless. Her back still pressed firmly into him, she felt his heart beating. *Breathe. Yes, you heard right. Mr. non-committal proposed to you in his awkward, Carlos way of doing things*. Carlos pleaded, "Say something?" *Breathe*. Not facing Carlos made it easier for her to express her feelings. Ginger managed to draw a breath and in a soft, calm voice she said, "You wanted to be friends, probably with benefits. I needed more and told you so. You bailed on me, emotionally. I always knew you had issues. In some odd way I think that's part of what I love about you. You are a complex person, Carlos Martinez." Carlos asked, "What about *your* new best friend with benefits?" Ginger gently removed Carlos' arm off of her. He did his best to control his panic and said, "I'm sorry. I am just so freaking jealous." She pulled herself away from the warm embrace of his body and turned to face him. "That's over. Every moment he and I were together; in the same room, it was as if I was cheating on you. My soul is attached to yours. I tried so hard to get you out of my head." Carlos placed his hand softly on her waist. His hands were warm and his touch radiated an orgasmic sensation throughout her body. "I was horrible, and yet, here you are. The answer to my dreams." Ginger had tears forming in her eyes.

"My beautiful, wonderful, Ginger. Will you spend the rest of eternity with me? I promise; I will commit my life to loving you, cherishing you, and caring for you."

"Holy father in heaven! You're serious!"

"Is that a Yes?"

"Yes. Yes! Yes!!!"

The rest of the RV clan had all but finished breakfast when Carlos dropped down from his hidden bedroom above the helm. All eyes said, "So?" "Pretty quiet last night, but it sounded like you got the job done this morning." Nick thought maybe he stepped over the line there, but even Monica said nothing. He continued with, "Yes, yes, yes!" but in a quiet voice so Carlos' guest would not hear. Now Monica pinched his arm. "Ouch!" "Idiot." Carlos ignored Nick and poured himself a cup of coffee. Ginger appeared, like a goddess of the morning. Even in sweats and t-shirt, she looked incredible. Carlos handed his cup to her, she kissed his cheek and took a sip before handing the cup back to him. She quietly said, "I'm starving." She whispered in Carlos' ear, "Eggs and coffee or me?" Their eyes met and a million virtual words flowed between them in a split second. *Control, Carlos; control. You'll have a lifetime with her.* Not much was discussed, and only a quick introduction was made to his friends the evening before. Carlos formally introduced Ginger and everyone greeted her warmly. Ginger took Monica's hand, then kissed her cheek. "Thank you for everything. I hope you will consider me a friend as important and special as I do you."

Carlos whispered something else in Ginger's ear. She blushed as she nodded and kissed him softly on the lips. "Guys, get a room." Now all eyes were on Joshua. No one expected a comment like that from him. Derek hi-fived Josh. Nick and Monica laughed. Carlos remarked, "We will, later. But first, we have an announcement. I asked this incredibly smart and beautiful woman to be my wife." Ginger chimed in, "And I said Yes!" Ginger looked at Carlos with the biggest smile. "Your dad is going to be thrilled." She saw the questioning look on Carlos' face. "Oh; he paid for the ticket out here. He and I had several intimate conversations. And, I'm not leaving the company, I'm transferring to the other side to manage a new division in Human Resources. Your soon to be bride is moving on up." "So, you're not quitting?" "Right." Ginger explained her conversation with Margaret and the later one with Martinez Sr. "So, you and my dad conspired to trap me?" He felt the sting of her stare and that of her audience as well. "I mean; I'm really glad whatever it is you two conspired with, that you're here with me. I suppose we'll spend time having lunch together now that we won't be working all day with each other. I think I'm liking the concept of this." From the front of the RV Nick

bellowed out, "Hey! I thought I was your lunch buddy."
"You're my friend, you all are. We've simply got a new
addition to the group." He received another questioning
stare. "Well, once in while we can hang with the guys,
right?" Ginger laughed, "Of course. I can't wait." She put
her arm around Monica, "I bet there's lots of stories we
can share about him. Let's do drinks one night next week,
when we're back home." Monica said, "You have my
number." "That, I do." Ginger pointed to Randy, "The
three of us." Josh said, "They're the Three Miss-keteers."
Derek bumped fists with Josh, "You're funny, dude. Who
knew?"

Everyone congratulated the reunited couple. Monica
kissed Ginger and then Carlos. "I'm really happy for you
guys. You better work on babies soon so I can babysit."
Now Carlos' face flushed a deep shade of red. "Babies?"
Nick took Monica's hand, "Babies? I like babies."
"Nickolas; you are so cute. Now, go away. Go play with
Josh and Derek and let the adults speak." She wasn't sure
if she projected too much attitude, and almost started to
apologize when Nick said, "I think I'm falling for you." He
let go of her hand abruptly, winked and turned to walk
away. She said, "Bye…"

Chapter 51

"So now what, big guy?" Carlos glanced over to where Ginger and Monica were whispering to each other. He assumed they were lovingly tearing him apart. After a brief moment, he returned his attention to Nick. "Ginger and I need time to reinvent ourselves as a couple. Daniel and Randy already said they wanted to spend time together alone in New Mexico. They are looking into catching a bus this afternoon. They'll fly back home early next week. I'm going to jump to the end of this Route 66 trek by taking Ginger to Santa Monica for a few days. We'll make flight arrangements to fly home from there. Can the four of you navigate this puppy back east?" Nick made a goofy face as he pondered Carlos' question. "For sure. We can do that." Carlos said, "Cool." *I better check my insurance coverage...*

****

Carlos found Monica sitting on a huge log behind the RV, strumming her guitar softly.

"Hey there, girlfriend."
"Hey yourself."
"Are we OK?"

"Sure, we're fine. It's just that I'm really still confused. My head and my heart are messed up."

"I'm sorry. But..."

"But you are in love with her and I always knew it. I am truly so happy for you."

"Nick gets out of control sometimes, but he really likes you. Actually; more than likes you. He needs an incredible woman like you to settle him down. You should give him a chance."

"You're right Carlos. I think will. He's trying so hard and I've been so mean to him."

Carlos put his arm around Monica. "I'm going to marry one of my best friends, but I need my other best friend to be there for me; like you have been these past few weeks."

"You're my best friend too, Carlos. Always."

They hugged for what seemed like a really long time before Monica pushed Carlos away. "Ok. Now, down to business. You stuck me with a crazy man who can't keep his hands off me, and his two sidekicks. Who's going to drive this monster vehicle?"

Chapter 52

The sun looked incredibly beautiful as it gracefully began to sink below the horizon. It's reflection in the calm pacific water created a serene effect on the few who still remained on the famous Santa Monica pier. Carlos and Ginger held hands as they watched the slow descent. The last of the day's surfers carried his board under one arm as he trudged out of the sea and across the cooling sand.

"This is exactly how I envisioned us at this moment. I know the real world awaits us back home, but this is my dream and I don't want to let go." Ginger looked as if she was feeling a little chilled. Carlos pulled his lady close into him. She said, "Thank you. I was cold now that the sun has gone down." Carlos leaned into her, taking in the scent of her hair. He kissed her gently on the lips. "I promise to always take care of you. In a few days we return to reality, but this is not a dream. This is a sample of what we can look forward to. We'll come back here as often as we like, or anywhere else you desire. We'll create new adventures." Ginger squeezed Carlos' hand. "What about children?" Carlos made that weird bewildered face again, like he did the other day in the RV when Monica had mentioned kids. He said, "Now, that'll be an adventure." She asked, "You do want kids, don't you?" He looked her squarely in the eye, his expression unsettled her. "I haven't really given that idea much consideration. But I'll tell you this; we will be the best parents ever. I mean, if my son looks like me and our daughters look like you..." Ginger grinned, "Then, we'll be in big trouble, mister. My dad swore he nearly had several heart attacks starting when I turned fourteen." Carlos laughed, "I completely understand. I imagine the same thing will happen to me every time you go to a bar or club without me." "Jealousy doesn't seem like your thing, Carlos. That emotion is never going to be part of our relationship. I am yours, and I can take care of myself." Ginger wiped a happy tear from her cheek. Carlos made the sincerest face as he told her, "And I am yours; forever."

"I love you, Carlos Martinez Junior."

"I love you, Ginger O'Connell."

Epilogue

The ceremony was sad in one way, but comforting in another. It had been eighteen months since the group's adventure crossing America. Derek's mom, during her eulogy for her son, remarked about Derek's time on the road with his new found friends. "You were all an inspiration of hope and solace for him. He had many good memories throughout his young life. He told me that in the short time he had to share friendship with all of you, you all added to the fulfillment of his life. He considered you his true brothers and sisters." She looked warmly at the campus friends. Her eyes glassy with tears. "I suppose that makes you all part of my family as well. Thank you, and God Bless."

Randy and Daniel got engaged the day after Carlos' and Ginger's Wedding. Daniel was offered an internship at Google during his last semester at Brooklyn College and recently was offered a contract to work for them in Manhattan. Randy began student teaching history at a Long Island middle school. They are planning a wonderful life together.

Joshua Cohen with some help from his dad, made peace with him mom. He cautiously told of his adventure away, placing more emphasis on his visit to the Jewish Museum in Tulsa. A few days after Joshua returned, his mom admitted that the trip had changed him for the better. She told him that he had matured and that the smart and handsome mensch she always knew was hiding inside, had now flourished. She told him how proud she was of him. Josh no longer plays baseball. He spends most of his time studying the Torah while waiting for his acceptance into a Yeshiva for Rabbinical Studies.

After a short and tumultuous relationship, Nick and Monica ended their romantic relationship, but still remain friends. Monica's trust fund allowed her to continue playing her music. She plays in clubs all over Long Island and recently was a featured Indy artist on Satellite Radio. Nickolas Caputo landed a teaching job at a community college teaching philosophy. Most afternoons during lunch, he can be found behind the cafeteria parking lot eating fast food and sneaking a few hits of weed.

Business as usual continued at Aerotech. The company had a great quarter and Carlos got approval to hire additional sales reps to help in his planned territorial expansion. Most days he has lunch with his beautiful bride, but at least once a month, weather permitting, he makes his way over to Brooklyn College and his favorite taco truck. He sits alone now, against the old oak tree. For fifteen minutes he lets his memories prevail. The music plays in his head as Monica strums her guitar and sings. Derek, Randy, Daniel and Nick all sing along. Passersby sometimes wonder about the guy sitting under the tree, smiling and singing quietly to himself.

****

Carlos Andres Martinez Junior took his wife's hand as they crossed the avenue. "Your dad invited us to dinner next Saturday night. I took the liberty of saying yes for both of us. I hope you're OK with that." Carlos pulled her close and kissed her cheek. "I'm OK with anything you arrange for us. Certainly, dinner with my dad." He paused for a second and then remarked, "I hear you're making waves in Human Resources." Ginger smiled, "I found my calling. These ideas come to me so easily and I love what I'm doing." "Evidently, so does management. But, not everyone is so much on board with your ideas." Ginger tilted her head then said, "Only one or two, who seem to care more about reducing work load than doing an efficient job." "Wow. You are a force to be reckoned with;

aren't you?" She replied, "I have my family's business to help look out for." Carlos grabbed her hand, "The bus is here."

The bus was not crowded, and they managed to get a seat together. "So, where is my dad taking us?" "I don't know, but he'll let us know by the end of the week. I was thinking. We should look to get a new place." Carlos made a face. She continued, "Well, I mean, this was your place, and it does have history that didn't always include *us*. We should start fresh. Perhaps a two bedroom. Our apartment now is kind of tight; don't you think?" Carlos looked at her hard. She could tell his brain went into overdrive. She waited in anticipation for his response. "I was wondering; are you in the mood for branzini over a bed of garlic and spinach? I could run into the market while you go ahead to the apartment and slip into something more comfortable." Ginger leaned against her man.

"You're avoiding the question."
"That I am."

They sat quietly; neither responding to the other's question. The ten-minute bus ride was nearing their destination when Carlos squeezed her hand. "Wait, you said you were not feeling well last night, some kind of stomach ache. Then you had a spell at lunch. Now you want to move?" Ginger grinned like a little girl. Her face glowed. She looked incredibly happy. "You're pregnant?" Ginger drew a breath and said, "I didn't plan to tell you on a bus, but yes." His face froze, she waited in anticipation. Ginger suddenly remembered his face that day in the RV when Monica mentioned babies. "We're going to have a baby!" Carlos stood up abruptly, pulling Ginger onto her feet as well. The bus pulled into their stop at the same moment. The other passengers, mostly regulars who recognized each other from their daily travel home looked on, as the crazy man and his stunning wife made their way off the bus. Carlos turned back to them just before stepping out of the exit, "I'm going to be a dad!" They all smiled and nodded. Some yelled "Congratulations."

As they made their way through the park, holding hands, Carlos was nearly skipping in place as he walked. Ginger said, "Branzini sounds awesome." Carlos stopped walking and took Ginger in his arms and kissed her. "I think we should get a bigger place. Maybe on the other side of the park. It's a nicer neighborhood, with more kids too."

"I love you, Carlos Martinez."
"I love you, Ginger Martinez."

Wayne Lasner

Note from the Author:

I hope you have enjoyed this adventure. Life can throw lots of curve balls. Overcoming disruptive situations can be difficult. But, with the support of family and close friends, and a healthy attitude, surviving these chaotic times can better be endured. Life is short. Sometimes it takes a little effort to keep relationships strong. Our group of friends from the story learned to lean on each other for support. They found personal strength from within the energy of the group, enriching each of their lives.

As I create new works of fiction, I hope to improve the reader's experience with each release. Your comments and ratings are invaluable to me. **If you enjoy the read, please rate your experience for this book on Amazon**. This will help with the success of my books. *From the Amazon search bar, type "Wayne Lasner" and you will see all available titles.* I hope to bring more new and diverse adventures to you on a regular basis. Keep a lookout on Amazon for new releases and visit my webpage **waynelasnerbooks.com** for information on future works. Also, blog me on my book website telling me what you like or dislike about individual characters or the story in general.

Wayne Lasner

Wishing you all: Peace, Health, and Happiness.

Acknowledgement

I write fiction because I love to create a story that pushes the reader's imagination. While creating the story and putting it to paper takes a good deal of effort and time, the real work is in the editing. Thank you Mark, once again, for your true dedication to the final product. You are the guy that makes sure everyone else can truly enjoy an easy and clear read.

To all my faithful readers, thank you for your support and encouragement.